Praise

'One of the things I love about M[...]
showing of life in all its complicate[...] ...nagers. Teenagers
can keep many secrets and that is dea[...] with brilliantly in this book. I also love
the bustle of the novel, and the strange way that lives connect.'

Jackie Kay, Author and Makar, Scottish National Poet

'Clough has created a vivid and distinctive voice for her tough-tender protagonist, Joey, who is driven by an intense need to answer the question, "who am I and where do I belong?" Echoing the contradictions in Joey's character, a powerful binary setting (the beautifully evoked ancient landscape of Cumbria, and the contemporary nebulous, shape-shifting world of social media) allows for an originality of style, form and structure which seems entirely fitting. Morph is a gripping and challenging YA read with real emotional heft.'

Ann Coburn, Author

'Set in the richly imagined landscape of the Lake District, Morph takes as one of its central themes gender identity and, in particular, transgenderism, and the complex issues that arise for family and friends – and the young subject themselves – in this drive and passion to imagine themselves differently and live a different kind of life. The material is handled with great sensitivity, without sensationalism, in a way which recognises that this is one aspect of identity, one dimension of living. The novel allows for many others and gains in wisdom and complexity as a result.'

Linda Anderson, Author

'Absolutely magical, and so beautifully written! Jill Clough has bravely taken on a controversial subject. She really understands teenagers' mentality and the problems faced by them and their parents. I found this a fascinating book.'

Jilly Cooper, Author

M O R P H

DATE DUE

2 7 SEP 2021	
1 5 OCT 2021	
	PRINTED IN U.S.A.

SWALLOW BOOKS

OF THE ENGLISH LAKES

www.swallowbooks.co.uk

This edition published in 2019
Copyright © Jill Clough

Second Edition

Jill Clough asserts the moral right to be identified as
the author of this work.

Typesetting by Rebecca Souster
www.rebeccasouster.com

Printed and bound in Great Britain
by Clays Ltd, Elcograf S.p.A.

ISBN 978-0-9575740-4-5

Author's note

We all develop an inner narrative – a shifting story that shapes our sense of self. As we grow up, we hold it to ourselves, not telling the story to people we fear will want to change it. The story becomes a secret. We might share it with a trusted other but not with parents – largely because they love us and want to keep us close. But we are designed to fledge.

My starting point for Morph was the sense of shock that parents experience when they encounter the absolute otherness of their children – that moment when the child is suddenly apparent as another adult.

When I was pregnant with my first child, I was gripped by the reality that another human intelligence was growing inside me, but I would never know its thoughts. The child was an unknown passenger, getting ready to alight. Once the child was born, I forgot. I believed it was my role to nurture and understand, influence, shape.

And that's where the plot of Morph began. It became a wider story about classification, but its starting point was the shock of meeting the stranger who is your child.

Jill Clough, 2019

For Georgia, Frances, Libby and Niamh

ONE
MIRROR

Zef's Blog

There's a stranger in the mirror.

The uterus inside the body says F not M. There could be other organs too – apart from spleen, liver, gall-bladder, stomach, kidneys and the rest.

This reflection looks like me.

Josephine Ruth Wilcox on my birth certificate, Ruth for Ma's best friend whose kid died in a car crash with her husband. You can't have a name without somebody's history getting snagged on yours.

Mollie Alison Underfell let herself be renamed Mollie Wilcox, why? It isn't like Ma now. Who was she then? Andrew Arthur Wilcox. He hates Arthur. Why call your first child Noah? Most of what happens in the human brain is unknowable.

You can't trust anything to stay private online. Even this blog feels dangerous.

Status: **Draft:** Edit
Visibility: **Public:** Edit
Publish: **Immediately:** Edit

The default means you broadcast to everyone, every-where. Blogging is internet graffiti. You choose from the drop-down menus instead of spraying the side of houses, bridges, but you have to take care every time, check and choose to stay private.

They used to call me Josie till I got hold of what I could bear. Joey's ok. For now.

6:44 Noah

Home pm, come climbing?

Jay-Babe get up.

Lazy slag xx

12:20 Bex

Matt's trolling me xx

Where r u

12:25 Joey

Noah coming, getting lift, ttyl? Xx

Thursday August 3

I lean forward for a sight of the road between the lads' heads. The hedgerows are all red and pink and blue and yellow and I think of Pa excitedly reciting the names, trying to get us interested, telling us why classification matters – rosebay willow herb, wood cranesbill, meadow cranesbill, campanula, yellow hawkweed, Herb-Robert. Some things stick. Pa has a passion for order. He won't like Noah's new hair colour when he sees it.

'Joey, are you feeling better?' Simon twists round from the front passenger seat with a smile. He's much politer than my brother.

Noah interrupts. 'I had a good look at the climbing lasses last weekend when we were at the wall and the only reason you don't climb is in your head, Jay-Babe. You're just too nervy. You got to do what I say.'

Noah's driving hasn't improved. I've only stopped feeling sick by looking straight ahead. But his words make me picture the great green and grey diamond slab of the Bowder Stone Rock, perched on its point like a fat man on one toe. Noah is convinced he can make me learn to climb. *Bouldering*, he calls it, telling Simon. Nobody knows quite how it found its way into Borrowdale. Perhaps it was dumped by a passing glacier. We've walked past it lots, Pa checking out flora. Some helpful Georgian leaned a neat staircase up the side.

I have my own private plan, though. 'I didn't put in any rock shoes.'

'In the boot. I took care of everything.'

At Easter Noah dragged me up what he called an Easy climb. It had literally been 'a drag'. He roped me, 'to be on the safe side', but drifted off the route so that we blundered into a capital D for Difficult. All of a sudden he was hammering pitons into crevices. Waves of anxiety flowed down from him like fog and I shook so much I couldn't get a grip. My ribs ached for days afterwards. Funny how 'get a grip' shifts its meaning.

Simon says that bouldering is meant to be good for all levels, by which he means 'novices too'. Noah thinks that just saying things will make them ok. I hate to think he may be right. On www.iwannagetoutofhere.co.uk, that's the advice. 'Picture it, talk about it, name it, do it, become what you dream.'

I visualise reaching up and out, farther than my body thinks is possible, my hands scrabbling for handholds. My mind won't bring up the picture. I can't till I know what the picture is. I think that's Catch 22.

I'm not doing it, anyway, not bouldering. I'm going to run up the Derwent fells. Already my feet anticipate splashing across the river, along the far bank and up into the forest, over slippery slate and scree, angling like fingers tracing the route. My ankles flex, working the hamstrings. Simon will make Noah wait for me. He appeared in our kitchen for the first time only a couple of hours ago, helped Ma to pack rolls for our tea, told Ma he'd make sure Noah wouldn't bully me. I'm inclined to trust him.

Noah doesn't get that when I run, everything makes sense.

By the time we reach the car park in Borrowdale, two or three cars are still waiting for walkers to return. The mountains make me think of giants turning over in bed. Their names are cumbersome, magical. I roll them in my mouth like sucking marbles – Ullscarf, High Raise, Glaramara, Bessy Boot, Dale Head, High Spy, Maiden Moor, Catbells. Whoever calls a mountain *Bessy Boot*?

Noah throws open the boot and tosses out shoes, rucksacks, the bag of rolls, water, slams it shut. The car shudders. He kicks a tyre, locks up, slings a rucksack over his shoulder and sets off along the path that leads to the Bowder Stone. Simon and I stare after him, at the small heap left on the gravel. Noah yells, 'Get a move on!'

Simon looks apologetic, picking up what remains. However did he become Noah's friend? My brother is all bluff and blag, whereas Simon – I can't analyse him right now. His grandparents are from Thailand, he said, and his mum and dad are Thai. Does that make him Thai? He's never lived anywhere but London, and whatever boarding school he went to, and Leeds. He met Noah at uni in Leeds. Climbing Club, they say.

Furtively, I sling my running rucksack over my shoulder. The woods smell of hot afternoon and high summer. Amazingly, it has been dry for several weeks in a row. Grass at the edge of the path looks crumpled and grey, but the trees are full of sap. I pat the rough brown bark of the nearest Scots pine. Pine is an old friend.

When we catch up with Noah he's muttering something about a pump.

The Bowder Stone looks tidy but its sides are glassy from the number of sweaty hands practising grips on its surface. I try not to roll my eyes. It must be like trying to climb up the side of a battleship, looking for safe holds while the whole

16

of gravity tries to pull you off. The staircase is a bizarre domestic touch.

Noah chucks the inflatable mattress on to the ground. It's transparent, a grounded jellyfish. 'Yeah,' he says, scrubbing his blond hair so that it sticks out like cut straw. 'I forgot the pump. We'll have to blow it up. You start, Jay-Babe.' I glare. 'Come on, it's exercise.'

There's a rubbery, dragging sound as Simon yanks at it, searching for the blow-hole.

'Don't give in to her!' Noah wrestles it away.

'Noah, I can do this.' Simon peacefully loops the mattress over his arm, but again Noah snatches it back. His face crimsons as the mattress slowly gives form to his breathing. The flaccid rubber stiffens into shape and he lugs it towards the looming rock. Then he turns, one hand already sifting through chalk in the bag at his waist.

'Tell you what, before you get on the rock, climb up the underside of the staircase. Easy. Used to do it myself. It'll limber you up a treat.'

'Is Simon going to video everything?'

'Oh, I will, yes. It's very useful, watching yourself. I upload videos when I've edited them, though I'm no good at finding music. Noah does that. Maybe you could help.' His phone sits snugly in his hand. It's much newer than mine.

'Si can video you too, Jay-Babe. Seeing yourself is the best coach.'

Your image in a mirror is reversed. I've never seen myself on film.

Noah and Simon forget me. The differences in their physique seem more than mere body shape. Noah's newly-broad shoulders, newly-bleached hair, and astonishing, deep tan are still as familiar as the palm of my hand. Simon, with his springing, glossy black hair, his narrow-boned body, his shining skin, seems to come from another world – Vietnam, Cambodia, Thailand, Mongolia, China, Japan – world-in-a-name that means as much to others as Glaramara means to me.

I've read on the net about ladyboys in Thailand. But Simon is Home Counties, Mr Polite.

We are all related, I've read that too. The genes that stream through generations, giving my body its shape, flow through Simon's ancestors too. Six degrees of separation, someone's idea. Mr Polite is kin to me – has to be kin to Noah, too. Unbelievable. I twitch.

'Did you get that, Simon?'

'Yes, though the focus could be better.' Simon's phone is enviable. I wish I could film the forest but when I slap my hand against my pocket I realise that my phone is sitting at home on a window-sill. I can picture it.

I strip off the jeans and rugby shirt that have hidden my running gear, and slip my feet into running shoes, supple as gloves. Soft air puffs on my shoulders and stomach. One pinch of flesh. I'll check the BMI later tonight.

Noah lands with a squawk and a bounce on the crash mat. Behind him, Simon steps up to the same pitch, swinging across the sheer surface of the outward-leaning boulder as if he has performed the movement a hundred times. His arms tighten to reveal the iron muscles of long practice, and he twists sideways to lodge the toes of one foot in an invisible crack, high above his hips. The other leg hangs below, a pendulum. His balance seems perfect. Noah leans back on his fists, saying nothing.

I recall another Noah. One year on holiday we built a dam across a small stream. A wild pony kept us company, trotting down to the water to snuffle and watch. We took an apple cut in quarters and Noah held out his hand, palm flattened, whilst the pony took the slice between its yellow teeth. Its lips were enormous, its breath hot when it was my turn. Noah held my free hand. He loved the pony's vast teeth, its swinging tail.

Now, he gapes as I leap away down the path, his yell swallowed up by the overarching trees. Moments later I slither through undergrowth to the Borrowdale road, next to the Derwent. A couple of startled tourists with cameras slung on their shoulders fall back into the ferns. 'Sorry,' I sing out. A twinge of guilt on behalf of Simon vanishes when I glimpse sunlight glittering on water. On the river's far bank is open woodland. I'll wade. Everything smells brackeny, pine-bright.

The Derwent runs fast and shallow between mounds of pebbles brought downstream by becks pouring down fellsides. Sunlight flashes and sparkles around my legs as I catch the occasional tiny hard pebble between my toes, curse. My shoes dangle from my neck. I shout, 'Hiya, hiya!' Sound spins in this huge, free space – sycamore wings on the wind.

I run parallel with the river until the path turns west, up the fell. This area has been mined for centuries and greenish-grey slates lie everywhere in sliding heaps or single, razor shards. The air is sweet and woody, with pea-green bracken erupting everywhere. There will be bilberries between the trees. I think of searching out the purple berries, but my eyes focus on the tantalising peaks along the skyline.

Then I am in the midst of the old quarry with its mountainous piles of grey waste and I hover, wipe the sweat from my eyes. At my back, the land falls sharply to the dale. The mountain hides the sun but the shadow in which I stand is warm. I look at my watch. I want to run the whole ridge, from High Spy to Catbells, then back along the valley, but I know there isn't time. And my navigation's not perfect. I forgot the compass.

Six-thirty. Forty minutes since I left the Bowder Stone.

It takes longer than I hope to reach the T-junction at the shoulder, where the path forks – left, up the fell towards Dale Head – or right, for High Spy. But I pause. A large bird glides overhead, west, so close that its streaky, dull markings are clear. It rides the air as easily as leaves floating on water. Brown, speckled with white, a white rump. Automatically the facts tick the boxes, when I spy a wicked, downward-curving beak. It's a curlew and I've never seen one flying before. It's silent. Curlews only sing in the spring. The bubbling call is the most haunting, beautiful sound I know. I don't play the game of coming back as another species. But if I could sing like a curlew I'd reconsider.

I flop on a bed of grass, all tufts and fluffs of white flax, gazing up at a sky where the wash of transparent blue gradually thins until – I strain to see – it reaches the horizon and is lost in the brilliance of the sun, which floats on a streamer of cloud, stains it pink. I place a finger on the throbbing vein in my wrist. It settles to a steady, slow beat. My shoulders, my spine, thighs, calves, heels, settle into the body of the mountain, nesting. Silence and sound magnify with every breath until the invisible stars sing. I am never going to leave this place.

Somebody shouts beyond the horizon. The sun has gone.

My heart leaps into my throat. Ten-past nine. They'll think I'm dead.

I scramble to my feet, straining to see the path. Though there are lights in the valley below, up here I'm almost in the dark. My knees turn to jelly. A band of ice tightens around my head. I simply have to put one foot in front of the other. I say it aloud.

Noah said there would still be light at eleven o'clock, but here, in the shadow cast by the fells, all shades of difference are indistinguishable. The path must be somewhere, covering itself with bracken and roots. I have to rely upon the picture in my mind.

Running downhill over razor-sharp flints, hidden boulders and stones takes all my concentration. Trees merge with waist-high undergrowth, branches lash at my ankles, I lose my bearings, stumble into chilled air. *River.* Winking surface, black depths.

I crossed it only hours back but I can't see below the surface. I can't tell what's safe.

I clench my fists, focus, glimpse a faint ribbon of grey. *Road.* A running figure slows, waves, calls. At once I hurl myself into the water, splash to the far side where Simon reaches to pull me up the slippery bank. 'You're soaked to the skin,' he says, stripping off his shirt. 'Put it on, I won't look. Noah's driving up and down the road, on the lookout. I'll see if I've got a signal yet. He's not in the best of tempers.'

Simon's shirt is comfortingly warm. He squeezes the river water from my running vest, carefully extracting the fine green strands of water weed that have hitched a ride. Noah skids the car into the bank. 'You do realise,' he says, noisily gritting his teeth, 'Pa will say it's all my fault. You'll have to tell him.' He shakes the faint glow of his watch-face under my nose. 'I can't get a signal and I didn't want to waste time looking for a phone box when we were working our arses off trying to find you.'

The journey home is taken at frightening speed. Noah pulls over to ring home. Afterwards, he's calmer. 'Ma will kill you but that's your problem,' he says, throwing himself back in the driver's seat. Simon, meanwhile, is foraging, enveloped in his spare sweatshirt. We both smell of whatever it is he uses to wash his clothes, fresh and green – like lemongrass, maybe. Lime. 'Here,' he says, holding out a packet of peanuts. 'Noah ate the last roll.'

'I'm not hungry, thanks, but water would be good.' Reluctantly I reach out, my thighs ungluing themselves from the deflated crash mat that Noah has spread on the back seat of the car to save the upholstery from my saturated shorts. Noah grabs the packet.

'Don't be nice to her, Si, she bites.' He tosses a peanut in the air, craning his neck like a fledgling to catch it. The engine roars. 'Gross, stale,' chucking the packet over his shoulder. The water is warm from its stay in the car. I eat a couple of peanuts. My stomach cramps.

Noah and Simon embark on a long and technical conversation about the videos. My pictures unroll against the dark. Occasionally Simon looks back, frowning. Noah accelerates through St John in the Vale, taking the wide bends so fast that I have to grab the door handle. A spurt of warm liquid soaks the gusset of my pants. It isn't river water leaking. My head throbs. If I were alone, I'd be pounding my fists. This body doesn't fit me, doesn't fit me at all. I'd like to rip out all my female organs, leave them on the bathroom shelf. If only.

We bump along the track and turn into the drive. The front door flies open and Ma's silhouette holds a towel. I hobble, desperate to avoid her but she's hard to escape. The towel makes me a toddler, swaddled. 'Come on,' she says. 'It's okay.' I want to cry.

She has been working at the kitchen table. It's August, it's nearly midnight and she's still at it, worse than Shirley, worse than anyone, waiting up for Ruth to arrive, finishing the third draft of her speech for Awards Day in September. Does she ever stop being the headteacher? Maybe Noah gets his wild persistence to be perfect from her. Pa staggers from his doze to switch on the kettle. He has been on the high fells above Ennerdale, his latest passion. My eyes feel huge and sore. 'Go on.' Ma shoves me lightly between shoulder-blades. 'Go and get a shower. I'll hear all about it later.'

'Later?' exclaims Noah, sweeping her into a hug. The swing of his rucksack sends paper, pens and cue cards flying. 'What on earth were you doing at school? It's August, it's holidays. I thought you'd be here when we arrived.'

I bypass Simon in the doorway, waiting for Noah to introduce him to Ma and Pa.

Ma knocks. 'I've brought you a hot drink and a sandwich, darling. You haven't eaten anything?' Her voice is strained and tight on the other side of my bedroom door.

'I'm not hungry.'

'Joey, can I come in? Please?'

Slowly, I throw Marmalade off my lap, turn down the volume.

> *Dance to your Daddy, my little laddie*
> *Dance to your Daddy, my little man.*

The lyric makes me think of being a child again, but not the child I was.

Marmalade tries to climb back, his claws deep in the pad of tissue above my knee. I open the door, half clutching him, half holding him away.

'Darling, it's half past midnight. Are you online? I brought this to help you sleep.'

I'm wearing a clean rugby shirt, and shorts. There's a long graze down the side of one shin and a blossoming bruise on the other knee. Marmalade takes a running jump at my arms, slithers, flops down upon his four black pads, yowls.

Ma takes one step into the room. She won't come further unless I ask. 'He seems very pleasant, that young man. He says Noah was a bit over-enthusiastic about climbing. You have to say no to your brother.' She waits for me to say something but there's nothing to say. She bites her lip. 'It's your period, isn't it?'

I count the planks between the bed and the desk.

'I hope you don't mind. I didn't mean to pry but your papers blew off the desk. I haven't read anything. Anyway, I left a box file in case you want one. For your papers.'

I see the box file, my printouts lined up next to it. Ma being tidy and helpful.

'Thanks,' I say. Probably I mean it.

'You'll talk to us when you're ready, won't you, darling?' She turns away without waiting for an answer. Marmalade streaks out. As she closes the door she says softly, 'Ruth's nearly here. It'll be great to have her, won't it? Bex'll be glad to see her too.'

I label the box *Research Sheets (Private)*. Ma won't look if it's marked Private.

Why the comment on Bex? She's my friend, not Ruth's.

There were three missed calls on my phone from Bex. Matt's no good for her. I should have rung but I don't know what to say.

Later, I drift towards waking and hear the sound of a car coming to a halt, a slamming door, voices. Ruth's here. Dawn.

Networking

Forum: what's the difference between self-talk and hallucinating?

Narrative: Mercury 23:01

I talk to myself all the time. Am I getting schizoid? Read something online about bi-polar?

Comment: Moderator Sue 23:01

I really don't think so, Mercury. Perhaps you ought to see your doctor instead of worrying on your own. You do need to talk things through with someone who really hears what you say so that you can get your life together.

Narrative: Mercury 23:03

Talk to you all the time thought you could help

Comment: Barbarian 23:04

I went to three gps in our practice and they all say different. You can't rely on anyone else. If your explaining it like you do, Merc, your not nuts.

Comment: Cybersnake 23:06

You have to take care. After uni I got on a management training scheme and they wanted me to do psychometric tests, other stuff. I couldn't stand it so I resigned, I had to go home till I could get fixed up with a job and somewhere to live and my parents wouldn't let it go. What was I going to do about my debt, references, employment reliability. It was like hell. You end up talking to yourself cos you're the only one understands. Except here obviously

---

Comment: Zenith 00:05

You get different answers according to what people think. I haven't told anybody – don't know what's trustworthy. It feels like I only trust you guys. But you could all be fakes.

Narrative: Mercury 00:22

Thanks a bunch, Zen, that really makes me feel great.

Zef's Blog

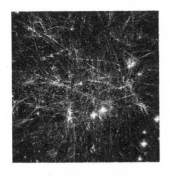

At school there's a take-it-to-bits human body in one of the biology labs. You snap out the heart, lungs and spleen and work out where everything goes. The one for the brain is too simple. You can't see how all the bits fit together. My brain feels like an exploding star – all those electrical connections and I can't track them. People make cyberspace maps of the connections between servers all round the world, I think. This one is beautiful.

Everything seems to be networked. I never thought of cyberspace as a place to map.

Different kinds of real? Marmalade sat on my head this morning to make me get up. His brain is like mine, wired for touching and smelling. I read online that human brains haven't evolved far enough to manage without touching and smelling.

Maybe Bex will talk for real at work today. When we chat online I'm sure it's her, but sometimes there's a time-lag. Online, you could brush your teeth, fell a tree, go running between chatlines. Would that change what you say, going off to do other things, talk to other people and the person on the other end has no idea? I don't think it's funny but I'm the odd one out. I am so glad Ruth is here.

Research Sheets (Private)

Ask PA? what does he know?

evolutionary biologist argues that, in addition to male and female sexes, more than two _genders_ exist in hundreds of animal species. Species with one female and two male genders include red deer who have two male morphs, one with antlers and one without.

Species with two male and two female genders include the white-throated sparrow, in which male and female morphs are either white-striped or tan-striped.

so you can't tell by looking which is which?

the highest number of distinct male and female morphs or "genders" within a species is found in the side-blotched lizard, which has five altogether

human morphs of gender,
who classifies???

Surfing

Total control

Join this site if you want to control your fate. Mould your body according to your will. Despise anyone who says different. Don't network with victims, don't take advice from those who tell you that you are ill, have a condition, are abnormal.

You are far beyond the normal. Nietzsche understood this with his vision of an elite and perfect humanity. Perfection is within your reach if your will is strong. Make your body conform to your vision alone. Focus all your talents and gifts to this end.

Join this site if you are strong enough for the truth.

Zef's Blog

Some guy in Korea reckons if you spend forever online your brain gets scrambled. If I were Korean I'd volunteer, get loads of electrodes attached to my skull so they see my brain all lit up. The man in Korea does research with kids.

An English professor put microchips in his arm so he could open doors without using his hands. Virtual *Open Sesame*, but the doors opened for real. So what I say online must be real, right? Like stories. Ruth spends every summer with us so she can write more scripts, like make-believe, like living in her head. But I totally trust her. Maybe it's because real people have to make her stuff come to life. Her mind must be full of camera moves and head angles and lines to say out loud. And then what she imagines, some actor says it differently and Ruth's idea belongs to someone else. Weird.

If only there was a way to fix words in place like bricks in a wall, so the meaning stays exactly what you want. I used to tell Ruth all sorts when I was little. Even though she's Ma's best friend, Pa doesn't seem left out. Would she understand Zef's blog?

Maybe art = make-believe. Bex's masks make you want to touch them but the ideas start in her mind, same as Ruth's scripts. It's all make-believe.

Like on www.iwannagetoutofhere.co.uk.

You got to dream it, picture it, do it, be it.

Friday August 4

'I'm bored not talking about it,' Bex said. 'You making yourself sick on purpose?'

She brought rolls and water for lunch and we sat on the grass in Maude's Meadow. I flicked a cigarette butt from under my leg. The grass by the benches was thick with stubs, made me think of flattened fungi.

Bex sat cross-legged, skirt tugged tightly across her knees, the beaded fringe trailing around her ankles. Shirley said Bex should send her version of the uniform to head office. She loved to offer career advice. Since Bex had been a Saturday girl for the past two years, Shirley was certain, she said, that Bex could get a designer's job at head office.

I pictured Bex in an office chair, with a computer and shelves and notices over the wall behind her head. She had painted her nails pale pink since yesterday morning and her fingers never stopped moving. The sleeves of her blouses always cover her hands.

I said, 'I could get bored not talking about your stuff.'

'If you roll your sleeves any farther up they'll get stuck in your armpits.'

'Noah made me eat bad peanuts. I threw up all over the kitchen table.'

'You don't eat peanuts, they're fattening, according to you. Bad monthly?'

I swigged water. 'Grim.'

'You're so not eating I could use your cheekbones as a frame for canvas.' A piece of tomato fell out from the end of Bex's roll and two ants rushed up to check it. I resisted the urge to touch my face. 'You wimped out of climbing yesterday.'

'Bouldering. We need to talk about Matt.'

'Look how far I can get my fingers round your arm.'

'He's still posting stuff, isn't he?'

'It's like you want to hurt yourself.'

'You have to do something, stop him.'

'Eat something, it's stupid. Every day I see you picking your food like it's full of grit. You haven't even taken it out of the bag yet.'

'I bet you haven't told your mum.'

'You're on that website again, that extreme health one, aren't you?'

'You're not listening.'

'It's sorted, Joey. For the moment. Please. I am not talking about it.'

Today, her eyes were framed by smudges of green and grey eyeshadow, darkened by black mascara. Her hand rested lightly on my shoulder. I counted the pulses in my throat.

'It's ok, Joey.'

I felt too tired to push. 'Ruth's here. Middle of the night.'

'I practically don't remember when she didn't come every summer.'

'It's like holidays, soon as she arrives.'

'She's almost like family, isn't she?'

Ruth and Mum met in a doctor's surgery when Mum was vastly pregnant with me, and Ruth was expecting her baby, the one that died. No, he was *killed*, in the car crash with his father. *Being killed* can't be the same as *dying*. I didn't want to think about it. I wanted to picture Ruth writing scripts for a living, creating a soap opera world that other people thought was real. Ruth was a magician. She and Bex always got on well.

Bex stretched back on the short, dry grass, balancing the roll on her stomach and spreading out her hair like an oriental fan, intensely black, in fine streaks of crimson and white from the left temple. It's art, she says. Bex makes me think of one of those Chinese or Japanese paintings where tiny women have white painted faces like dolls. Bex is not much taller now than when we were ten. I'm five-eight and she makes me feel huge. For a moment I pictured Matt, his long blond curls tied back for rugby, bulging muscles curved around Bex's tiny shoulders. Giant and princess, I used to think. I pictured his string of posts, the jokes, the smut. I used to like Matt when we were younger. He used to be funny, even kind. I read online that dolphins can turn on one another, torment and rape like humans.

'When's your Ma making chick pea curry again?'

I lay back on the grass, glad of the cool grittiness of the turf, and the high threads of cloud hanging like fleece on a fence. 'What colour blue would you call the sky today?'

'Pale wash cerulean, hints of cobalt.'

A faint breeze carried sounds from the high street – chat, the clatter of cups on saucers outside coffee shops, phones beeping. Everyone sets tables on the street. The shop was as hot as a kitchen by midday. All the suffocating fabric made it seem even hotter. Expensive clothes smell marginally more pleasant than cheap ones. Bex got me the holiday job. We saw more of each other in the shop now than we had done at school for months. 'Noah keeps on about climbing. I tell him to bugger off.'

'I bet he eats like a horse. You'll never manage a climb if you starve yourself.'

I lifted my hands and stared through them at the sun. Sometimes your hands against bright light are see-through. 'I eat enough for running.'

'Yeah yeah. Mum's coming here in a bit.'

I pulled my skirt up above my knees. Bex said, 'Are you wearing lycras?'

'I can't bear this uniform crap. It's ok for you. I feel better with running gear underneath. This floppy stuff gives me the creeps.'

'Sequins over a sports bra. Shirley quite likes you. You do know that.'

'She's got something on her mind, I know that.'

Bex pulled a red streak of hair before her eyes and carefully separated the strands. 'How long's Ruth staying this summer?'

'Ruth's going to ask about you and that online stuff.' A pigeon cooed nearby, and the doors of a bus wheezed. Somebody, on a bench too close, coughed and spat.

'What's this Simon like? You like him, I can tell.'

'What colour hair are you wearing for your mum's wedding?'

Bex fumbled for her roll. 'I'm saving up. Thought I'd have the colours a bit more muted.' I laughed. 'Are you coming or not? You're invited. Mum and Jack said to ask you. She thought your Ma and Pa might like to come too. And Ruth. If she wants.'

'What have you done to your arm?'

She flipped to her stomach, black hair fanning forward. 'Brambles in the garden, weeding. For the wedding. The party's in the garden.'

'The new house.'

'You'll see if you come. To the wedding. You'll have to wear –.' Her eyes glittered through her fall of hair like Marmalade's in long grass. I sat up, shredding a crumb for the ants. They sped away, busy busy. 'You don't have to wear a skirt. Mum and Jack won't mind. Jack's going to be the coolest stepdad.' She pursed her lips, nipping the edges of her roll with sharp, precise movements. 'Bet you could borrow something from the shop. Shirley will lend you something. The skinnier you get – has she asked you, yet, about the show?'

Suddenly she giggled, 'Shirley-girly. Girly-Shirley,' and started to pelt me with crumbs.

We ended up rolling around, like in the old days. White crumbs speckled her black hair. She shook her head violently before grabbing the other half of her roll. 'You used to eat. I exactly remember when you used to eat lots. Now you just poke things round the plate. And you're obsessing about running, do you know that? Grips and pull-ups and bleet tests.'

'Bleep.'

'And what's that about?' She eats like a cat, as if each bite has to be approached with the tip of the tongue before getting pulled into the mouth. Except that cats are picky, not cautious. Bex chose the rolls, she must know they're not poisoned.

Before falling asleep last night, I unfolded the map of Borrowdale, and traced the route of the Borrowdale Fell Run. Seventeen kilometres over Great Gable, Dale Head, Scafell Pike – it wasn't the distance but the heights, the slopes. Running down is often harder than the ascent. The fastest runners do it in less than three hours and the slowest take no more than six. I'd settle for finishing. I needed more practice off-road, in the hills. Running on roads makes you think you're better than you are. Bex doesn't get me and running. 'Come in spacegirl, are you with me?' Bex prodded my arm. I took a bite, swallowing down the mush of bread and ham with a slug of still-cool water.

The only time my body fits is when I fill up my senses with walls and sheep, waves of bracken, heather and scrub oak and tormentil and eyebright, gills that taste of peat, skylarks, stonechats chit-chitting at one another. It's a landscape shaped over centuries. That's why I might like to be an archaeologist. Landscape tells the truth and you have to get to grips with it. I've learned that from Pa. Landscape's not just nature, it's us shaping nature and if we understand how it used to be we might get better at the shape of the future.

'What did Noah do when you ran off?'

'Simon sorted him out.'

'So is he nice to you?'

'What's the pay for that show?'

'Ask Shirley.' Bex wrestled a book out of her bag. Bright yellow and brown butterflies chased each other through a buddleia behind the bench. I watched them disappear in the foliage. I could be a butterfly. I'd like the life-cycle. I pictured winding a cocoon around my body, nobody able to see me change.

Bex pointed. 'What sort of butterflies?'

'Comma, maybe. Clouded Yellow. You are so not interested.'

Bex's eyes flickered whilst her fingers riffled pages as if they knew how to read and were finding the place. You could film Clouded Yellows speeded up and get the whole life-cycle in a few seconds. You could film a rock for years, and rain, snow, sun, night, day would flit past but the rock wouldn't change.

'What's Ruth writing this time?'

A pigeon, tight-breasted as Shirley, played landowner round some office types eating sandwiches on the grass. The girl twisted her legs sideways, short skirt creased tight across her backside, a shiny red plastic skin. The men sprawled, cans between knees. One guy wound his tie around his forehead, untied it. He had stubby, restless fingers.

'Ask her.' The sun was suddenly too hot. Butterflies lifted casually on the breeze, a handful of leaves thrown carelessly into the air. Dried earth caught at the back of my throat.

'You're still in a state about Noah and that climbing stuff.' Bex turned a page.

Running, you think about what's around you, where you're going. You have to notice the lie of the land. And you can lose yourself utterly. But climbing ... that Easter with Noah, all I could think was how lost I'd have been without his rope. At least I got myself off High Spy. You have to do it yourself, in the end. DIY is how you live and die.

Bex was reading like a cat casually hunting. She flicked pages, skimmed, underscored with her finger, as though she were preparing to pounce on the author and demand to know what was happening and why.

'What's the book?'

'As if you care,' not raising her head. '*Metamorphosis*. A man wakes up one morning and he's turned into a giant insect. It's by Kafka. It's really famous.'

'Oh. What's the point?' Bex plays Book Roulette. She takes out books from the library at random and returns them if she's not sucked into the story by the end of the first twenty pages. She says the librarians know her name. I used to go into the library with her. I knew she wanted to carry on reading. 'What happens?'

'I'll know by the end.'

'Thought you wanted to talk about Matt?'

'Leave it, Joey.' Bex looked up with a dark frown.

'Hello girls.'

'Hi Mum, Joey's coming to see you and Jack getting married. She'll borrow a *frock*.'

Zef's Blog

We say we are friends on www.iwannagetoutofhere.co.uk but trusting them isn't like trusting Ma, Ruth, even Noah. Maybe there's Cybertrust as well as Cybertalk. I say more to Cybersnake than Bex but I never touch and smell Cybersnake. Sometimes it's like dreaming, online, it feels real but you know there's another sort of real somewhere too. The guy with the electrodes would work it out.

All the people I chat to are somewhere in space. Online I'm connected to millions of people. It's like putting a dot in the universe and the dot is me and we're all dots who meet in cyberspace. Maybe there's Cybermeeting and one day we'll live in cyberspace. Touching and smelling will be microchipped. But I live in physical space too. Ruth's in cyberspace when she writes her scripts. So is Bex when she imagines her masks and then she gets out the stuff and makes them in real space.

Maybe we all have split minds, or two minds and that's why people say 'I'm in two minds.' One mind is in cyberspace and the other mind has to deal with fingers and tongues and aches and pains. When Bex makes her masks she makes a bridge.

I'm not an artist or a writer. But there's something free in cyberspace, makes me feel easy. I can make myself what I want. Can I bridge that to physical space?

Bex and me. Two dots with a dotted line between us. It used to be a solid line.

Chat

Joey	You're sure Matt can't track you now you've changed your settings
Bex	I've gone through the privacy stuff over and over
Joey	Can you depend on them?
Bex	Jack would kill him or Mum would.
Joey	But you're not gonna tell anyway you said
Bex	Don't want them knowing
Joey	Pa says Jack ought to have been a national park ranger not policeman.
Bex	Suggest it, he'll want something new to do now he's retiring, mum says.
Joey	That craft stuff he's been doing, your new house?
Bex	Your Ma says she'll help with food at the wedding, she rang Mum.

Saturday August 5

Shirley picked me up in her black Range Rover and we drove through Windermere to the hotel, for the show. The car stank of her cologne but I had Noah's mints. I kept thinking about the money and what I could do with it.

Noah said it was hysterical that I was going to be a model and somebody would video the show. Ruth gave me advice. 'Don't look at the camera. Tell yourself it's not there. If you find yourself looking at people in the audience, stare at the forehead, between the eyes.' She made me practise. Noah pranced around the kitchen but I didn't blink. Ruth told Ma that I was a natural. Usually when you look at someone you expect them to look back. I practised looking at Simon's forehead. I wondered if that's how actors manage all the different parts, if they pretend that nobody sees them. Looking without seeing, you could be private in public.

Shirley and I were shown into a long wooden-panelled hall by the events manager. 'This is a first for us, you know. Our ladies are terribly excited. The view's wonderful, isn't it? We're so excited.' The badge on her lapel bobbed up and down. Her red jacket was too tight and stuck out over her hips. The patio doors were open, and women in tight jeans perched on the terrace wall. The manager introduced us.

Two or three glared at me but I didn't care. Shirley said she would give me the equivalent of two days' full-time work. I wondered what she was paying them. The cool smell of lakeside vegetation drifted up. If I really couldn't bear it, I could leap over the wall and disappear in the shrubbery.

Bex reckoned Shirley had been planning the show for months – make-up specialist, hairdresser, a photographer who turned up with two cameras and a tripod. Shirley said, 'I've been thinking about the best angles for the video,' and posed in the flimsy model she'd picked for herself, pinky-green. She'd have worn it in sleet. She meant to be on the video.

In the dressing area, the women stared and I stared back. One of them said, 'What's your experience, love?' She had a harsh accent, Liverpool perhaps, and the tops of her arms were stringy. During the drive Shirley said that a wide age range for models was important. Clients with money to spend had tough, tanned skin, from years spent on cruise ships going round the Med and the Caribbean. Shirley made sure some models looked the same.

'I'm holiday staff. Shirley's.'

Another voice said, 'Well, dear, you ought to look at yourself seriously.' An older woman pushed me towards one of the full-length mirrors that swung on heavy wooden stands against the panelled wall.

I saw this person in black jeans and red and white striped rugby shirt, trainers, hair cropped short, bony jawline, level black eyebrows. The woman behind me tilted her head. Gold and silver streaks feathered her fair hair, which lay snug as a cap on her small head. It was creepy to be standing so close to a stranger who'd already taken off half her clothes.

'You see?' She gestured at my scowl and smiled. 'It's that male-female look. It sells. There's a word for it.' She clicked her fingers impatiently, earrings swinging like silver lanterns. 'You'd do quite well, modelling. You've that bone structure – look at yourself – oval face, tidy cheekbones, broad forehead. Wait till make-up has finished with you.'

'Don't put ideas into her head,' said the Liverpool woman, yanking a tight sweater over her head. Her bony, tanned back glistened in the mirror.

The woman behind me frowned. Carefully I removed her hands from my shoulders. 'It's kind of you to bother,' I said, 'but I'm only here for the pay.'

'Suit yourself. You could pay your way through college, had you thought about it? Your straight up-and-down figure.' She turned away. 'I run the agency. Daphne, that's me.' A gold-edged card lay stiffly in my hand. The print was gold, impossible to read. 'Do you know how to walk?' She laughed when my eyes rolled.

I had to be dressed. Shirley's energy filled the room. 'You can't wear a sports bra with my clothes. That bra flattens what you've got completely. Get it off, pretty please. There, you see? Small tits, hardly anything, perfect. These clothes need a hint of boob to fall right.' She approached with something purple, flimsy, full length. 'You'll have to take off your jeans. Did you bring any black panties with you? White'll show. Anyone got spares?'

Daphne foraged in her case and held up a black thong.

I went behind a screen. The string cut into my crack, shoved the tampon further in, and the triangle at the front barely covered my pubic hair. Girls at school wear thongs all the time. Lads wear jock-straps for sport. Ma won't touch Noah's. She makes him put them into the washing machine himself. Sometimes she makes him drop them into bleach. Now I knew why our washing line was full of sensible briefs and boxers and shorts.

After that, the make-over. My face was turned this way and that by a girl with purple nails who plucked invisible hairs from between my eyebrows, squinted at the box of colours and creams and decided what angles to paint on my face. I began to picture Bex's face, screwed up tight as she assembled the framework for the mask, laying whippy pieces of willow over my face, measuring and fixing. 'Fur, a few pheasant feathers and I'll felt the Herdwick so it creates a different texture. Maybe some simple feather stitching?'

'You look fabulous,' said Daphne in her smoker's voice. Shirley turned me into a walking clothes rack, moaning that I didn't have pierced ears. She made up for it with bangles, scarves and necklaces. The only way to cope was to be someone else, as Ruth said.

Daphne made me stalk up and down the hall between the rows of heavy, padded chairs, and then out to the patio. 'Stand against the balustrade. Perfect. She isn't moving an inch, is she? You wouldn't like to smile, would you? Good, you're a natural. She's great, Shirley. That defiant look. Camera will love it. Now back here. Walk this way.' Daphne wrenched my hips sideways. 'Walk on,' with a slap to my bottom. 'Walk from the hip, use the whole of your thigh, we want the skirt to swing. And back again.' She watched me move as though she were my athletics coach. 'Practise at home, Joey. Put a mirror at the end of your hall, walk towards it, watch yourself.' I imagined Noah's commentary and winced. 'You should come when I'm looking at the video. It's useful, seeing yourself on film.'

I lost all sense of what they dressed me in.

It went on for hours. There was music and Shirley with a microphone and a break for tea and slivers of cake and then the ladies wanted to see some of the clothes again. The photographer ran between tripods. I glanced at him and he gave me the thumbs up.

Two cameras, two angles, so maybe it was like having both eyes form a single image only he couldn't superimpose one upon the other without muddling the pictures. Perhaps he could do something digitally clever, morphing one into the other. You only see your back with a mirror, never as others see you. Nobody sees you from back and front at the same time except your, with the mirror in your hand. Even then, your reflection is reversed. Doppelgängers aren't mirrors. Maybe you don't recognise your doppelgänger.

I couldn't count the clients. I had to concentrate on looking between their eyes. Most of the chairs were occupied, which seemed to please Shirley, and the air reeked with perfume. I tried shallow breathing. They weren't looking at me, anyway, only the clothes. We've a clothes-horse at home. It's collapsible and Ma keeps it in the utility room.

I got into Shirley's car in a stupor. At least her car smelt of car. I pictured women in huge four-wheel drives or long limousines, coasting through narrow roads to houses set far back in landscaped gardens, or to luxury apartments with limestone cladding, bright windows and wrought-iron balconies overlooking lakes. Our windows needed cleaning.

Shirley was deep in fantasy about future shows. The thrum of the engine and her non-stop commentary merged into a hum that made my eyelids heavy. Every time my head drooped I jerked awake, remembering a jostle, a flick across the arm, collisions with a wooden rack. They really didn't like me, apart from Daphne. And I ached. My legs weren't used to walking so slowly and my back was stiff. Ma wouldn't have bought any of Shirley's stuff. She wears the same clothes – trousers, tee-shirts, blouses, sweaters depending on the time of year, jackets with sunflower patterns, or plain gold. She keeps black for disasters. One jacket is bright yellow with black ribbons, in case. If it's hot she wears a skirt instead of trousers. At her school, they know who she is. How Ma is with clothes feels ok to me.

We were not the only people to have spent the afternoon by Windermere. A long line of cars inched forward. Shirley switched off the engine a couple of times. Pa might be home when I got back. He has a suit for the office, stiff jeans, metal-capped boots, scabby fleeces, woolly hats and stained helmets, wet-weather gear against hurricane and tornado, a whole cupboard devoted to snow stuff, all of it probably expensive enough for the rent of an affordable flat. Having the right clothes is a matter of life and death, Pa says. People die on the fells. The traffic queue unclogged itself and we moved into third gear. Fat lambs bounded up a fellside. My legs twitched.

Girls at school want to be fashion models, register online with agencies, take photos on their phones. One girl's photo went to so many phones she had hysterics and her parents tried to sue the school. But the phone isn't the problem, it's the way people use it.

'Soon get you home.' Shirley's voice made me jump. 'Time to wake up. Modelling's more tiring than people think.' She kept glancing sideways, trying to see my face. I stared through the passenger window at the hedgerows, farms, the outlying houses of the town. 'You'll be glad of a bath, I expect. I can't wait. I've been sweating like a pig.' She meant to be kind. 'You did really well, Joey. I've put a bit extra in the envelope. Glove compartment.' I snapped open the small locker in front of me and found a white envelope, sealed. 'That's right.' Beneath the perfume was a sour taint. Shirley was tired, too. I wondered, with a start, if I smelt stale to her. Noah does battle with his body odour. Bottles and sprays line up on his window ledge. Man-smell is different from woman-smell. I can't capture my own smell. People smell different according to mood. I have smelt fear.

'Thanks.' I opened the envelope and saw several banknotes. I realised that I had been a fashion model, all afternoon, and if anyone at school found out there would be trouble.

Shirley reversed up the track leading to our house. I caught sight of Ruth waving, covering her nose. A slime of exhaust was settling on hawthorn berries and rosehips. Ruth opened the door of the car, holding out her hand. I was stiffer than I knew. We waved as Shirley's car leapt away, and the stillness of the evening welled up.

'Why didn't she turn round here like everybody else?' Ruth was already going inside. 'Your mother's been given two tickets for a poetry reading tonight. They've gone out to supper. I don't know where Noah is, or Simon. He's an unexpected friend.'

I looked across the valley. Long shadows undulated down the side of the fell. I seemed to be standing with one leg bent, like a stranded heron. A lamb bleated. We had passed fields full of sheep, one ewe barely upright with the fierce tugging at her teats of two nearly full-sized young. I wondered if the lambs ever went to a ram for comfort. Rams would have been taken off after the tupping and driven away until next season. Fertility rituals.

Pa said this morning there's a male pygmy hippo that changes the ratio of X and Y chromosomes if it's kept in captivity, to produce more female offspring. Apparently this makes his life easier with less competition from other males. Designer hippos.

I swear Ruth is psychic. She didn't ask how it went, she didn't ask what I wanted for supper, she didn't tell me about her day. Whilst I was in the shower she went into my room and took everything away to wash. She left a tall glass of fresh lemonade, full of ice, beside my bed, and opened all the windows to fill the house with the sounds of the evening breeze, our rowan trees swaying, and the house martins chattering in the eaves.

Zef's Blog

Man wakes up as bug, little legs sticking out through the pyjamas.

Caterpillar/chrysalis/butterfly. I do not want to do my university application.

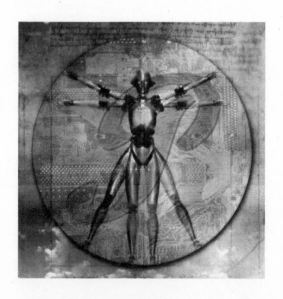

A professor inserts microchips into his body and feels his wife's movements on the other side of the Atlantic. A volunteer with fingertip implants tries to sense how far away things are, through vibrations, like bats. Deaf people have microchips inserted.

Mutation or transformation? human/cyborg/transhuman? Maybe I could email that professor. What would I ask?

Research Sheets (Private)

http://www.ucas.com/students/applying/howtoapply/
personalstatement/presentation

Practice personal statement

You can enter up to 4,000 characters (this includes spaces) or 47 lines of text (this includes blank lines), whichever comes first. You do not have to use all the space provided. When you save text, the system will tell you how many characters are still available or if you have used too many characters. You can preview your statement after you have saved it.

I want to study archaeology because I am interested in exploring human nature through artefacts and hope to be involved in original research as a student, using scientific methods. In a gap year I hope to gain experience as a volunteer, and have already visited several archaeological digs, to find out what people do on site. I enjoy analysing evidence. In my spare time I go fell running, often over land which has been farmed or mined for many centuries. I am fascinated by the information the land holds and how this can help us with conservation or sustainable development in the future and this application is a total waste of time. My mother is a headteacher so the last thing in the world I am going to study at university is a subject where I'll end up teaching. My father is a biologist and conservationist. He works for a wildlife charity. I am quite interested in wildlife but I'm never going to study sciences. My brother is already at university doing economics. This application might divert my parents' attention until I'm ready. If I go to university they'll be sure to want to help with fees etc, and I don't want their help. In case. I want to stay in the Lake District. I remember enough of living in London to know I never want to live in a city. I need money to sort myself out, so I can choose. I've just got disgusting work experience as a fashion model. The money is far too good. At school they say that going to university is one of the most transforming experiences anybody can have. How do they know? Transforming starts inside.

Saturday evening

'Supper's almost done.' Ruth switched on the television and put the remote into my hand. 'Whatever you want. There was a black thong? Not yours, I guess. It's in the wash.'

She made pasta with anchovies and garlic and chillies and heaps of grated parmesan and I sucked up spaghetti like a kid until I saw that I had eaten almost half the portion so I stopped, and carefully spread what remained around the bowl. There was a trickle of oil on my chin. Ruth poured herself a glass of red wine. I went to the bin to clear the plate.

'I'm just doing a spot of work,' she said. 'Is that ok with you?'

She threw me a cloth for wiping down the table. Our table had lots of burn marks and knife indentations from when we'd painted and cut out and carved and done experiments when we were kids. The smell of old, stale wood was really comforting, a bit oily, a bit aromatic. It helps you to know where you are, who you are, family old things.

I laid my head against the cool wood, inhaling it, remembering our London kitchen in the basement, with light filtering down from above, and a tiny yard where my sand-tray from childhood and Ma's pots of lavender silted up together.

'I guess you must be worn out. I hoped you earned a big fat fee. I'm just going to sit here with my notebook. I'll put on some music.'

'Dreary walking up and down, that's all.'

'You managed ok, I reckon. The woman looked happy.' She loosened a vinyl from its cover. 'Brahms piano music ok?'

'Ok.' I wandered towards the sofa at the other end of the kitchen.

Ruth returned to the table, opened her notebook, took out a pencil, and instantly slashed at a page. I half-expected her to tear it out but she gazed intently, flipped over the page and began to write. She has a tiny laptop but says she prefers to write by hand when she stays with us. Things come out differently, more concrete, she says. I watched her through half-closed eyes, her ash-white hair falling forwards over her face. Noah and I used to try to distract her when we were younger, screaming or banging a door, but nothing would make her react. She had gone into an invisible room and closed the door.

I stretched out along the sofa, wedging myself into the crack between the seat cushions and the back. The sofa was old, too, but not from living with us. Pa had picked it up at an auction soon after we moved here. The sofa sat before the long window with its back to the kitchen. You could be out of sight but still in the room, if you wanted it like that.

The big metal kettle on the slow hob sputtered and hissed and a pencil faintly shushed over paper. The deep, dark cushions of the sofa swelled to enclose me. Images from the afternoon wafted under my eyelids like fragments of a dream. The faint after-odour of onion soup drifted towards the open window. It must have spilt on the hob.

The pencil slowed, stopped. There was a heavy sigh. My eyelids flickered. Other people's lives invented, other peo-

57

ple's lines written, other people's feelings, dreams. Where do stories come from? The pencil started moving again, fits and starts, crossings out. I floated. After a while Marmalade was heavy on my belly and had been there for ever, gently breathing up my nose. I opened my eyes and looked into his. He clawed me with his best love, stood up on his stiletto paws, turned round several times to massage my guts and flattened himself when he was satisfied. We closed our eyes. I dreamed in the rhythm of his breathing, asleep and not asleep. Dimly I knew that he patted my chin with his delicate hooked paws and carefully inserted a claw into my nostril. At one point I saw through a slit in my eyelids that he was staring into my face whilst flexing his paws on my shoulders. He wanted something. Then I slid down into dreaming again, mirror, coat-rack, whitened knuckles, a great grey boulder, Bex, a white dress, a scratch along a bare white arm –

– and the door clattered open and Marmalade and I were clutching one another. He tried to wriggle free, shoving with his hind legs but I hung on until he gave in. Ma said hello to Ruth, and someone slapped open a cupboard door and switched on the ceiling lights.

'You can't see a thing in here, surely to goodness.' That was Pa. 'Let me bring you –,' still banging about – 'here, perfectly good desk lamp we never seem to use. That's better. Ruth, you aren't even using ink, for God's sake.'

I fingered the cat's ears, feeling about for his catty thought. He has an exceptionally bony skull. Inscrutable. *Where does inscrutable come from?* A bottle clinked, glasses, the scrape and drag of the kettle being moved to the fast hob, somebody muttering. Marmalade belched up a fishy, rank blast of air. The vibration in my back pocket meant incoming text. I wriggled the phone free but my eyes were still gummed up and the back of the sofa cast a shadow over the screen. *This phone is dying.* There are faster phones.

22:32 Bex

Where r u? chat?

22:33 Joey

Asleep. log on soon my
phone's crap x

Pa was complaining and Ma was defending Noah, as usual. 'He's ok, Andrew, we have to trust him. If he messes up, that's his choice.'

'Not if he keeps on expecting you to do all his laundry.'

'Oh come on. That's trivial. It's easy to put it in with our stuff, anyway.'

'I've two spoilt shirts.'

'He's devoted to all of you.'

Ruth's calm voice, followed by a splutter from Pa. 'You are ever the peacemaker, Ruth, and you can come again. Only you weren't here for the unending rows at Easter.' I heard Pa's smacking kiss and Ruth's protest. 'You'd have liked the poetry reading this evening, Ruth.'

Someone rustled the pages of a newspaper. 'Mollie, there're some terrific sessions this month. I haven't been to the arts centre yet, this year. What about next Wednesday?'

'What's the date? Next week's hopeless, it's the day when

we get the big exam results in school and I'll be in it up to my neck getting the stats right.'

'What's up with Joey? Noah's no help, is he?' Pa's lowered voice made me shiver and I tightened as the door to the back porch slammed open.

'What's that rubble by the gate? I nearly broke my ankle.' My brother, raucous.

Bottles chinked. 'You look as if you've had enough, Noah. Andrew, watch out.'

Glass shattered on the tiles.

'It's never enough after a Saturday night. Full-on. Si, don't, I'll do it, my mess.' The scratchy sounds of broken glass being gathered into paper, muttered curses and laughter.

Pa sounded surprisingly calm. 'You know the way the garden slopes? We thought we'd build up soil, support it by a wall, get a decent veg area. I was going to get Harry from the farm up the back, he lays walls like other people lay hedges, but Joey wants us to build the wall. We thought it was a worth a shot, didn't we Moll? I arranged for half a tonne of stones to be dropped at the end of shift. Didn't expect it today, not a Saturday. Good though. I like the idea of building a wall.'

'God knows we've got enough stones of our own but it would be a real turn-off to dig them out just to build it. Joey's downloaded a plan from the internet. Don't give me that look, Noah. It'll be perfectly good. We can all muck in. I love the idea of our own dry stone wall.'

'You're never relying on something from the internet.' I heard the thump of a discarded boot, Noah's usual scorn, even to Ma.

'I remember a summer when Joey spent a week building a dam in the stream at the back and the field flooded. You were only too glad she found something she wanted to do, Moll.' Ruth sounded cheerful. 'You had to step in, Andrew.'

'I'd forgotten that. I had to bribe Harry.'

'It was a pretty effective dam.' Ma's voice was dreamy.

Simon said, 'The dam must have been rather large.'

'That's my sister's big fat ego for you.'

I squirmed into the sofa, sweating. Marmalade leapt off with a reproachful thud, padding out of view. I could fill a page of notes on being out of place.

'That's not fair, Noah. She knows what she thinks. That's different.'

'She's your little girl, you mean.'

'My son, she's better informed than I am about some things. I wish she'd come out when I'm on field work, like she used to. She was great company on a trek, soaking up everything I told her.'

'She's good at running off.'

I bit hard into the back of my hand. Marmalade made a stately return and I inhaled his fur. He smelt of cows, oil, the barn at the top of the rise, grass.

'Don't be trivial, Noah, just because she wants different things from you. I'm looking forward to wall-building. Ruth?'

'Sounds good.'

'Joey seems to be a very unusual person, very strong -minded.'

'Don't get your hopes up, Si.'

'Noah, go to bed, take a shower, something.'

A teapot was filled. Pa said something I couldn't catch and Ruth said, 'You'll have to come to terms with it, Andrew. She's practically eighteen. It's her life.'

I couldn't keep still any longer and tried to sit up against the weight of Marmalade.

'You've woken up.' Ruth peered over the top of the sofa. 'We made too much noise. I should have warned them.'

Ma leaned over with a glass of red wine in her hand. She looked flushed. 'How did it go? You must have been exhausted. You don't sleep on a sofa.'

Pa executed one of his scissor-leg moves across the arm of the sofa, hurtling into position as if he was playing musical chairs. He scooped my legs across his lap and seized Marmalade. 'How's my girl?' he said, patting my knees. 'My little glamour starlet, my fashion cat.' Marmalade shrank his skull to escape through Pa's arm.

'Truly, how was it, darling? Did you hate it? But you survived.'

'She's tense as anything, sweetheart, you're not well, are you? Should you have gone today? She didn't need the money, she's got her allowance.'

Noah's voice. 'Sweetie-pie.'

Simon said something and Noah said, 'Well, all the girls do it, fathers, little fingers.'

Pa drew a breath, but Ma got there first. 'Noah, drink some water, will you?' She reached down to smooth back the hair from my forehead. Her fingers were cool. 'It's not about money, Andrew. It's about independence.'

'She's independent all right. She doesn't tell us anything.' Pa's face was kinder than his voice.

'Of course not, would you? I never did. Give her a break. She's probably worrying about the results, anyway.'

'I am still here, you know.' I got myself up. Marmalade pushed into my legs as I made for the door, stumbled into Noah.

'Look – hey Jay-Babe, it came out all wrong.' His face was serious and the contrast between his bright blond hair and dark eyebrows was oddly touching. Maybe that was how Fi wanted him to look. She would have been the one to bleach his hair.

'Do I look sorry for myself?'

We scowled at one another. Noah shrugged. 'Have it your own way.' He turned away, muttering under his breath. I didn't want to hear.

Marmalade was waiting at the foot of the stairs and bounded ahead, pausing to check my progress. I pulled myself up the stairs by the banisters and fell into my room.

Even if I could tell them, Ma and Pa, they would never understand. I could hear it now, their unspeakably reasonable conversation. *We must have done something wrong when she was a baby, we didn't respond properly. There's something in the genes we haven't accounted for, is it in our DNA, yours or mine, your parents or mine? Or the chromosomes. I shouldn't have gone back to work so soon. We didn't ask enough questions when she was born. She never liked dolls. She never liked cars and guns.* Bit by bit they'd go over and over the story of me as they saw it and bit by bit I would be eased out, like the stubble-skinned pink corpses we find on the drive, under the eaves where the house-martins nest every year.

The room was suffocating. I trudged to the window, flung it wide. A blush still lay on the horizon, water-colour alizarin crimson, staining the hills. Bex's notebooks were full of colour washes, textiles swatches, free-flowing pen and ink designs. She shaped what she saw. A bird floated down into the valley, into the rising shadows as the long flank of the fell heaved itself into the sky.

Chat

Ruth   Where are you?

Joey   In my room.

Ruth   Why chat, why not knock on door? Cup of tea?

Joey   Need to talk to you.

Ruth   Kitchen?

Joey   This, please.

Ruth   I'm only upstairs in the attic.

Joey   I need to write it down.

Ruth   Ok.

Ruth   Joey? Still there?

Ruth   Shall I just come down to your room?

Joey   I don't know what gender I am.

Joey   Knew it was a mistake.

Ruth   Sorry. How long have you felt like this?

Joey   Forever. A long time.

Ruth   I'm not sure what it is that you don't know. That's
          clumsy. I don't want to misinterpret.

Joey   I know what I feel.

Joey   I don't know what to do.

Ruth   You haven't talked to Moll and Andrew?

Ruth   I'm making my usual pilgrimage to Orrest Head in
the morning. Come too?

Networking

Narrative Zenith 01:31

Just told someone sort of in the family, can't bear to think of seeing her in the morning. What do I do? What if she tells my parents? Don't think she will but can't sleep.

Comment: Laylo 01:40

It's the middle of th nite and no one thinks strate then but hang on in there

---

Comment: Maz 01:50

It wouldnt be normal not to get in a panic so dont worry about it get some sleep like Laylo sez. We will all still b here 4 u!

Comment: Moderator Sue 06:30

You can ring me if you want to. Talking to someone close is good if you want to come out. We all start somewhere.

It won't be a mistake. Whatever her reaction was, don't lose belief in yourself. What was her reaction btw?

Zef's Blog

I wrote the unsayable. I'd never have said it to Ruth in the room.

If I hadn't read it online I wouldn't have.

It feels now there's another person, not me, in Ruth's mind. I've put a new idea into her head and I can't control it.

It will be far worse telling Ma. Noah. Pa. Pa will never get it.

Zef's Blog

It's barely light and I have not slept.

Marmalade never passes judgement.

He came in at four o'clock to say hello, curled around my legs, smelt me, stayed.

I'll die if anything happens to him. Her.

My mind leaked out of the ends of my fingers, through the keyboard, into cyberspace. It got loose. I don't know how it happened.

I will have to count stairs to get out of this room.
It'll be ok if I hold on to Marmalade.
My Life As A Cat.

Might just as well have **Published** this.

TWO
WALL

TWO

WALL

Research Sheets (Private)

Building a dry stone wall in seven easy steps

1. To make the foundations, clear and level the ground.
2. Sort the stones into small, medium and large. Measure the longest stones. The width of the wall will be slightly less. You use these stones to make the wall stable.
3. Mark out the area: lines of string drawn tight, stakes, chalk lines – whatever comes to hand.
4. Start building. Each layer consists of the long stones laid crosswise (tie stones) and smaller stones jammed between as close-fitting as you can get; like a jig-saw. Choose each stone as if it were special.
5. Build up layer by layer, with larger stones bridging the gap of the stones below, like any brick wall.
6. Make sure the wall tapers slightly inwards so that the top is narrower than the base.
7. Finish the top with heavy, flat stones. You can stand these on end for a neat, solid effect.

I can feel each stone in my hands, heavy and certain, the wall taking shape. Harry can keep off

Sun 6 Aug.
This wall is Mine.

Sunday August 6

Marmalade sits around my neck like a scratchy collar. He doesn't like being walked down the stairs but I need him. Ruth is already in the kitchen. I go to the cupboard and poke around for sardines, Marmalade's treat. I rip back the lid and set the tin on the table. He fishes out chunks with his paw and drops them on the table so that little smears of rainbow oil spread across its surface. Then he gulps at the fish as if we have been starving him.

My fingers stink of sardines. Ruth is clearing up from last night. I hear her placing the mugs with precise clinks on the dresser and slotting dishes into the wooden racks. I stare fixedly at notches in the wooden surface of the table. I remember that one, Noah made it, though he says he didn't. Ruth speaks and Marmalade dashes to the utility room, the cat-flap.

'It's a wonderful morning. It will only take two ticks to get the coffee and bacon rolls sorted.'

'Don't mind.'

I can't stay still. Already the sky is blooming with a steady, glowing light. I wish I were with Marmalade romping in the field. Suddenly Ruth throws the towel on to the draining board and pulls me into a hug. She's soft and solid as a cushion. I feel the floor beneath my feet.

She gets business-like, prepares the picnic. Her eyes are lowered but her expression is normal, unfussed. She sends me to the utility room, 'Small rucksack, do you think?' and wipes the sardine streaks from the table.

I stand looking through the open door into the garden, catching sight of Marmalade's stripey rump in the hedge. Suddenly my throat closes up.

As we drive over the crest of the hill, we see Windermere's crooked expanse, with mist still sitting on the surface of the lake. We take the usual track looping up the fellside to Orrest Head, Ruth talking to herself as much as to me about how easy it is to break your ankle on a track you know like the back of your hand, a track that you could walk up in flip-flops. She pauses at a turn in the path, beside a row of memorial benches. We stare out over the lake, glimpsing the great expanse of water between shards of mist. 'I reckon I've been up Orrest Head at least thirty times.' I shrug, feeling the light frame of the rucksack settling between my shoulders. 'You probably think it's man-made.'

'The route up Scafell Pike is man-made, I guess.'

She likes the comment.

By the time we reach the top of the Head, the mist has drifted to the edges of the lake like fluff on eyelashes. The water is a steely blue, already spotted with motionless white sails. Maybe there will be more breeze at water level. Maybe sailors treasure the moment, the waiting.

I breathe in the sappy smell of early-morning grass and try to imagine Ruth standing here on her first walk. I wish the skylarks were still spooling their songs across the sky. The fledglings will be trying their wings. Then I shiver, seeing all too clearly in my mind's eye the photograph of Ma and Ruth, swollen-bellied, bursting with laughter. There's a presence at my shoulder, looking at the view, someone who could have come into being alongside me.

I don't believe in ghosts or hauntings. Doppelgängers? Would I see myself reflected in the lake, my true soul that I don't believe in and might be gazing up at me like in myths?

Ruth shifts from foot to foot, turns west, north. Across the lake the green mass of woodland invites the eye, and once more I shudder. My stomach yawns. Women must like that sense of unborn child in the womb, they must actually want it. The organ is located in my guts. I have the anatomy but not the nature.

Already I am looking for the words to tell Ruth why my gender lives in my head, why it has nothing to do with sex. At school they say if you can't find the words it's because you haven't done the thinking properly but that's it. There are things that words can't describe.

Ruth pivots on her heel to take the rucksack from my hand and sit on the bench. She pats it so that I will sit down. The coffee smells surprisingly ok.

'Bacon roll?'

'I won't, thanks.'

She hands me one of the little red pottery mugs that usually swing from the spokes of a metal stand on the worktop. 'I don't like drinking coffee out of plastic mugs if I can help it. Since we weren't coming far I thought Mollie wouldn't mind. I left a note.'

She looks so different from Ma. She is nearly as tall as Pa and naturally broad. Ma has short dark hair, a square jaw, a slight build. Ruth's shoulder-length hair has been almost white for as long as I can picture her. She's not fat but solid. Her face is a long oval with a pointed chin. They must have seen one another as opposites in that waiting room when they were pregnant, about to see the doctor. Pa is tall and sort of skinny, still, despite all his work outdoors. Noah's shoulders are only developed by deliberate pumping iron and he is no more than two inches taller than me. He doesn't much care for that. Ma says I have Pa's build, and Noah is more like her. But Noah is changing his body shape.

Ruth's difference is more than physical. She tends not to ask many questions, and Ma never stops though her questions are often about life and the universe. They have the same habit, though, of looking at you straight. They both listen hard.

Right now, sitting alongside Ruth on the bench as the sun rises up the sky, and with an early hawk balanced on a thermal, making its mark on the universe, my mind grows quiet. Even my shoulders lose the hunch. Ruth gazes out at the lake and the trees below us flex their branches in the blossoming light. The coffee is more bearable than usual. Its bitter taste and spicy aroma seem to define the sharp, intense nearness of pine and heather.

'What you said online last night. I thought I ought to reassure you that I'm not going to talk about it – not even to you, unless you talk first. I don't want you walking on eggshells.' I picture walking on eggshells in bare feet and my toes curl.

Ruth picks up the flask and holds it on her lap. She screws and unscrews the lid with one hand, not seeming to notice.

'Ma says you don't put us into your episodes.'

She sets the flask on the ground where it topples, rolls to a standstill. 'I don't ever intend to do that, no. We're a scriptwriting team. If I have an idea about a character, what that character might do, I put it to the others. We toss it around. Any new character has to fit the scenario.' Ruth writes about people living in a new village, somewhere near Nottingham. 'After a while it gets hard to know who had the idea in the first place.' She swallows a mouthful of coffee. 'You start believing the character's real, because there's an actor.' She eyes me through the steam from her coffee, and I rest my own mug against my lower lip. I used to hate coffee but drinking it with Bex I've come to put up with it. 'What I do, what we all do, is give characters a secret life, like a voice nobody else hears. It means that there's always tension, always the potential for an argument. Like real life, of course.'

Ruth's eyebrows are golden brown. Ma says her hair used to be golden brown too. When did the colour change? 'You mean like me.'

'I was thinking of myself, as a matter of fact.' She reaches for the roll, fishing out a slice of crisp bacon, crunching it in half. 'I've come to realise, as I've got older, that whenever I'm talking to most people they're busy thinking about something else. I do the same. Except with close friends. With close friends, you listen.'

I jump as she suddenly looks intently into my face. 'I suppose.'

'You've told Bex how you feel.' She states it so calmly that I can't find words to reply. An empty water bottle lies under the bench. Ruth nurses the empty red mug, her eyes still focussed on me. 'You haven't talked to her. I thought she was your closest friend.'

'Yes.'

'You trust her.'

'Course.'

'I just wondered.' I cross my feet. Startled, I see that I have not laced the trainers properly. 'I couldn't sleep for a long time last night. I kept remembering you as a child.'

An itch frets under the arch of my left foot and I yearn to snatch off shoe, sock, make the blood run red into the turf. Furtively, I roll my foot against a stone, finding a sharp edge. 'If I was in your series – if you were writing words for me to say – for someone like me – what would you write?'

'Who's like you?' She plucks the mug from my hand. 'Are you going to finish this?' Dregs of lukewarm coffee splash across her lap but she brushes them off. 'I couldn't write words for you. I couldn't do it.' She looks genuinely surprised. 'Maybe that's not quite true. I guess I would leave you silent a lot of the time. Watchful.'

Watchful. If she'd grown up being me, she'd have been watchful too. 'What's that thing when they put thick black lines on published stuff? Like censorship?' My fingers tighten around the edge of the bench. It's spongy with age. A fingernail catches at a splinter. I feel like she's got a clue for me, only neither of us knows what it is.

Ruth looks alert, curious. Her eyes have brightened. 'Redacting.'

'But the words are still there, underneath.'

Ruth reaches for the thermos with the toe of the yellow-striped trainers she has worn for years. 'The words are still there but you've made sure only certain people can read them. You're thinking so hard I can almost hear the cogs.' I want to ask her about the dead child, the man she married whose name I do not know. 'You don't want to live a censored life. Do you?' She opens the thermos, pours dregs into her mug, tests them, upturns the mug.

'People sort of don't read straight. They interpret.'

'You're a bit nervous about that.'

'Maybe.' My epitaph could be Maybe.

'I am beginning to think you must be one of the bravest people. Much braver than me. I merely remember that once

I had a family and now I don't.' I cough to cover my exclamation. Her shoulder tightens but she does not look at me. 'I lock up the memories I don't want to think about. I picture a wooden box, a kind of treasure chest.' She tilts back her head, closing her eyes. Sunlight turns her hair red. 'Sometimes I lift the lid and take out a picture. It has to be at the right time.'

'When's that?'

Ruth reaches towards me, I shrink, but she is capturing the silky thread from which a tiny spider suspends itself. Carefully she sets it down on a chunk of greenish slate wedged under the bench. 'I was wondering what made you get online to me last night.'

The hawk stoops, soars again, thwarted. Birds chatter in the trees below. The mist has lifted and the far hillside is every shade of green you can imagine. Bex knows words for green that artists use but I sense there must be far more shades of colour than ever can be turned into words. What do you call that kind of green-into-gold that's entwined with green-into-bluish-purple on Claife Heights? It's so real my heart wants to burst.

Ruth clears her throat. 'Like I said, I couldn't sleep. I couldn't put you out of my mind. There's one more thing I need to say.' Someone far off laughs or shouts – so far away that wind and the warmth deaden the edges of the sound. I cannot tell whether Ruth has heard. She sits very still, hands folded in her lap. 'Lots of people dish out advice but they don't live your life.' The hawk is perfectly balanced on its column of air. Below, on the lake, white sails flutter. Ruth might be talking to herself. 'It's a bit odd if you are going to send me messages when I am in the same house but if that's what you prefer.' I could drift like a hot air balloon, a cloud. 'I'll try and reply sensibly but you can delete, anyway.' Say and unsay. I straighten up. Deleting chat isn't straightforward at all. Chatlines are stored out of sight, somewhere in cyberspace, on that map of exchanges. 'If you aren't going to eat the roll, let's go down to the lake and feed it to the ducks.'

The far hills spread themselves against the horizon like ripples on a purple tablecloth. The lake heaves and glitters, and voices coming closer resonate between the trees. Ruth wraps the mugs in a cloth and stuffs them back into the rucksack together with the flask and the plastic bags. Do I understand the one more thing she had to say?

I kick at the stone that was my scratching post. 'Thanks.' Ruth hands me the rucksack and gives me at the same time her quiet, familiar smile. We stand aside to let the new arrivals pass. They nod, say hello. I follow Ruth, down the curving track through the trees. 'I bet he's not out of bed when we get back, your brother.' Ruth slows, stops in the middle of the path and uncertainly I come alongside. She bites her lip. 'Is it still ok to call you Joey?'

A vast blue sky waits for me to say something. 'I guess.'

At the bottom of the hill, Ruth says, 'I thought about doing some gardening later.'

I say that I am going to lay out the plot for the dry stone wall so I'll be in the garden too. I bend, pick a chunk of rock out of the embankment beside the path. The rock is rounded, cold and solid in my hand. Sometimes I run with stones in my hand, for weights. I lift it to my nose. It smells dense, earthy, of itself. I wonder if climbers have lots of different words for how rocks smell. I carry it in my hand all the way back to the car.

Ruth says as we climb in, 'You could try telling Bex.' The idea makes me stiffen against the seat. I fumble with the seatbelt. 'I feel she'd understand.' As she moves to help

I want to shake off her hand but she knows, snatches her hand away.

Under my bed are two cardboard boxes full of old school files, all sorts. I have to finish the draft of my personal statement for university. I have to clear out junk, make sure I keep my research stuff somewhere different. It occurs to me that Ma could poke about in it if she wanted to but she won't. I know she won't.

Research Sheets (Private)

www.ethicsinanewworld.org

Tony Radice on Posthuman Ethics and a postgender world

The more we investigate the complex interplay of biology, environment, and our evolutionary characteristics of creativity and playfulness, the more likely it is that gender diversity will increase to the point that classification of individuals by gender will become irrelevant. Already, the inhabitants of cyberspace use multiple virtual selves, creating modes of knowing that were previously unrealisable or even non-existent. I predict that the outworn model of human development posited on a single, perfectible identity will be replaced by one where self-actualisation flourishes in a myriad forms. Today's youth are probably already living in this postgender world, creating our posthuman future.

→ side-blotched lizards – 2 sexes, 5 genders.

→ Thailand – 3 sexes? M, F and transsexual?

trans-sexual = crossing from one sex to another?

trans-gender = male in female body/vice versa?

5 morphs of gender for lizards so what
about people? NO BOXES to tick?

Zef's Blog

Daphne wants my number. I don't want to talk to her.

Ground cleared, wall area marked out, shallow trench dug out. √

Simon helped out a bit yesterday. He's got a lunchtime shift. Ruth weeded all day, filled the recycling bin. Then I attacked my stuff, shoved into boxes what I don't want to throw out, not quite yet, put them in the loft and rummaged. Next to the water tanks, I found another box I'd forgotten. Two paintings I did when I was 8. Ma is sentimental about our stuff, though she says she has burned all her past and nobody will be able to write her biography when she's dead and famous.

Noah could never be bothered with anything that didn't involve scissors and a knife, but I used to spend hours at our table, painting and drawing. Noah was good at making stamps from pieces of sponge, potatoes, anything he could cut up. Prints from another life. I laid them out in a row on the loft boards.

Then I found one of those cheap lined exercise books. I must have got Ma to buy it for me, and a few of the pages were filled with drawings, with writing round the edges. I was trying to be a scientist. I went through a phase of writing lists, too. I listed all the things in the kitchen. Then I found the pages where I wrote a holiday diary when I was seven. I wrote in careful letters between the lines. There was even a paw print. You don't get paw prints online unless somebody digitally inserts them.

Inside the back cover was a faded photo of Noah and me. I was blinking into the sun. Noah was holding my elbow. As I looked at the photo my left shoulder twitched. Noah had tried to put his arm round my shoulders but I wasn't having it. I wrote about being on holiday in a narrowboat. I know it's me in the photo, but it looks like a stranger. A connecting thread from then to now marks ten years of living in the same evolving body, the body in the mirror that isn't me.

Networking

Forum: applying for university

Narrative: Zenith 22:22

Stuck on my personal statement. Anyone know website –
ideas to copy and paste into application forms? Waste of
energy when there are more important things.

Comment: Cybersnake 22:23

I know I was messed up about what happened to me after
uni but uni was great so go ahead and take it seriously
because you get away from home and start being you.

Comment: Moderator Sue 22:30

Try not to be influenced too much by what other people

say, Zenith. Family can be terrific if you trust them. Have you told them yet?

Narrative: Zenith 22:31

I want to find out about testosterone.

Comment: Cybersnake 22:45

Have you been to the dr?

Comment: Barbarian 22:56

Try www.getting-personalforuni.org/

Comment: Moderator Sue 23:01

Zenith, what do you really want? Your posts confuse me.

Zef's Blog

The exercise book sits on my bed. My heart is beating faster than usual. I ought to be working on an assignment but I can't concentrate. The memory has streamed back so vividly that I could be there now, seven years old, peering at the window beside a narrow bunk where my reflection blinks back at me. Ma comes to pull the blind down for the night. I lie inside a wooden box that now seems to smell of kitchen table. And all night long a voice sings in my head because I know why my drawings show me in shorts. I don't have to be like the girls in my class at school. Girls sit around or skip or bring out their dolls. Boys run and run and run, up and down steps, round the girls on the grass, sometimes with a ball, but even if there isn't a ball they run. I'm better at running than anyone in my class. You can run much better in shorts than a skirt.

Marmalade coils around my legs, bindweed, trying to trip me up. I don't have a secret stash of sardines. Maybe I still smell of fish. How could I explain him to anyone outside our family? Our cats have all been called Marmalade, Pa's idea, from when he and Ma were first in London and a cat adopted them. Its life was short and when it died, they went to a refuge to find another. Pa said that it was Marmalade in his second incarnation, though the new cat was a queen. Morphs of gender.

Noah was kind when I was little. Sometimes he let me beat him running.

Chat

Bex	Come round tomorrow night?
Joey	You never said a word all day.
Bex	Never sure who's in the shop.
Joey	Miss Paranoia. Matt won't come.
Bex	Our new house is amazing.
Joey	What does your mum say about Matt?
Bex	My room you will be astounded our stuffs tiny here
Joey	Do the girls like it?
Bex	Susie's ecstatic, Tess isn't saying
Joey	Jack must be counting the days.
Bex	Asleep on his feet! You will come?
Bex	BTW Susie and Tess will ask what you're wearing. For the wedding

Wednesday August 9

Bex and Matt were ok till Bex brought the photos to school last term. Jack had been working on the renovation for ages and the house was taking shape. He'd sorted out all the planning problems, Bex said. Lots of people looked at the photos, said she ought to post them, like Extreme Makeover, before and after, stuff like that.

Matt said he'd post them for Bex, she said no, they started to argue and I had to walk away along the corridor. But their voices rose and a crowd got round them, blocking the corridor till a teacher shouted at them to go to their lessons and other teachers came out of their classrooms to see what the fuss was about.

Bex said that she didn't want other people looking at her photos. She didn't know who they were. Matt's shoulders got bulky like he was ready to tackle and you could see him taking deep breaths. He started a rant about privacy settings and Bex said she didn't trust anyone's idea about privacy except her own and Matt said he supposed that meant him too, and he snapped his hair out of the sweatband, shaking long blond curls over his face. Afterwards one of the girls said he looked dead sexy, like a lion and I said it was the lionesses that do the hunting but nobody listened to me. The Bex/Matt bust-up was far too interesting.

Matt said Bex had shown the photos to everyone in her history class anyway.

Bex said there were twelve real people in our class and she still had the photos in her hand and nobody else could show them off on her behalf and she practically spat at him, she was so angry. Matt had taken a step back that he didn't mean, you could see from his fists.

What started out with Jack making an old house into a new one turned into a fight about privacy, only it wasn't just that, it was about Matt telling Bex. It got totally out of control, a campaign with people who didn't know Bex or Matt and who weren't even at our school posting garbage online about Bex, because Matt was going to be captain of the rugby team. Matt posted garbage too. He and Bex'd been around one another for over a year and then, because of an argument over posting photos that weren't even his, he gave her a kicking online, to spread it about. It was more than a squabble about privacy.

I met Caroline in town, soon after Bex broke up with Matt, and she started to ask about Bex and Matt, only she choked up. 'Bex isn't saying anything. I shouldn't be asking.'

Now I was going to the new house and a month ago I wouldn't have waited to be invited, I'd have been helping Bex to pack up, move. The new place was only about twenty minutes' walk away from ours, like the old one – just a different direction, different part of town.

It was a still, calm evening, one of those times when the wind can't make up its mind, moves there and back again like a tide on the turn. Half a dozen children were throwing a ball, their voices echoing off the buildings around the green. Two old guys sprawled on the grass with their huge rucksacks propped against each other like extra bodies. Two women leaned on their bikes, chatting. The grey stone had a pink tinge. Garden walls are different from dry stone – lots of old mortar, plants creeping in and out. *Our wall will hold the plants.*

I stopped, poked the wall beside me with the toe of my shoe, dislodged a small landslide of dead mortar. Somebody shouted and I jumped, but no eyes turned in my direction. I stared across the green at the two women who were swinging helmets as they talked. Bex and I used to wear school uniform, till we went into the sixth form. Now we were back in uniform again, but in the shop. Uniforms are supposed to average out the differences between people. They hide them, too. I never thought of that before.

Our tutor at school said we needed to think strategically. I don't understand what she means. She posted something on our tutor room monitor.

I am part of the problem and the problem is part of me. The most likely way of changing the problem is to change me.

She said it was one of the best ways of gaining control over a situation. Yeah.

My eyes hurt. My ears ached. Ever since Saturday my entire body had been groping for clues as to whether or not Ruth had spoken to Ma. Maybe I told Ruth because secretly I wanted her to tell Ma, for me. Maybe I thought she *would* tell, even when she had promised not to, because she was Ma's best friend and thought she should. Maybe she had already forwarded to Ma my chat messages, cut-and-paste, maybe it was already out there on some website. Maybe she'd let on to Bex already, getting ahead of me. My epitaph, *Maybe*.

I leaned against the railings. I had walked all the way here without working out how to tell Bex, without finding how Bex and I would stand face to face, and I would tell her. 'I'm not a girl.' Face to face, I'd say it. I tried to picture her face as I said it.

'That's not our house, silly.' Susie's face looked tiny under a huge pink cycling helmet that twinkled like a tiara. She was a small version of Bex.

'New bike?'

'Jack gave it to me. He said it's an unbirthday present, my birthday's not till September. Tess's got one too and her birthday isn't till October.'

'It's a wedding present, too, maybe?'

'Oh yes, I suppose it is.' She stood astride the new pink bike with her face beaming. Pink ribbons fluttered from the handlebars, shin and elbow pads were pink, and even her small feet, firmly on the pavement, wore pink trainers.

'You're very pink today.'

'It used to be my favourite colour.' Her face went pink. 'What's your favourite colour?' I didn't know. She shook her head, looking exasperated. 'I'm on look out, come on.'

'How old is your unbirthday? I forget.' I stepped out of the way so that she could manoeuvre the bike.

'Nine, silly. You do know.' She placed a hand on my arm to steady herself. 'Tess isn't eight till October so I'll be two years older than her not one year, just for a bit. You are getting me a present, aren't you?'

94

I never ask why there were so many years between Bex and her little sisters. There are things you don't ask. The question forms but an alarm rings in your head. Susie's wheels glittered ahead and I chased along the pavement behind her. I've known them practically their whole lives. 'Your helmet flashes!'

Susie would think I was old. 'It's so just what I wanted.' She had a high, clear little voice, turning heads on the other side of the street. Somebody laughed. 'They're diamonds. They're not really but I pretend they're precious diamonds.' She twisted on the saddle to cast a look at me and steered artfully around the corner to stop dead beside a gate. 'This is our new house.' Her grey eyes watched me with bright, intense expectation.

At first, it looked like any old house, with a door in the middle and windows on either side. But it was different. The front door was painted a deep chestnut brown. The windows on either side of the door had stained glass panels, not old-fashioned but modern-looking, birds with flowing golden-brown feathers, pheasants ready for flight.

'Joey!' Susie sounded reproachful as she shoved the gate open with the wheel of her bike and crunched up the green shale path. Were they Honister Slate Mine chippings?

'It's amazing.'

'It's the best house ever.'

The garden looked old-fashioned, with tiny little hedges made into neat squares and lavender growing in the middle of every square. Susie leaned on the handlebars, her eyes brilliant beneath the over-sized helmet. Insects hummed, and bees hovered and dived around the bobbing heads of lavender. A couple of butterflies perched. *Bex hasn't properly told me about this house. Photos don't show it.*

The air was cool in the shadow.

Caroline's little house could not have been more different but I had always liked it. It was a bit like a toy house, in a small grey toytown terrace. There was a tiny yard at the back that Caroline filled with wooden planters for growing herbs, three tiny bedrooms upstairs, and the front door opened straight on to the street. Caroline's an artist and her hands have a life of their own. Sometimes she'll be talking and looking at you but her fingers are busily working away, pummelling clay or stitching at something very precise in an embroidery frame or twisting wire. She lives by graphic design. Once she borrowed a ladder so she could whitewash the house. Bex and I had to stand at the bottom of the ladder to stop it from slipping. The little sisters were very little, at the time, and we kept having to shoo them off.

Tess hardly ever speaks. She looks like a tiny Caroline, a sort of bud, closed up, small face in a frame of dark hair.

I didn't see what Susie did with her bike. She stood in the doorway with her tiara in her hand, yelling, 'I've got Joey, Joey's here!' and leapt across the threshold. Noah and I used to have a competition to see how far we could get along our hallway from the front door, in one jump.

There was an impatient wave – a small hand insisting that I should hurry up. I tripped over the step, fell onto my knee. Small amber and terracotta tiles made a mosaic floor in the porch. *Caroline's style. They've been making this house together.*

'Come on, come on.' Susie's piping voice issued its commands. Was she always this bossy? I saw pale golden floorboards the length of the hallway and, to my left, a huge wooden stand for coats, the same wood. On my right was a curved wooden cupboard, gleaming so that you wanted to stroke it. It looked as if someone had made it who loved making things from wood. I stroked it.

Then Bex was there, and Caroline, and Jack slicking down his thick grey hair from a shower, the muscles tight at the angles of his jaw. 'Do you like it?' He had the soft Cumbrian accent and big frame of a farmer, from growing up on a hill farm. He always seemed to wear the same out-at-elbows rusty-coloured jumper. *If only all the blokes in the world were like Jack.* Caroline's hands and lips were pressed tight as if to stop the laughter from bursting out. Bex stood behind them with a gleam on her face that was new to me, unsettling.

Jack said, 'Are you doing the guided tour before tea, Bex?' and we set off, with Susie hopping from foot to foot to make her trainers sparkle. Bex opened the door into the main living room. Jack had taken out two floors of the old house to make a great room like the hall in a stately home. At an upper level, all along one side, was the kind of gallery you think minstrels must have played in. Wooden railings, the same mellow-yellow wood, edged the gallery. And fixed to the wall below was a ladder. Bex sent me up the ladder first.

At the top it wasn't just a gallery, it was a whole other room with a big circular window. You could look out to the garden and the low fells on the other side of town, or you could look down into the living room, at the huge open fireplace and the stacks of logs already in place. Up here there were chairs, a table, lots of drawers, artists' stuff.

'It's Caroline's!' stupidly pleased with myself.

Bex's face was still polished. 'Jack made it for her. He didn't ask her, he just did it.'

Susie appeared through the door at the end of the room. She must have used the boring stairs and hurled herself at me, trying to swing from my hands. 'Jack's been ill so he could do it a lot faster,' she said, walking up my legs. I flipped her over into a somersault.

Bex frowned. 'Don't say that.'

'Why not? It's true.'

Susie was ready to be somersaulted again but Bex seized her wrists to pull her away.

'You haven't mentioned Susie's hair.'

'She had her helmet on.'

Susie buried her face against Bex's shirt. Bex mouthed so I said, 'Nice hair.'

Susie twisted round to give me a suspicious, anxious glare. 'It's really nice isn't it?'

'You've had your plaits cut.'

'I'm going to be a fell-runner, same as you.'

Now she wanted to show me her room.

'Go and tidy it up then, and tell Tess too. Go on.' Bex pushed her sister through the door to the landing.

'What's that about?'

'What do you think? She wants to be like you.'

I had nothing to say. We left Caroline's gallery and stood on the landing, where Bex patted another of the doors. 'It's oak, Jack loves oak and he found a whole lot of people to do this. He says town's full of craftsmen dying to do a decent job instead of hack-work.'

I pictured Jack in his rust-red pullover, Caroline's glowing face, his arms gathering them in. Bex would be gathered in too. I wanted to go home.

Susie clattered behind a closed door, talking to herself.

'Where's your room?'

'In a minute.'

'Jack seems ok.' There was a story about Jack I didn't really understand. He had stopped work, had been about to go back but didn't. Bex said he was ill but I couldn't see it myself. He didn't stay in bed, he didn't stop going to Caroline's and then he and Caroline were going to get married. He wasn't ever going back to policing though he loved it.

'Yes.' Bex pulled her hair into the familiar black and crimson screen, and again I sighted the faint white and red lines on the inside of her arms. Maybe she'd been trying out tattoos. A small pulse ticked at her throat, and she smelt of roses. There were roses in a vase.

My throat was dry. Now was the time to tell her. 'Jack's not my idea of a policeman.'

Bex stroked the banister on which we were leaning. 'Well he won't be a policeman so you won't have to think about it.' Something sharp in her tone made me draw back, but she seemed not to notice. 'Anyway, if he hadn't been off work, the house wouldn't have been done so fast and he and Mum might not have been getting married this year.'

The moment vanished as Susie flung open her door with a bang and I had to inspect her room. It was a child's room, I suppose – a wide window ledge filled with small soft toys, neatly lined up, a table by the window with bottles of poster paints pushed into a cluster where she had been painting, and a small set of shelves where books were lined up in height order. No pink. The floor was of polished wood and a simple blue and white striped rug lay beside the bed. 'This is nice,' I said, trying not to sound surprised. 'No pink.'

Bex laughed. 'It's already changed several times and I expect it will again. Last week all the toys were on the bed and Susie could hardly get into it. She had a pink bedspread too but she's kindly given it to Tess.'

Susie said stiffly, 'Jack gave me the bike and the pink stuff so it would be rude not to wear them.' Her mouth was set in a stubborn fullness.

'When did you stop being pink?'

Susie drew back her shoulders. 'I can change my mind if I want to.' I could see an elaborate explanation evolving before my eyes.

'Let's go, we've lots to see still,' Bex said, yanking me by the wrist out of the room.

From the landing you could go into Caroline's gallery and other rooms – a family bathroom, a big room for Caroline and Jack, another for Tess. The ordinary staircase at one end folded back on itself to reach the third floor. Bex quickly threw open doors for me to see each room but all the while she was urging me along towards the end wall where a series of handholds made a climbing wall up towards a navy-blue Alice-in-Wonderland door. For a moment I couldn't breathe.

Bex's eyes glittered behind her hair. 'Jealous? You can go first,' pointing at the holds.

Someone – Jack? – had shaped each piece of oak so that it snuggled into your grip. He – she? – made allowance for the polish, that could make the holds lethal with use, by shaping deep indentations and finger holds so that you could jam your hands thoroughly into them. I climbed. At the top I called, 'Ma would have a health and safety fit,' but Bex had disappeared. Her voice sounded from the other side of the door.

'Wait on, Joey, I'm unlocking the door,' and it swung inwards to her room.

'It's a tower!'

'Isn't it a miracle?' She was full of glee. I realised that there was a door at the other end, to be reached from the third floor landing. 'It was Jack's idea.'

'You don't like climbing.'

'I said I wanted to be able to pull up the ladder behind me.'

We went outside to the top landing. The only other room at this level was a small bathroom. Two doors led to enormous storage areas under the eaves.

Jack had used every inch of space. In our house the loft is where everything is shoved that we don't know what to do with but can't lose. You climb up a wobbly metal ladder you have to haul down and you're in danger of knocking yourself out if you don't manage it properly. Sometimes it slides down like a weapon. Pa says he'll replace it one day when the birds have stopped singing and the lakes have run dry. Ma says she'll pay someone to do it but somehow it never gets high enough on her list of things to do.

'What do you think?'

'It's awesome.' We stood alone at the top of the house, hearing the sounds of a meal being prepared below.

I could tell her now.

Caroline called. 'Come on, tea's ready.'

Bex stared at me, frowned as I opened and closed my mouth like a fish in a tank. 'Tea!' came the call again. Bex shrugged, swung towards the staircase. I stood with my hand against the wall, closed my eyes. I might as well have been underwater, gasping for air. My throat ached. I followed Bex down the butter-yellow stairs to the ground floor and the big dining kitchen.

'It really is a dream house, don't you think? You see things on the telly but this just is.' Bex had been waiting in the hallway and now bowed me into the kitchen as if I were an acquaintance, not a best friend.

Tess came to the table, ate like a bird, all picky and fast, and literally hopped away without saying a word. Susie kept up a rapid flow of chatter, regardless of Caroline and Jack's questions to me about school next year, about what next after school. Caroline explained her latest project and Jack said Bex's exhibition was the best wedding present she could give them. I promised to come to tea again, soon. The words slid out easily. Bex might not want me for a friend when she knew. They might not want me either.

Bex took me upstairs to show off the dress she was going to wear at the wedding. I was to wait at the bottom of Rapunzel's ladder until she called me. She was much faster up the wall than I expected, standing away from the holds like an expert. When she shouted, I was clumsy on the climb, pulling myself hand over hand towards another chance to speak, another moment.

Bex's dress was very plain, the colour of cornflowers, sleek and short, a close-fitting sheath. Round her shoulders was a wispy blue shawl thing. Her shoulders were bare, creamy white. I couldn't remember the last time I had seen Bex's shoulders. The dress had long sleeves, like gloves, with a different, clinging fabric that flowed gracefully over her wrists. I had nothing sensible to say. 'Bluebell.'

'What? Look here.' She held up a carrier bag with the shop's logo. 'I brought stuff from the shop for you to try on. Take it home, make Shirley happy, make Mum and Jack's day, choose something smart that you can bear. It's ok, Shirley said we could borrow it. She's thinking free publicity.'

'They won't notice me.'

'I'll notice. So will your Ma. Your dad could come too. I'd love Ruth to come.'

We stood face to face. Light from the setting sun streamed through the windows, deepening the blue of the dress, the pallor of her face. I swallowed, breathed deeply. The room smelt of roses. The words began to rise up into the back of my throat. *Bex, I think they got my gender wrong. Bex, I don't feel right in this body. Bex, what do you think?*

Bex turned to look at herself in the mirror, playing with the lacy drape of the shawl. 'I dyed this to be the same colour as the dress. What do you think?'

In the mirror, her eyes looked up and down the reflected bright dress, the shawl across her white throat. She smiled as she lifted the shawl against her cheek, allowed it to settle into new folds.

Behind her blue reflection, my dark eyes stared back at me. I saw the faded shirt, the tense set of shoulders, the lock of black hair flopping over the sun-brown forehead, the shadow behind the lady. A dummy, worse than, a block, a stone. Its mouth opened, shut.

'What do you think?' Bex's reflection grinned, turned away. She stooped to pick up the bag at her feet and the moment vanished, again. 'You're hopeless. Take it, take the stuff, I picked things that Shirley likes. You'll be ok with them.' She flung it towards me. Slowly, I picked up the bag like she was giving me suicide pills. 'She wants you to do more photo shoots. You won't have to buy anything. I'd like you not to wear a rugby shirt. Joey?'

The green was empty and cool as I drifted home. The sun had gone behind the hills and houses but colours were staining the sky in a wash of blues, pinks, greens. Everyone at home would be flopping about, wearing the house like comfortable old clothes. How would Susie and Tess feel about their amazing house when they were seventeen? Bex was becoming the princess in the tower. I don't know how to talk to princesses.

I stopped at our garden gate and leaned over, contemplating the foundations for the wall. There was a lump in my throat again.

Chat

Bex	Have you tried them?
Joey	Jack says he knows a dry stone wall expert ☺
Bex	You haven't opened the bag.
Joey	Jack ought to be a woodsman
Bex	Did tess speak to u?
Joey	Susie never stopped.
Bex	Cn i come to yours friday
Bex	Get your ma to do chick pea curry?
Joey	If I must
Bex	Is Noah behaving?
Joey	I've stopped listening
Bex	Bet having Ruth around helps? And Simon?

Zef's Blog

Marmalade let a shrew loose under the bed. I had to lock him out, find a box, catch the shrew, bypass Ma on the stairs, set it free into next door's garden. Pa says nature's full of surprises but Marmalade's a predictable shrew-catcher and so am I.

Bex, I need to be a boy. I say it into Marmalade's ear and he says, what's the fuss? Only these aren't the right words. *I need to be a girl who can be a boy and a girl. I'm a different morph of gender.* Bex never used to frighten me. I have to be in the same room to smell her reaction. I don't like it when she asks about Ruth or Noah. I get the feeling she and Ruth text each other and I really really don't like it but I haven't any evidence. It's me being Mr/Ms Paranoia. This blog is my honesty box.

Marmalade howls outside the door and I have to let him in. I wish I could stop him catching deadstock but I can't.

He wants to poach on my chest or the keyboard but when I throw him off he leans against my feet.

Me+Marmalade = get-hunting.

Bex, I have to tell you something really important about me [insert blank for answer]. I got the wrong label when I was born [another blank. I can't imagine it.] I've been brought up as a girl so I probably look and sound like one but in my heart and mind I'm not a girl [and she says?]. Doctors call gender dysphoria but I don't feel ill, not really. Well, I'd like to rip out my bloody uterus of course but doesn't everyone when it's period pain?

Research Sheets (Private)

Bex, I have to tell you something really important about me. J

Oh really? Dark secrets? B

Ok, I'm listening. B

Well, not exactly dark. J

I think I got the wrong label when I was born. J

What do you mean? B

Well, it's sort of hard to put into words. J

I've been brought up as a girl so I and sound like one but in my heart I'm not. J

Well you've started me thinking now so you'd better get on with it. B

I don't think I get you. What do you mean? B

I feel mixed up, guy/girl somehow. J

Joey, I've known you forever, you're not remotely like a guy. B

I sort of guessed there was something different about you. B

It's very confusing. J

You're all uptight, what you say doesn't make sense. You ought to talk to someone. B

How long have you felt like this? B

I'm trying to talk to you. J

Not totally sure what I am inside. Parts of me I'm ok with. J

You should be talking to an expert. B

And so on and so on. On and on and on.

MISERY

My holiday diary

We went on a narrowboat. Noah and I liked it alot. It was all painted nicely. Noah and I did lookout for the boat. Noah and I jumped off the boat onto the path. Lock gates were really exiting. We drove the boat in the gates and daddy wound the handle to close the gates and then he let the water in and we floated upwards.

I was as good as Noah at jumping then he got cross. My legs are smaller than his and I liked the smell of the water. It was cool. There were lots of flowers on the path. Daddy wrote a log about plants and trees on the path and said he was going to put it into the house magazine. On Wednesday when we were watching for a time to jump boys came on the path on their bicycles. One of them could ride on his bicycle without holding the handle bars. He could balance. He cycled backwards and forwards in one place without holding on. One of them said Did we want to jump on the bank so Noah whispered. We didn't want our parents to see or hear. I could feel his heart beating. My head was pressed into his chest. He jumped ok and it was my turn. The boy who was best on his bike said "Bet your brother will fall in" and Noah said No Way but I jumped and I did it and the boy said bet you fall in going back so I jumped back and I didn't. And then mummy heard and she got cross. But Noah thought it was funny the boy called me his brother.

Thursday August 10

Ma dropped me off for work. She was spending the day with Ruth going zig-zag over the passes to the Roman fort at Hardknott.

At breakfast:

'Joey, my darling, you look like a ghost.'

'She's on her extreme diet kick.'

'At least I'm not stuffing myself with steroids.'

'Will you two stop it?'

'Moll, I'm working from home today. Do you want me to source plants for the wall?'

'Is it your driving lesson after work, Joey?'

'Oh yeah, what time's your test, sweetheart?'

'Is there any more bread, please?'

'I used it making sandwiches for Mollie and me to take out, but I'm defrosting rolls in the microwave if that's any help.'

'I could rearrange my schedule, sweetie, give you some driving practice.'

'It's ok, Pa, thanks anyway.'

'Plants would be great, Andrew, if you can find the time.'

As I got out of the car by the shopping centre, Ruth leaned from the passenger window to mouth, 'Doctor'. The shadows under her eyes had gone. My eyes were raw.

Ma drove off like she always does, on a race-track. She loves her car. It's bright red with two broad white stripes running from bonnet to boot, and she fizzes as soon as she sits in the driver's seat. She bought it when she got the private school job. It's her image, Noah says.

Our headteacher drives something black with shaded windows. He's always there when I get to school and when I leave, so perhaps he sleeps in his car. Perhaps he's a werewolf, really, a kind-hearted one with a passion for collecting litter.

'Is it a boy or a girl?' That's the first question parents ask when a baby is born, but I read online that for one in every 4,500 births the gender isn't clear. Like me? A baby's birth can't be registered till it has a gender.

There are five morphs of gender for the side-blotched lizard. Cyborgs have no gender, or if they do, it's not what humans understand.

I wandered up the steps of the shopping centre, past some graffiti that had escaped

~ white heart jen ~

through the sugar cloud around the Pick 'n' Mix stand, and towards the main exit. The girl in the tight red skirt was wobbling on high heels, struggling to raise metal shutters in front of her shop. There was a scab on her ankle. The takeaway shop smelt of fresh bread. People queued, eyeing the hot sausage rolls, the flakes of pastry scattered on the paving like fish scales. A greasy paper bag fluttered, was recaptured. Someone with a tidy mind.

My mind was about as useful as an empty paper bag. I was ok at putting one foot in front of the other. I would be ok for the driving lesson. I felt queasy at the thought of seeing Bex when I hadn't told her.

The flower stall girl was dunking today's fresh deliveries into buckets of cool water, filling the air with the scent of freesias, lilies, roses, carnations. I stopped to inhale the giddy scents of cut flowers, green stems, cold water. The flower girl caught my eye, squinted.

Tourists dawdled on the high street waiting for shops to open and the cobbles gleamed where someone had thrown water to clear a patch of vomit. Tables in the sun outside a coffee shop – Bex's black hair swinging forward over her book – town clock striking the three-quarters. The flow chart crumpled in my bag. *You should be talking to an expert.*

I leaned against the bookshop window to watch Bex reading, thumb and forefinger flicking backwards and forwards between pages. Maybe she reads the story back to front. Maybe when Ruth and her team design stories, they create a timescape like the ordnance survey map. *Here's a crisis, this symbol means two people sitting on a bench with true confessions and this sign is for the fork in the road that the character keeps trying to return to, because s/he took the wrong turning. But this is a time map, haha, no turning back.*

Mental note, make a map not a flow chart. I love maps. You don't need words on maps, you follow the symbols, used your compass, look at the lie of the land. I watched as Bex flicked backwards, put down the book. You can't live your life backwards.

A beep, and a text from Noah. Peace offering, unusually polite. Would I like to go out with him and Si tonight. Simon has started to look sideways at me and it throws me off balance. He did it again this morning in the kitchen, not a sizing-up look, more considering. He had a word in his mind, was measuring me for it. Hope it isn't *redacting* or *inscrutable*.

As if she had heard the beep, Bex looked up, saw me, waved, pulled out a chair.

'I don't suppose you'll share a blueberry muffin.' She gave me the knowledgeable smile through the swinging veil of black hair. My stomach yawned. 'I thought not.' Laying the book on the rickety table, she went inside. I picked up the book to read its title and flip through the opening pages. Bex reappeared with a small tray, balancing mugs and a muffin. She set down the tray, snatched the book from my hand and put it into her bag. It was another of her handmades – old denim lavishly oversewn with layers of bright fabric, hand and machine stitching, buttons, sequins, braid. It looked extraordinarily expensive and delicate, as if tropical flowers grew on it. Ma bought two of her bags.

'I've never heard of this novel.'

Bex had produced a knife and was slicing the muffin like a loaf of bread. 'One for you and six for me. I like the title.'

'The Getting of Wisdom.' I shook my head. 'It looks old-fashioned. What happened to the other book?' I poked at my slice of muffin. 'The man who woke up as a bug?'

'I finished it. He died, before you ask. Anyway, you only read factual books. Which top? Which top for the wedding?'

The legs of my chair squealed on the pavement. 'What?'

'You haven't opened the bag.' With a neat gesture, she placed a piece of muffin between her lips. 'There's a red top you ought to wear, you'd look fantastic, but I put in something basic too. Shirley's going to ask you to model the new stock, you know that.'

My lips were sticky so I must have eaten. 'Are you really going to art school?'

Bex took a spoon to the cappuccino froth at the bottom of her mug, licking it with a precise pink tongue, cat-like. 'You could read instead of obsessing about your muscle-weight ratio.' She screwed up her eyes. 'You look terrible. Have you given up sleep as well?'

'Shirley's going to twitch all day.' Bex gave me a look almost as straight as Ruth's, but I did have a point. Shirley was taking delivery of a vanload of new stock. Yesterday she had printed out the email from her boss, reminding her to organise the weekend sale of current stock, and make room for the winter range.

The sun was warming the metal table, winking on the surface of spilt coffee, patting the backs of my arms. I closed my eyes, hearing the low, comfortable hum of the town on a fine summer day – a cluster of grey houses, sprinkled in a fold of land between the high rounds of the Howgills and the mountains where I pined to run. The moment was ripe. I opened my mouth, the town hall clock whirred into action and Bex was scooping up her bag before I could speak. 'What?' she said.

The little back office steamed. Shirley's face was red, beads of perspiration dribbling down her neck. 'The stockroom's jammed so tight I can hardly get in. You'll have to take turns if I'm going to get through all this stuff. I've been here since half seven, did you know.' The mug of tea at her elbow wobbled dangerously. 'Everything needs new tags. You'll have to reorganise the rails. There won't be room for both of you together. Joey, you start please.' She nodded at me as if we shared some special understanding.

Bex rolled her eyes and slid off to the shop while I squeezed into the stockroom. Its one high, tiny window had been painted shut, and the smell of fabric heated by strip lighting was worse than a charity shop. You couldn't breathe without fibres clogging your airways. I had to strip off my lycras after half an hour, cringing as the skirt glued itself to my damp legs. The automatic labeller kept slipping in my hand.

'Joey? Fug in here, my God. I suppose I'll get someone to unstick that window. I need you, come quick.' Shirley's voice was shrill.

I fumbled for where I'd slung my lycras across a rack. 'What is it?'

'There's a situation out here. I don't know what to do about it. Come *on.* I'll take over.' She had been spraying cologne again. Passing her I had to share the air and felt sick again. She wore an outfit from the new stock, **Autumn Glory, Harvest Gold** and **Berry Red**.

The high space of the shop was practically Antarctica, by contrast, and at first I leaned and breathed. The shop was almost full. Punters poking-about had sent slippery skirts and blouses into heaps below the racks. I scowled. I would have to put them back on the hangers.

I couldn't see anything odd. An old man in a green waxed jacket leaned with closed eyes against the wall, wearing a dress with red and purple flowers over one shoulder and another, all green and orange birds, over the other. For a moment I wondered if he was ill, if this was the crisis, till a woman pushed through the heavy swing doors from the changing rooms, snatched off the birds and flowers and left behind a plain turquoise dress with straps. He struggled to extract from the inside pocket of his jacket a stuffed antique wallet.

Bex stood behind the counter, facing a middle-aged man and woman who didn't seem to be buying. She had pulled her hair completely over her face, clamped her arms.

I picked up several stray hangers, went crabwise between the racks, trying not to jostle customers or dislodge yet more stuff and stepped behind the counter to join Bex. Her body was rigid and she smelt all wrong. The hair on the back of my neck prickled.

The man had short, densely dark hair and a shadow across his cheeks that made me think "designer stubble". Noah's special razor for designer stubble is his latest toy. Bony jaw, perfect white teeth and a smile at Bex as if he knew her, reaching out across the counter with his hand palm up. Silky cream shirt, cuff unbuttoned, tan. It probably *was* a silk shirt, a bit like some of our stock, a close, grainy weave and slightly uneven colour. It looked much more expensive than anything Shirley would sell.

I couldn't imagine how he would know Bex. From the corner of my eye I caught the slight rise and fall of her chest and the slightest waver of a strand of black hair. At least she was still breathing.

The woman was pale where he was tanned. She would never have bought her clothes at Shirley's or attended a fashion show in some hotel. She'd have gone to one of the boutiques down the hill, with price tags big enough to feed a family of four for a couple of months. She was skinny, with a wide leather belt tight around a fine milky shirt, like his.

He had a soft, surprising, local accent. 'I know it's not our usual arrangement, seeing you now, but I must give you *some*thing. Julia and I, we want to mark the occasion. Make it special.' He had the sort of voice that could curl up in your ear and stay till Christmas. He left his hand on the counter, leaned forward. The smell of musk and something spicy filled the air as his chest rose and fell. There was a heavy gold ring on his thumb.

The woman said, 'I don't understand.' Her small-boned face was defined by straight dark hair cut into a long bob. That was expensive, too. Something about her was naggingly familiar. 'Your father wants to give you something special. Not like for your birthday or at Christmas.' Someone had punched me in the solar plexus. 'Of course, he's a bit concerned now, with your mother marrying again after all this time.' Her dark eyes were fixed on the tanned hand with its gold thumb ring. The thumb twitched and she added, 'Sorry, not concerned, I mean, interested. And he's interested in you.'

I counted to *five, seven, ten, thirteen. Father.* The hubbub in the shop turned into sound effects in a play. Bex grabbed her hair with both hands and pulled it tightly back from her forehead. Only her eyes moved, to glance at me. 'Would you mind serving these customers please? Shirley's asked for help.' She vanished between the high racks of clothing. A couple of startled customers turned back to their chat. *Nineteen, twenty, twenty-one.*

The counter was cluttered by pink and green leather purses, racks of bracelets, ear-rings, catalogues for winter, for the loyalty card, the credit card terminal, a basket with trinkets priced at a fiver to tempt. *Father.*

The woman fingered her necklace, another designer item of intricate gold links set with something glittery. 'You're a friend.'

My head bobbed. I couldn't stop it.

The man turned his eyes upon me like he was seeing for the first time anyone other than Bex. He had pale blue eyes with large dark irises, flecks of green and black in the blue.

'Dominic Ainsley. Rebecca's father.' He waited a beat. 'You had to work that out. I'm sorry. Julia, my wife.' He was shaking my hand before I could back off, his skin hot and dry. Hers was cool and hand-cream smooth. 'Perhaps you could help. It's not easy.'

The woman and I stared at one another. *Thirty-one, thirty-two.*

'She's not called Ainsley.'

The woman tugged at her necklace. 'She was born an Ainsley.'

The man laid his hand on her arm, and she went still. 'I expect you know all about the wedding. I wish them all the luck in the world.' He paused to smooth back his hair, letting the creamy silk cuffs fall down his upraised arms. Not

just tan but muscle. He works out. *Forty-three, forty-four.*
'I gather that Rebecca will be a bridesmaid – well, all three
girls I imagine.' He gave me a thin smile, took the woman's
hand. 'I'd like to give her something to mark the event – jewellery, flight to Florida, whatever she fancies. I wish I could
give something to Caro but I realise that's tactless. I hear
Jack's a real character.' He tucked the woman's arm through
his. *Fifty-five, fifty-six, fifty-seven.* 'And something for Su-
sannah and Tessa.' A pause. 'I've never seen Tessa. Not even
a photo. I don't know what she'd like.'

Sixty-nine, seventy. I got rid of them. I took his email
address, mobile number. 'I'll ask Bex,' I said pointedly. The
woman gazed at him like a girl waiting in the school corridor for the lad she was desperate to get.

At lunchtime Bex and I went to Maude's Meadow. It had
stopped raining and Shirley had calmed down. We sat in
silence. Bex looked blank as I turned bread roll into crumbs
for the pigeons and after a while she joined me. 'Don't ask,'
she said.

She opened *The Getting of Wisdom* whilst I spread out
my map of Scout Scar. I had decided to mark out a route to
run rather than just turning right or left as the mood took
me, but I hardly saw the contours. A small wind lifted the
edges of the map. I saw Jack, with his work-marked hands
and sawdust in his hair. In my mind's eye Tess ran across the
room, wrapped her arms about his waist, leaning into him.
Dominic and Julia Ainsley made me think of city, business,
interiors, Bond Street. I'd never been to Bond Street. Bex
snapped through the pages at great speed, no backwards
scanning.

On the way back to the shop after lunch, Bex stopped
dead in the middle of the road. 'I see him once a year, in
October, by arrangement. An afternoon.' When a car horn

blared I leapt for the kerb, but Bex was still rooted. I had to run back, drag her to the pavement.

The afternoon was endless.

But the text made me smile, almost.

15.39: Noah

> Hey Jay-Babe, wot abt pix?
> Fab film at Warehouse, my
> treat

The Warehouse is a café-cinema, with half a dozen huge sofas. I had only been once before, maybe a dozen or twenty people watching the film. Driving lesson, then sitting in the dark, filling up with other people's stories. I texted to say yes. Bet it was Mr Polite's idea.

Shirley kept Bex in the stockroom all afternoon. By the time of closing up, Bex had pinched a couple of scrunchies and tied her hair into bunches. The skin was drawn so tight across her cheekbones I thought her eyes must hurt. It came to me that the woman, Julia, didn't want Bex's father to get back with Bex but he was going to anyway.

Bex and I stood on the pavement as Shirley locked the doors.

'I've got to stay late, driving lesson.'

'Were you thinking of walking me home?' Clutching her denim bag like a cushion, Bex reminded me of Tess hiding behind her mother. I felt a pang of fear.

Zef's Blog

When I get into the car for my lesson I never smell panic from the person before. He keeps the car fresh all the time. Mr XL-Drive-To-Success.

He's like shepherds I've seen at the Rydal sheep-dog trials and they read each other's minds, shepherd and sheepdog. Last summer we saw four shepherds, seven dogs and a quad bike bringing down the sheep off the fells above Haweswater for shearing. All we heard was sheep bleating, and the shepherds whistling, or calling out in language I couldn't catch. But the dogs did. Nobody got in a state, the sheep simply poured down the fell-sides, like foam by a weir, and the dogs were masters of the universe. When the shepherds whistled they flattened into the heather, getting longer and thinner, and their noses all pointy. It was like Marmalade shrinking his skull and doubling his weight when he feels like it.

Maybe dogs and cats living with humans change, reacting to us. It's the other way round from man into bug. I love seeing a sheepdog riding a quad bike. He lets the shepherd ride too, sits bolt upright, so much enjoying himself, so bright and beady-eyed. The dog looks as if he's waiting to take over driving when you tell me Dad. They say you have to pay a fortune for a sheepdog puppy. It's like the shepherd's mind passes into the dog's, and the dog is a part of the shepherd that can run free and fast. I wish I could go hunting in the field with Marmalade.

When I drive, I sit up on my perch, all bright-eyed Me. I have to work out what to do from Mr XL's finger twitches or arm-folding or looking out of the window. If I pass my test I'll be me+car. He says I'll pass. He says, 'You drive like a lad not a lass.' Apparently I don't fart about, I drive at thirty not twenty-six, I reverse without getting in a lather and I don't frighten pedestrians. When some clown tries to beat me up I don't bat an eyelid. Then he says, 'Maybe you do drive like a lass after all.'

I could become a cyborg, a driving instructor, me+car.

Me + quad-bike would make room for Marmalade.

I would be a cat-keeping cyborg though he'd rather hunt alone. I wonder if me + laptop is cyborg. I don't see why

I have to be Either/Or. Pa had to say F or M for my birth certificate but he didn't know at the time that he was wrong.

Found this on wiki

A **cyborg** (short for "<u>cybernetic organism</u>") is a being with both organic and biomechatronic body parts. The term was coined in 1960.

The term cyborg is not the same thing as <u>bionic</u>, <u>biorobot</u> or <u>android</u>; it applies to an organism that has restored function or enhanced abilities due to the integration of some artificial component or technology that relies on some sort of <u>feedback</u>. While cyborgs are commonly thought of as <u>mammals</u>, including humans, they might also conceivably be any kind of <u>organism</u>.

Marmalade could be cyborg too, if he had a replacement valve in his heart? or special metal claws instead of his own?

I downloaded *Metamorphosis* and it's disgusting. They hate him, the man who turns into a bug. The family shuts him away and pretends he's not there, he's invisible. That's worse than the void. Maybe one day people will get made into cyborgs so they don't cause trouble.

People get cochlear implants so they can hear and then other people don't have to bother to learn sign language. Touching the void.

Chat

Bex   Why is it called touching the void?

Joey   Two climbers somewhere in South America, very high mountains, one breaks his leg coming down and the other carries him then there's another accident.

Joey   It's a book too.

Bex   I've heard of it. True story.

Joey   Fantastic photography, climbing. This guy, if he didn't cut his friend loose they would both have died, they were roped together.

Bex   So he cut the rope? I remember that.

Joey   And the friend survived, the friend wrote the book, not the one who cut the rope.

Bex   The one who cut the rope, he must be in hell. Some kind of friend.

Joey   Did you tell your mum about your dad?

Joey   I got rid of them, that's what you wanted?

Bex   How long is Simon staying at yours?

Zef's Blog

I've been thinking about Matt's party last year and Oliver, his friend. He's not a bit like Matt. He tried to get off with me and I wanted to have a go. We were in the garden shed. But I couldn't get it in. That's three times I've tried, and he was decent, patient. Never again, never. The weight of his balls in my hand was almost comforting, and the skin behind was soft. His breath was fresh. He put my hand on his balls. I suppose he thought it would make it ok for me.

Maybe the sex was all wrong between Matt and Bex. Everybody does it except me, obviously. That picture came back to me – Matt's huge arm around her shoulders, his hand curving down towards her breast and the way she flicked his hand sideways. She always flicked it sideways. I need a map not a flow chart.

I try to picture myself with dick and balls. Maybe they're tucked inside anyway. Whatever's in this body I don't want anybody taking a knife to it. I've watched the videos about surgery. Implanted microchips might be ok, though it would depend on the program and the controller.

Research Sheets (Private)

One morning, when Gregor Samsa woke from troubled dreams, he found himself transformed in his bed into a horrible vermin. He lay on his armour-like back, and if he lifted his head a little he could see his brown belly, slightly domed and divided by arches into stiff sections. The bedding was hardly able to cover it and seemed ready to slide off any moment. His many legs, pitifully thin compared with the size of the rest of him, waved about helplessly as he looked.

"What's happened to me?" he thought. It wasn't a dream. His room, a proper human room although a little too small, lay peacefully between its four familiar walls.

Gregor's family hated him, shut him away, threw rubbish into the room, said he wasn't Gregor any more.

They left him to die on his own.. **VOID?**

Bex's real father is creepy. Why did he marry Caroline look-alike?

Friday August 11

Ma was making the chick pea curry. She'd spent the day in school but by the time I got home she had already chopped up garlic, chillies, fresh coriander and the chickpeas had finished soaking. The kitchen was full of spicy smells. Ma finished whizzing up the chillies with tomatoes to make a paste and added these to the pan where the chopped garlic sizzled. I watched her throw spices into the pan, counting as she went. 'One tablespoon turmeric, one coriander, one cumin, one paprika, one cayenne pepper, one teaspoon salt.' Noah questioned the extra cayenne and received a dismissing wave of the hand. Ma's chick pea curry was a wonder of the world because you couldn't find it in a recipe book – not her version, anyway. She had worked it up over years and Bex loved it as much as we did.

I scooped up Marmalade and buried my nose in his neck. He grumbled, telling me the biscuits in his dish were crap.

A fine mist sat on top of the town – the sort you could walk through into bright sunshine on top of Helvellyn, and then you would see nothing below except cloud. Bex did not come to work. I texted and she said she wasn't well but could she come to supper. The shop had been full but we sold nothing much so Shirley was cross. The 'Sale Tomorrow' sign meant people dragged stuff off racks, looked at price tags and slung the garments back.

I turned Marmalade on to his back and stuck my nose into his belly. He smelled of fields, flowers, earth. I could measure how much better his day had been than mine.

Noah shambled in from the utility room and leaned over Ma's shoulder to poke the curry.

'Did you want some of this tonight?'

'You know my wetsuit, what happened to the bag?'

Ma slapped at his hand and he laughed. Sweat stained the underarms of his thin shirt. I pictured Simon as I had seen him half an hour earlier, his hair freshly washed, his chinos neat. He wore a fine white cotton shirt of a kind you don't see in this country – a job lot, he said, from an uncle in Thailand. Ruth said they were enviable. He and Noah hadn't done much climbing yet. They'd been too busy working at the pub. I tried to imagine assisting behind a bar. Noah showed me photos on his phone of him and Si at the pub, flashlit, red-eyed, reflections glinting in the beer puddles on the counter, glasses cocked.

All day Shirley kept saying, 'If this sun doesn't shine it'll close us down,' and the flesh quivered at the top of her arms when she pulled her ponytail tight and smoothed her eyebrows. Bex would have said something like, 'But you've had so many phone calls since that show.' And Shirley would have brightened up.

Today, Shirley wore another outfit from the new range – black and yellow with lacy bits at the neck and flutter on the arms. I didn't want to stare too hard in case she asked me to wear it on Monday. Shirley plucks her eyebrows viciously.

All day I rehearsed my opening lines.

'It's like this, Bex. I don't feel right. I have to try living as a guy. It might not be truly me, but I have to find out'

Try again.

'If I don't try out life as a guy I'll never know. I'll never be sure of myself or what I could be'

And Bex says?

'Really, Joey? How terribly exciting'

'Really, Joey? You're not safe.'

'Really Joey? You're not the person I thought you were.'

'Really, Joey? You're on your own with this.'

The kitchen windows steamed up. I leaned forward from the sofa and lightly drew the symbol for railway lines. Marmalade gently nibbled my earlobe and patted my face. I had not been paying attention. I groped for the brush to groom him again. Her.

Voices in the hall and Marmalade squirmed away. Ruth shook out her coat and patted the spider-light net of mist on her hair. 'I met Bex at the bottom of the hill and we walked up together.' She set down a bulging bag by the sofa. 'This is what I meant. I'll pass it on to you next week, I'll read it over the weekend. It's good, that library.'

Bex put out her hand but Noah, bouncing on the balls of his feet, grabbed the book that Ruth held. '*Two Worlds and Their Ways.*' He stared at the cover. 'Sort of cultural study?'

Bex shrugged off her damp denim jacket, face going pink, and held out her hand again. At once Noah seized the jacket, slung it across the back of the nearest chair.

'Where's Simon tonight?' Ruth's large hand covered Noah's fingers.

He gave up the book. 'Evening shift. My day off.'

'You could lay the table.' Ma's voice sounded remote.

'I'm going to the climbing wall anyway.'

'Do you want supper or not? I'm keeping some back for Simon.'

Noah went to the door and swung from the lintel, red-faced. 'Glad he's a hit, Ma.'

'This book's typical of her style. It's completely out of fashion but I read her for the dialogue. It's so sharp. The plot happens backstage, somehow.'

They had obviously been talking all the way up the hill. Out of the corner of my eye I watched, grinding my teeth, for undercover signals that Ruth had said something about me. Bex was my friend. Ruth was our friend. it shouldn't matter. I tried not to glare.

Ma gave Bex a hug and Pa hung up her jacket on the coat rack, along with a new bag decorated with curving rows of buttons to make a rainbow. Perhaps she had spent her day off sewing on buttons. Noah leapt to Bex's side, drew out a chair and patted the seat. 'Bex?'

'Oh, I won't take your place.'

'I'm off in a couple of minutes.'

'Do you want me to save supper? Do you want to eat now? Noah, are you listening?'

'Maybe I'll go a bit later. I'm only going to the climbing wall.'

I stood by Ma at the worktop, picking up a knife to chop an onion for relish.

'Nice and fine, please. No chunks. Wine vinegar or yogurt? You choose.'

Tears were soon running down my face. Ma took the knife out of my hand. 'Why don't you check out the dough for the chapattis? It's settling in the fridge, the one in the utility. This one seems to be full of beer.'

Bex and Ruth and Pa were deep in conversation. Ruth casually put out a hand and rasped it over the dark stubble on Noah's chin. He laughed, ran out of the room. I heard him taking the stairs three at a time. Bex seemed to have got over whatever made her ill.

In the utility room I clutched the heavy, cold ball of brownish dough in my hands. Ma used wholemeal flour. These windows were clear of steam, framing the garden and the green of the hillside beyond. Three freshly-shorn sheep, unnaturally clean and white, stood nose to nose midfield. Along the top of the hill was a faint line of blue sky, pushing up the cloud as if it were the lid of a box. It might even be a clear evening. If I could stand like a tree with wind swishing through my head –.

'Joey, you're not kneading it are you?' Ma's voice, slightly plaintive. 'Don't warm it up, darling. I need it cold. Just poke it with your finger to see if it's getting nice and elastic.'

'Noah's gone out, thank God. If I could wire him up to our boiler he'd heat us for the next two winters. Wine, Bex?'

'If that's your elderberry and blackberry, Andrew, don't overdo it.'

'Ruth, this is my best.' Pa held his glass to the light. The wine was a deep purple red, completely clear, the colour of ripe blackberries.

'Can I try?'

'If you like.' Pa poured half an inch into a glass and passed it to me with a cautious expression in his eyes. I wetted my lips, surprised by the tang of alcohol. A dry, ripe taste rolled across my tongue, intensely blackberry.

'Ok?' Pa's face was slightly anxious. I loved the colour.

The last time I tried red wine was at that party, the last time I tried sex. The drink seemed like a good idea, but one glass of red wine merged with the night. I lost myself in the noise in Matt's house, its windows wide open, bedrooms heaped with bodies and coats, boys peeing in the kitchen sink, wine stains on the pale green carpet, and the garden, where I had gone to hide, overgrown and murky. I blundered into the garden shed with its rotting boards and rusting metal windows, and that was where Oliver found me. Later, Bex came looking, too. She held my head when I threw up, Oliver crouching alongside, wanting to help.

'Andrew, don't.' Ruth beckoned for my glass, for Bex's, and Bex caught my eye. She grinned. I twisted in the chair and knocked the glass flying. Shattered glass spreads as if you've set off an explosion. Fine red droplets sprayed across the tiles.

Ma said, 'Go easy, the curry will take at least another hour to ripen.' I was already in search of broom, dustpan, mop. 'Wear gloves, Joey. Don't get glass splinters.' I muddled about at floor level with the mop, listening to the burr of chatter above my head, Ruth's mockery, Ma's commentary on her day in school with a teacher getting neurotic

132

about results, Pa rumblings about planning laws, rogue landowners, fly-tippers, national strategy for water. I gathered the glass fragments into last week's *Gazette* and stuffed the spiked, red-stained package into the bin. Pa patted my shoulder and rattled about in the corner cupboard.

'Monopoly?' The money had blotched and the cards were curling. Bex said she hadn't played since years ago at our house. I couldn't remember even that.

We could have gone upstairs to my room, as we used to, or along the track into the fields or through the hedge and up the fellside. We could have talked. I could have talked.

Ma set the deadline for the game or it would have gone on all night. Ruth won. She laughed at Pa's expression as he counted the few notes left on his side of the table. I had the top hat still in my hand and sent it spinning as Bex tidied the stacks of cards. Ruth said it was a good thing Noah wasn't here and Ma said that he took after his father and Andrew used to be a devil and look at him now, not sulking at all.

Bex asked, 'How did you two meet?'

Ma spooned steaming curry over neat mounds of wild rice. I divided my portion into what I would eat, what I would spread around the plate. If Noah had been here, I would have spooned half on to his plate.

Pa said, 'We met in London, would you believe. All those millions of people and I found Mollie.' Ma's eyes were watering and she put down the ladle to dab them with the tea-towel. 'We were at that dreadful seminar introducing research methodologies and I thought, utter bullshit, completely useless.'

Ma snorted laughter into her hand. 'You were in the wrong building.'

I wanted to shake them but Bex's eyes were bright. 'Your seminar was literature and Andrew's was science.'

'Spot on.' Pa reached over to pat the back of Bex's hand.

'Yin and yang, sort of,' said Bex.

I watched Pa lifting the fork to his mouth, putting it down without eating because he had to say what he had been thinking about soap operas/political correctness/conservation and what's happening in Ennerdale. Pa's skin had acquired its summer tan, except for the white lines > o _ o < at the corners of his eyes. When he pulls on swimming trunks to dive into Windermere you can see that he seems to wear a short-sleeved tee shirt of white skin. He thinks sun-bathing is a waste of time.

Ruth asked how Caroline and Jack had met. Bex was already halfway through her curry and had put out her hand for a second chapatti. She did not see me at all. Her face was relaxed, soft. I watched Pa, Ruth, Ma, all looking at Bex. The light tones of Bex's voice wove in and around the sounds of chinking cutlery, creaking chairs, laughter, breathing.

'It might have been when Mum got her studio in Southey's Yard. She wanted advice about safety – you know, keeping a computer there, not having break ins. It wasn't Jack that time. Community policing isn't his thing. He's been a custody sergeant. You know.'

'We know.' Ma produced a sympathetic echo. I didn't know, but I couldn't spare the energy for somebody else's secrets.

'There was a town hall conference, I think, and Mum went. Start-up businesses, something like that. I think Jack may have made a presentation.'

Pa said, 'He's a resourceful man, Jack is.' How would Pa know anything about Jack? Even if they had anything in common, Pa wouldn't have noticed. He sees insects or plants, or *truly remarkable* small mammals. He peers and pokes and holds his breath, lifts up twigs and fronds with the end of a pencil till he has tracked them down, no hiding places. He sees lichen, or mosses growing in unexpected places or birds watching their broods learning to fly.

Bex finished her mouthful. 'Jack came to ours and replaced a broken window. He was lovely.' She ran her hands up and down her arms. There was a fresh red mark just beneath her elbow. I used my fork to separate a few chick peas that had not disintegrated. Then I lined up slivers of red chilli between them like stringing beads. Pa eyed my plate. I pushed it across the table.

Ruth wound a fine blue scarf around her head to keep the hair from her face. She looked like a wise woman in an old painting. 'Will your mother keep on with the design business after the wedding?'

'I guess. I think so. Jack's made her a studio anyway. You'll see it when you come.'

A vindictive little voice piped up loud and clear in my head. *Bex is my friend not hers. Her child's dead, she's poking her nose in.* My chair toppled. Had I spoken aloud?

Pa's chair scraped on the tiles. 'What's up, poppet, you can't sit still tonight.'

'I need to check the routes. My test.'

'You gave your curry to your father. Was something not right about it?'

'Oh heck, I promised to give you driving practice this weekend.' Pa rounded the table, setting the chair on its four-square legs, seating me with a thrust of his bony fingers. He began to probe my shoulders. 'There's no rush, sweetie.' He found the pressure points, kneaded. 'You are so tense.' Wine and curry gave his breath a rich, invasive headiness. 'Maybe you're still gripping the steering wheel too hard. I'm going into Borrowdale on Sunday, you could drive if you like. That would be great practice. You could do a spot of running.'

'Could I come too?' Ruth got to her feet. 'I wouldn't drag round after either of you but it would be a wonderful chance to walk up Dale Head and look at Newlands. I love that view of the valley from the top. I could sit there for hours. I wouldn't put you off if I were in the back seat, would I, Joey? I'm not a backseat driver. Maybe Bex could come too.'

The wicked goblin in my head flexed its talons. Bex said, 'Thanks but I have to help Mum. She's practically licking the floors in the house to make everything perfect.'

Empty plates were pushed to the end of the table to make room for the map of Borrowdale. Ruth and Ma sidetracked themselves into plotting for next week, and Pa talked to Bex about early retirement and Jack. I half-listened. The silky man in the shop yesterday was prowling somewhere through the dark, with his woman hanging off his arm. How could he possibly fit with Bex? Or Caroline? Why did Bex come tonight, anyway?

Noah brought Simon with him in a dark, damp rush of energy. Noah ate Simon's reserved portion, found a cheese alternative in the fridge, opened another bottle of elderberry and blackberry wine for sampling purposes, plucked the book from where Ruth had placed it. 'Who's this writer, Ivy Compton Burnett? Never heard of her. Let's walk Bex home.'

Simon's eyes gleamed. He wanted Noah to get up at four o'clock next morning to do a quick climb in the Coniston fells before the afternoon shift, and grabbed a map from the shelf, spreading it on the table. 'Look, we could climb from the road, Tilberthwaite Quarry, or the Coppermines Valley. You've probably done it loads but – maybe Joey would come too. What do you think? You could run?' He smiled as if he meant it.

Noah folded the map with a smack. 'She'll have work to get to. She starts before us.' His eyes sparkled at me with a competitive glint. 'Even her twinkly-toes wouldn't get up and down the Old Man and back here all buffed up for the shop by nine o'clock.'

Ruth said, 'It was very overcast all day. Isn't rain forecast for tomorrow?'

'I want to know when we plan to get on with that wall. I don't want the heap of stones left too long. Creatures will move in. Andrew's ordered plants and I'm ready to be inducted into wall-building. Are you working all day tomorrow, Joey?'

'Sorry I can't help. Someone coming from London.' Pa clattered the plates into a ragged pile and wandered towards the dishwasher. Noah leapt at the door-frame for pull-ups.

'I must go home, shop tomorrow.' At Bex's words, Noah swung himself to land neatly beside her and reached for her jacket, easing it on to her shoulders.

Simon tugged his sweater over his head. 'It's so unlike London. I forget there's so much oxygen here. Come for the walk, Joey? It's a wonderful night.'

Ruth tried to catch my eye but I wanted to kick someone. Noah.

Ma stretched out on the old brown leather sofa at the other end of the kitchen, feet on the window sill. 'Bring a bottle, Ruth, there's a love. August is too short.'

'Won't you come too, Joey?'

Ruth stood for a moment watching me, the lines of her mouth drawn tight.

'No thanks.'

Ma's arm appeared over the back of the sofa to tug at the bottom of Ruth's shirt. Pa closed the dishwasher and returned to the map of Borrowdale, fetching some of his Ennerdale papers to lay alongside. He was talking to himself.

Slowly I made my way to the utility room. I needed the dark.

Gentleman Noah and his good friend Mr Polite, escorting

my best friend home. My entire family treated Bex as if she were one of them. Us.

The door to the garden was ajar. Mist had brought the plants alive and the air smelt of high summer, concentrated lavender, clematis, sweet peas, jasmine, honeysuckle. Marmalade slid from somewhere, his tabby patterning at one with the shadows, and wound himself around my legs. *He loves me, he loves me not, he loves me. He loves me.* I bent to scratch his neck under his collar where he likes it and he arched against my calf with a thunderous purr. I could not imagine what Noah and Simon and Bex were talking about.

Together we went, Marmalade and I, to the top of the garden. I pushed through the small gap in the hedge, scrabbling into the field beyond. My hair was full of leaves and twigs. Marmalade's eyes caught the light of the moon as he poised, every hair of his coat quivering. Although it was close to midnight I could see individual stalks of grass and the closed heads of daisies.

I love the long, slow evenings and short nights. The pale half-moon was watching from the sky, its momentary halo staining the feathered clouds. Trees massed under the fells, and walls were thick black lines, curving into the distance. It was windless. My head cleared.

Family ties are tough as a spider's web strung out between bushes. Spiders set traps. Victims don't get away unless they are super-strong. The clouds shifted and the loosened moon stared down at me, its gaze outlined by the widening pool of inky dark as if someone had blacked its eye. Maybe there'd be no rain tomorrow. Marmalade hissed. Even in this dim light I knew his hackles had risen. The fine hairs stood up along the backs of my arms.

I went back inside to look for Yin and Yang. Anything to distract.

Networking

Forum: gender and behaviour

Narrative: Zenith 00:33

Is anybody else reading stuff online about gender imprinted on you when you're a baby?

Comment: Moderator Sue 06:21

Zenith, what are you reading that makes you ask?

Narrative: Zenith 06:22

I could put up some of the weblinks. Am I just my parents all over again? Am I their reprint?

Comment: Moderator Sue 06:24

We wouldn't make it past the first 48 hours without a parent.

Comment: Barbarian 08:21

this is doing my head in. don't giva toss about parents gotta think about me, you.

Comment: Gozo 08:54

This dosent look a lot of fun. Just live it man, don't squeeze it to bits.

Comment: Cybersnake 08:56

Zenith's on to something it's like having 2 people inside you, the one your parents think about, and you

---

Narrative: Zenith 09:02

I've been on a couple of gamesites for months now, playing as a guy. Seems to work OK.

Zef's Blog

I looked again at the photo of me aged six. I was six when Noah said he wasn't getting into the bath with me anymore. He didn't even want to have a shower if I was in the bathroom, but Ma told him not to be so silly. When he got in the shower he put his hand over his willy.

Ma had it all worked out, when she was going to tell me The Facts Of Life. I was nine. We went to the park and sat on a bench. She bought me an ice cream. Ma tried to find out what I already knew. I watched the children on the swings, kicked my legs, chose a chocolate flake for the ice cream, it's as clear as yesterday. She talked about menstruation as if I was interested but it wasn't going to happen to me.

That summer I knew that Joey was Zef too. That was the year I found a book in our holiday house, full of illustrations and speckled brown pages. The children in the book lived in the old days. They called their parents Ma and Pa. It was like a secret code for being different till Noah did it too.

The next year we moved out of London to the Lake District instead of having a holiday. It was like my whole life becoming a holiday. I started a new school and I met Bex. I never had a true friend before. In London I hung out with other people, but not seriously, not someone making me feel I could unwrap my heart.

Surfing

The ancient Chinese subscribed to a concept called **_Yin Yang_** which is a belief that there exist two complementary forces in the _universe_. One is Yang which represents everything positive or masculine and the other is Yin which is characterized as negative or feminine. One is not better than the other. Instead they are both necessary and a balance of both is highly desirable.

Yin is soft while Yang is hard. Yin is stillness while Yang is movement. The sun is yang while the moon is yin. Female is Yin while Man is Yang. Mountain is Yin while the river is Yang. Intuitive is Yin while Logical is Yang. Winter is Yin while Summer is Yang.

Yin Yang is whole? You can't be one without the other?

THREE
SCAR

Zef's Blog

On www.ethicsinanewworld.org, this guy says in the future some people will still choose to be male or female, some will choose to be both, some will choose to be neither. Some will choose what we haven't invented yet. Maybe people will choose to be made of different stuff or fused with stuff in ways we can't begin to imagine.

The guy's forgotten **parents**, how they want what's best, so they think. I found an old news item about a couple keeping the sex of their baby secret so s/he could work out gender for him/herself. But you don't work out how to talk all by yourself. It's not like we're imprinted, as if we were sheets of blank paper and somebody with a great stamp marks you for life. Maybe you imprint yourself, looking at yourself in a mirror. Do babies look at themselves in mirrors? Yin and Yang? Like the you in the mirror, and the you looking back, being together 1+1=1.

Peter Pan cried when his shadow was chopped off.

Yin and Yang means no extremes, everything balanced. You and your shadow together forever? What if the shadow is dark? Some parents love their children to death.

Research Sheets (Private)

shadow self – Carl Jung/psychologist

The shadow is a moral problem that challenges the whole ego-personality, for no one can become conscious of the shadow without considerable moral effort. To become conscious of it involves recognizing the dark aspects of the personality as present and real. This act is the essential condition for any kind of self-knowledge.

To confront a person with his shadow is to show him his own light. Once one has experienced a few times what it is like to stand judgingly between the opposites, one begins to understand what is meant by the self. Anyone who perceives his shadow and his light simultaneously sees himself from two sides and thus gets in the middle.

anima = male side of female + vice versa but what if you aren't M/F in the first place?

Tuesday August 15

I'm running through exhaust fumes, away from people clotting the pavements, away from the dreary smotheration of the shop, up All Hallows Lane, up Beast Banks, my legs pumping steadily, my breathing slow and deep, deeper as the air sweetens. The roads glisten. I dodge a passing car, sprint across slippery grass, and swerve left into the Brigsteer Road.

Ahead of me stretches the rippling, upward swerve of the road over the bypass, towards Scout Scar. I shake the damp from my hair. The trees lean across the road, leaves gleaming. You could swim through the green air. Water drifts from eaves and branches, mutters in the small gully at the side of the road where the line of houses peters out. The hum of traffic fades. A steady pulse beats in my wrists.

Ahead of me, the mist thickens as I run into a haze of water on my Scout Scar. Sunday dog-walkers think it's theirs. Pensioners, wandering along to the iron dome of the Mushroom for the views to Morecambe Bay, think it belongs to them. Lads drive up here to party, chucking out cans and takeaway packaging. But the Scar cries out for runners. Online I've read that humankind has evolved to run. I can outrun dogwalkers. If ever I'm cyborg I won't let the machine be greater than me, not like the bikers zooming round the bypass, old men in their black leathers thinking the speed limit is for them to decide. I am evolution.

I skim up the hill, towards the old racecourse that swoops around one side of the Scar. The blisters on my hands from all day wall-building on Saturday don't exist. I am here-and-now where I'm light as a feather, leaping with the preen and stretch of a dancer – that guy from Havana whose dad was a builder – imagine a builder in Burneside boasting about his son the dancer. As if. Carlos Acosta, Carlos Acosta – the name swoops and bounds. I'm a hare at full stretch, a rabbit skittering under a hawthorn away from the beady eyes of the kestrels. The trees stream behind in my wake.

I played at mountain goat going up High Spy on Sunday, after driving with Pa. The path leads steep and true, marked by pyramidal cairns, and I leapt on top of every one of them, being a heron. At the big circular cairn on top, three walkers leaned on their rucksacks, gazing at the view. I smugly shucked off my rucksack, chewed a bit of fruit cake, threw water I'd collected from the Dale Head Tarn over my face and shoulders, planted my foot against the cairn as if I owned it. We are made of the same stuff, formed by earth, wind and water.

Monday had been suffocating, grey, grey, grey. I rehearsed questions. *Bex, tell me about your father, about him and Caroline. Why's he so creepy?* Only you can't ask your best friend if she thinks her dad's creepy. Her face was immobilised behind the make-up. Cars get immobilised too. I made myself busy. I wanted to know everything.

Clouds closed in, but the air kept Sunday's heat like a wet sponge. Bex was robotic with the customers, smiling as if the machine were switching her on. We took lunch at different times. On the way back from a quick canter round Maude's Meadow I saw that man again, with his woman, coming out of the shop. Bizarrely, Bex had made the time to paint her nails deep purple. Shirley said she was trying it out for the wedding.

But today, running out of the shop is like bursting out of an old skin. Twenty minutes and my brain twitters like our house-martins – me – free – meee – freeee – meeeee –. A faint green-blue line thickens and thins along the horizon and the raincloud shape-shifts, drifts. Straddling the narrow stile, I conjure the map of the Scar, writing the paths on the air with my finger, and decide to cut across the Allotment, avoid the dog-walking paths.

When I get to the Scar I'll lie on my back and spy on the birds. I'll use my running jacket for padding, on a limestone pavement that's not shattered by frosts. The words for broken limestone are better than swearing – clint, clitter, gryke.

I throw myself like a swimmer into a shallow green sea. The turf beneath my running shoes bounces with life and I think, *of course, it's growing*. Sheep graze here, sometimes cattle. *They* decide. Pa knows who *they* are, it's part of his patch. Today it's my patch. My quads and calves swell and contract with perfect ease. The calf muscle is gastrocnemius. I looked it up – a word that works your mouth, a muscle you mustn't tear.

My feet know the route, but today I'm turning off to a different, narrower path. I pause to orientate myself by the radio mast ☒. I have to keep the mast on my right and go straight ahead, more or less. I know where I am.

I love running my hands through wet vegetation and

smelling the full-on spending-spree of summer. Here's the narrow track, branches sagging – hawthorn berries, still green, and a rowan where the berries cluster in reddening handfuls. The air swells with heat and hordes of small flies that enjoy the air as much as I do. Little blue bell-shaped flowers grow in the cracks of the rocks. Pa says it's mostly limestone on the Scar. The blotches of lichen are usually white, like paint that's dripped off the end of the brush on to the grey stone. I recall the splodges on the Bowder Stone and imagine giant insects scrabbling for purchase on outward-leaning rock. Beetles on limestone, there must be some. I've stared at videos of climbers on the Bowder Stone, but the way they're shot you can't always understand what you're seeing till you look again, like those puzzles where you're supposed to guess what the objects are when your eyes and your mind don't line up. One day I will climb the Stone.

Raucous voices somewhere too close, dogs barking, and there's a man on the track in front of me, spreading his arms wide and he's saying, 'Well look at this, look who's here.' Unthinkingly I throw myself off the path, the ground drops – something clutches my foot in a wicked spike – blackthorn, knotted, wicked.

'You're in a hurry,' says Matt, looming above as I unlace, wrestle to extract my foot. There's blood on the sock. Not a man but a lad with a liking for victims. 'It's the freak,' he calls, and two or three others appear behind him with a couple of dogs bounding and yapping.

'They ought to be on leads,' I say, rubbing my foot. I can't believe the blackthorn has punctured trainer, sock, skin. My heart races and suddenly I have to shove my foot back into the trainer whether it hurts or not.

'What's the freak say?'

'This one gets in my way,' says Matt, hair swinging in knots. I can smell the booze and something else, a twanging electric tension that says 'run'. He's furious.

I plunge into bracken that towers over my head in sticky, wet fronds. Behind me there's a yelp from a dog. Matt shouts, 'We know where you live.' Branches scrape at my bare arms and my punctured foot throbs and I ricochet between the crowded trees, struggling not to panic until I have to slow down, panting, and angry with myself. He's only Bex's ex.

I don't know where I am. If I get to higher ground I should be able to work it out. I strain for the sounds of dogs, people, car horns. Nothing. Fractionally the mist clears. Layers of grey cloud race across a watery blue till the mist exhales, obscuring everything. There's a name for cloud like that. I can always look it up. Why did Caroline marry a creep? Bex got snarled up with Matt. Maybe it's in the family, attracting creeps.

I can't imagine my Bex Woods being Rebecca Ainsley. Rebecca Ainsley could be her shadow, her doppelgänger, her other self. Who does he think he is, turning up out of the blue, calling her Rebecca? My foot throbs. It's good. It stops me brooding.

There's a glimmer of sun between branches. If I find open ground I'll see my shadow – run ahead of it, towards the west, towards the wall, reach the top of the Scar and know exactly where I am. The eerie picture of chasing ahead of my own shadow makes me shiver. My phone beeps.

18:59: Bex

Where did u go?

The signal disappears.

Breath catches at the back of my throat. I set off at a trot but the ground fights back. Fragments of limestone split by matted roots spring up underfoot.

On the high fells you see the wide perspective. I used to think Matt was a sweet guy.

Bex didn't want anything to do with me today so why the text now?

Suddenly there's a cairn. Where there's one there's sure to be another. On maps you sometimes find, "Pile of stones", and this looks exactly like that, dishevelled. But that's what cairns sometimes are. People randomly chuck stones as they pass, adding to the heap, saying *I was here*. There's a man comes on the Scar all the time to make stone circles. I wish someone thought of stringing a rope between cairns. I could go hand over hand to the next. The mist swirls, thins, tears apart to reveal a line of trees further up. This must be right. I wish someone like Ruth was at the other end of the rope, reeling me in. Ma.

I grab for my phone to check again and there's signal so now now now

19.14: Joey

on scar signal crap wr r u

Press send but it won't send press press stupid cheap phone.

The mist sneaks back. I haven't been able to reach Bex for days. I stop dead, turn around. Scout Scar's not big but the trig point's two-two-nine metres. Where's the path?

Bex will think I'm sulking. What's she meant to think? I ran away.

The mist billows and deflates like gigantic breathing in a closed space. Something monstrous is taking shape beyond the edges of my vision. I can't hear the dogs. The phone says it's seven twenty. I can't even ring home to get someone to ring Bex for me.

Bex's eyes glitter through her hair but when she scrapes it back I don't know her anymore. Ever since her father came into the shop, she's stopped seeing me. Maybe she's not seeing anyone. I pull the phone to my nose, glimpse the thinnest bar, phone Bex. Three, four, five rings. Hush my breath. *The owner of this number is not available. Please try later.*

Perhaps there's a kind of cataract for the mind – a slow-growing film that obscures the light. The mist exhales again in huge, grey surges, spreading its droplets along my bare arms, and again I shiver, unable to name the fear.

Suddenly the mist relents and there below me sits the old grey town. If I run straight down I'll reach the road. There will be signal. There's got to be.

I should have learned. Scout Scar in mist is as treacherous as Haystacks, everyone's favourite mountain that sounds like a Sunday picnic but it's a mountain, can't be trusted. There is no straight down. I won't break my neck but hours could pass whilst I wander round. If Bex were watching she might laugh out loud. I'd love to hear her laugh. Days have passed since she laughed. Her face is in the mist, less and less distinct. I'd clutch at her shadow.

A wall lifts up at the top of a rise and I scramble towards it. I am so glad to touch something constructed. And even as I see that it isn't a wall, I know that I've been here before. Pa brought me, years ago, when he was conducting a survey with farmers. It's a kind of ruined house. Rings of stone might have been rooms. Here's a solid platform that looks like an altar. Strangely, the signal comes back loud and clear and my text sends itself and seconds later my phone rings. I drop the phone. Stones slither with me into the pit as I scrabble after the sound, but my fingers find the phone too late. *Missed call.* Is Bex merely replying to my attempt at calling her?

The signal ebbs and flows as I dial her number again and yet again the voice politely intones. *The owner of this number is not available. Please try later.* The home phone is answered. Pa tells me to get to the road and he'll pick me up. Unnerved, I hurl myself regardless down the uneven path that grudgingly reveals itself and arrive at the road merely minutes after Pa has drawn up in his ramshackle Land Rover.

'Ah, those cairns,' he says cheerfully. 'Kids build them for fun. I told you, walls and cairns look as if they mean something and half the time they don't.' He asks if I've noticed that some of the limestone lichens are orange and green, not just the white they are meant to be. He's looking for patterns. Have I noticed the improvement in the flora since the Welsh Blacks started to graze on the Scar? He seems quite unfazed by my getting lost on our doorstep, so to speak. He's still living in Sunday-time. I've been shunted to a parallel universe and I can't hear him. His fingernails are ragged from digging around. My foot aches. At the bottom of the Brigsteer Road he suddenly brakes, and plunges under the passenger seat for a hairy, grass-filled blanket. 'Put it round your knees. You've gone green. Is this all you've got to wear?'

18.59: Bex

Matt help ☹

20.11: Joey

he's on scar?

Zef's Blog

Matt posted a series of gross comments about Bex. It had to be Matt though the person putting up the posts called himself DicDoc. Nobody else would have got so many details so nearly right. I smelt the rage on Matt today, on the Scar. Thorn in the flesh. It's a saying I'm beginning to understand.

I found the weblink too easily. "The Whoreshop that Jack Built." Matt copied a photo of one of Bex's masks and digitalised an image that everyone would know was Bex, with the mask on a pretend-nude body so it wouldn't be tagged as porn. But if you knew Bex's masks you'd see straight off it was porn. One hundred and twenty-four people I'd never heard of had plastered offensive remarks underneath.

Everyone has that nightmare of being outside, with no clothes.

I ran round the house banging on doors like we were on fire and Simon and Ruth came out straight away. Pa was sitting at the kitchen table talking to himself. He was preparing a lecture on protective herd behaviour among the Galloway cattle in Ennerdale, his pamphlets and maps spread everywhere. Ma pushed him and his papers to one end. Ruth collected her laptop, and Simon pinched Noah's. He doesn't use a password. Pa carried on talking to himself.

We sat at the table and started posting. We filled the screen with comment after comment about Rebecca the artist, Rebecca who was exhibiting her work with artists of national renown, Rebecca who was the best friend of, Rebecca whose costumes were the most highly praised, Rebecca who ... Rebecca was a Saint and the trolls were pushed back into their caves.

Ma went into the garden with her phone. I heard, dimly, 'Thanks, Peter, it's not good timing but I knew you'd want the information.'

Ruth posted a comment about the magical powers of the witch-woman. The image on my screen was now all mixed up with reflections from the kitchen lamps. The mask-headed creature had become a mythical beast in a world of shadows.

Pa thought we were making too much fuss. I knew that Matt could deny everything. My foot hurt. Noah came home pissed from his shift and Pa told him off. Then they chatted about how I got lost on the Scar. Noah went on about GPS on his phone. Ma said maybe I needed a smarter phone but I can't afford a contract so???

If you could put microchips into people's brains could you reprogram them?

Networking

Narrative: Zenith 23:32

Give me a clue. What do you say to the doctor?

Comment: Moderator Sue 23:33

What do you want to happen next? Try to imagine the outcome you want. Picture yourself in two or three years. Ask how the doctor can help you get what you want. Be the guy in that game you like, maybe.

Comment: Cybersnake 23:46

I'd be freaked trying to be a fantasy.

Narrative: Zenith 23:59

Are we all completely sure this forum is secure? Nobody reads it do they except us?

Wednesday August 16

Shirley's voice on the phone sounded as if she were locked in a box. I said I'd do without pay for coming late to work but she said I'd been a blessing doing the database and what was an hour, anyway? 'Hope it's ok, Joey, the doctor. Hope you're ok. See you about ten? But they're all the same, doctors. You just have to be patient.' She laughed hoarsely at her own pun. I thought if she knew she might change her mind about me being a blessing.

The practice where we're registered has lots of doctors so they need multiple rooms. It's a big house, over several floors, and it smelt today of new paint and new wood. My appointment was with Dr Hallgrave but I had no idea what Dr Hallgrave looked like. Once I got past the glass doors my eyes flickered till I found an engraved list, sweated, scanned, looking for the name and the floor, hoping nobody would try to be helpful. Out of the corner of my eye was a receptionist whose face looked familiar. Instantly I knew she was Matt's mother and hunched my shoulder. I'd been in their house with Bex a couple of times apart from the party. She looked ginger with make-up. Maybe she'd found out about Matt's posts.

The waiting room is huge, sectioned off into corrals. I suppose they have to organise us somehow. Outside each doctor's door about a dozen chairs are set out, six facing six, across low tables covered with magazines. I shuffled around the tidy chairs, not catching anybody's eye. Dr Hallgrave's name was at the farthest end of the waiting room.

The chairs had the rooted look meaning Do Not Disturb. I sat by a woman who was resting her handbag on the magazine in her lap. The skin of her hands was wrinkled, covered in brown spots. She had stiff white hair and you could see from the perfect waves and neatly arranged curls on her forehead that it had been done recently but it was flattened at the back. Not a wig. I could see the pink of her scalp. Her coat smelt old, like a charity shop. Maybe the charity shops smell like that because of the old people's clothes in them. I am never getting old. Ruth's white hair is thick and glossy. Old people's hair must lose its spring.

I heard breathing, sniffling, the rustle of fabric, pages turning. Bursts of laughter floated up from the floor below. The staff were having fun.

The old woman lifted her bag with both hands, as if it were heavy with treasure trove, and the magazine slid off her lap to the floor. She gazed at it over the top of the bag and then turned her head in my direction. The whites of her eyes were threaded with red and a sort of teary goo had settled in the sags of skin beneath them. I groped after the magazine, but she shook her head. 'No love, thank you.' Her voice was surprisingly deep.

I spun the magazine with a flick of my wrist to the heap on the table, starting an avalanche of magazines. Somehow she snagged the last, though her hand shook, skin folded up thin as paper, transparent. I pinched the back of my hand. My skin bounced back. *I'm never going to be old.* 'Have a mint, love?' There was a gleam in her eye. I had to take one.

Then she handed the tube to the girl opposite, who perched on the edge of her seat with a baby on her knees. The girl looked the same age as me but I'm no good at ages. The baby had a sad little cough, and snot ran from its nose in a fine stream over its lips and chin. The girl dabbed a thin white cloth at its nose like swatting flies, and the baby cried and turned its head sideways, shoving its little blue bobble hat over its eyes, so it cried more. *It'll be a boy. She'd not put a girl baby in a blue hat.*

'What time's yours?' said the old woman to the girl. A blue knitted elephant lay on the carpet under the table. I picked it up, flapped it at the baby. The girl's skin was stretched tight over her cheekbones and blue shadows fingered her eyes. *Whoever wants a baby?* The baby's skin was peachy. I never sat so close to a baby before.

'We're nine thirty,' said the girl in a flat voice.

'What about you?' The old woman was talking to me again. I tried not to wriggle.

Ma and Ruth must have taken us, me and Ruth's baby, to the doctor for injections and stuff. Seventeen years ago. Maybe my skin was peachy, too. Maybe I dribbled snot in a clear stream over a scabby chin. I never asked Ma what clothes she put me in. She could have given me Noah's baby clothes. I'd have been happy. In some parts of the world, I'd have definitely been safer in boys' clothes. Women come in for rape and pillage wherever. Female babies get exposed, abandoned, sold.

The old woman and the girl started to talk about the new supermarket in the town, and the troubles of the farmers' market, how there were too many betting shops.

Maybe in another country I could be a guru, a soothsayer, a gatherer of herbs. I groped for the brilliant ideas that had flooded my mind at six o'clock this morning. All sorts of people were involved in my growing up – Ma and Pa, Noah – the boys on the towpath, Caroline ¬– Miss Smith at primary school in London, Sue and Barbarian, Ruth. Even Bex.

Maybe in another world Matt would be transformed into a giant bug, with a bulgy body and stupid wriggling legs. And all the cruel bastards who had posted about the image of Bex would be squirming maggots and a huge booted foot would stamp down on them. A cyborg foot could be pitiless. That would be more satisfying than a brain-scramble.

A door swung open and a figure framed by sunlight called a name. The old woman shoved herself upright, carefully placing her bag on the table so she could grasp the edge of her chair with both hands. The doctor came right out, picked up the bag and said, 'Hello again, Mrs Goodison. How're you keeping? Come on in.' She looked about Ma's age, had a clear, soft voice and a Scottish accent. The rest of us were invisible. I picked up *Lancashire Life* and contemplated the torn edge in the middle. The baby whooped, suddenly joyful. The digital seconds of my watch flicked over, over, over. Five minutes, seven minutes. *How long's an appointment?* I ought to get back to the shop.

Suddenly sunlight streamed through the opening surgery door and Mrs Goodison put out a foot, passing her hand across the door jamb. She caught me watching, smiled. Her teeth were yellow. Strong arches of bone sprang above each eye and her nose was a beaky jut. She could be a man in woman's clothes with an old woman's hair-do. S/he edged around the door and shuffled towards the lift, fingers still tracing the wall. I tried thinking of her as him. It wouldn't work. I'd got something wrong there. Some people's gender you just know is M or F however they look – Pa, Noah, Bex's dad, Jack. Ruth. Bex. Unless it's how I look at them. There's a check-out operator in one of the supermarkets whose lapel badge I have to stare at to know it's Him not Her and even then I'm not sure.

The doctor's door closed. The girl mopped the baby's nose. 'What time are you?'

'Nine twenty.'

'Oh.' Her face fell. 'I'm nine thirty.' The baby's head jerked. It had no neck.

'Do you want to go before me?' I felt noble.

'It's ok. Will you be long?' Strands of wispy bleached hair fell into her eyes.

I half-got to my feet. This was a waste of time. 'You go first, it's ok, your baby.'

'Oh no, she's all right,' said the girl, readjusting the baby's coat and tiny green shoes.

'Josephine Wilcox?' It was too late to escape. I wasn't ready.

I thought all doctors had photos of their families and boxes of toys to distract children and pictures of flowers and trees and maybe a seashore. There was hardly anything in this room, apart from her desk and a couch, and medical stuff. Everything felt neutral.

Behind her desk there was a picture, after all – water on pebbles, like in show-homes. The doctor gestured to the chair that was next to hers, pale brown upholstery.

'I don't think we've met before.' Behind her the computer screen flickered and went to screensaver. Water on pebbles. 'Are you usually called Josephine?'

'Joey.' My voice came out in a croak.

'How can I help you?'

My mind went blank. She leaned back in the chair and put her feet evenly on the ground. I stared at her shoes, orange leather with yellow flowers. Her legs were surprisingly tanned.

'My shoes were a bit of an indulgence,' she said, angling one foot, setting it down again on the brown ridges of the carpet. I was startled into looking at her face. She smiled. 'What are we here to do today?'

I thought wildly, what does she mean? A clock tick-tocked. I hadn't noticed a clock. Outside, an engine revved and a man laughed loudly. After my shower this morning I stared at myself in the steamed-up bathroom mirror, working out what to say, like, if I had a dick and balls I could be a skinny lad, couldn't I? I've no breasts to speak of and my quads are good from running. I've no hips, I don't want to go on living like this, I want to be a guy, I think I want to be a guy and she was still smiling at me, looking a question and I knew I'd got to speak or the blood would burst out of my ears. 'I do lots of running.'

'Oh?'

My chest hurt. 'People keep saying I'll knacker my knees.'

She leaned forward slightly. A faint flowery perfume drifted in my direction, with undertones of antiseptic. 'How old are you, Joey? Sorry, I know it'll be in our records.'

'Seventeen, I'm seventeen.'

'Are your knees giving you problems now?' I shook my head. My fingers gripped my knees, prodding bone and muscle and ligament through the layers of crumpled skirt, tight lycra, skin. 'It sounds like wonderful exercise. I wouldn't want to stop you.'

'You think it's ok?'

'I think it's great if you love running. Where do you run?'

'On the fells if I can.'

She looked at my trainers. 'My husband's a fell runner too – he's not to be stopped.'

'So it's ok.'

'I'd think so, yes. I'm just going to look something up, if that's all right.' She swivelled on her chair like someone who

167

enjoyed it. 'I'm looking at the statistics for knee conditions. Running on roads is what does the damage.' She looked back over her shoulder. 'Do you run on the roads?'

'Sometimes.' I had to clear my throat. 'To get started.'

'So you thought you'd check it out?' She faced me again, with that expression of helpful interest. 'Might I give you some advice?' I felt stupid. 'You could join a club, a fell-running club, if you don't already belong to one. Local clubs train their members well.'

'I suppose.' Membership, M/F, there's no way out. The room dimmed. Cloud would be settling down upon Scafell Pike, Wetherlam, High Street, Blencathra.

'Is that a problem for you?'

'I'll be eighteen soon.'

She was giving me that intense head-tilted look again. 'Was there something else?'

I shrugged. She leaned sideways, took a pack of tissues from her handbag, laid it on my lap. A fat, disgusting wetness hung off the end of my nose. I fumbled, couldn't get the packet open. She took it back, extracted a tissue, placed it in my fingers. I counted the beats of my heart, breathing through my mouth like a kid with a cold but filling up with frustration. No man would cry in a doctor's surgery. I clung to the frustration and the tears dried.

When I raised my head she was still waiting. She had a thin, brown face with freckles and bright brown eyes and she wasn't smiling anymore. Her hair was cut in a short bob. To draw her face you'd make fine lines >>o _ o << beside her eyes, and faint purple fingerprints beneath them. Tissues sprouted stiffly from a box on the desk.

She followed my glance. 'NHS tissues are thin and horrible,' she said. There were green flecks in her eyes. Shreds of tissue fluttered to the floor. 'I try to keep nicer ones.'

My throat hurt. 'It's clear in my head.' She nodded. 'I've been thinking about it for years and years.'

'Take your time.' Another nod.

'Ten years ago we went on holiday on a narrow-boat.' I couldn't tell her the whole story. She'd think I was still a kid. 'My brother and I were mucking about.' The careful writing in the diary was as clear in my mind as if the diary itself lay open on her desk. I thought she was going to speak but she merely coughed quietly into the back of her hand. 'Something happened.' A baby wailed in the waiting room, stopped. 'That girl with the baby, she's next, she's after me.'

The doctor gestured for me to go on but I was stuck, swallowing hard. 'Up to you.'

The clock ticked. 'Some older boys saw us. Noah, that's my brother, got talking to them.' They *said* his little *brother* couldn't *come*. You could make a dance out of it. 'They wanted him to meet them later but they said his little brother couldn't come.' Remembering the joyous leap in my heart from that time made my heart skip a beat.

'Yes?'

'The little brother was me. They thought I was his brother.' She sat with her hands in her lap. It was like running over a sodden fellside. You sink to the ankles with every step, slow motion, and the ground heaves and shifts. 'It made me feel – it was great.'

'Could you tell me a bit more about that?' I could have told her I was a murderer and her face would still have looked sympathetic and alert. Maybe the cogs were whirring inside.

'I felt all wrong before and then it felt better. I felt better.' She looked at the wall. Workmen built that wall. Somebody whistled. A train rattled at the station. Birds sang. 'I think when I was born. There weren't tests.' A gut-wrenching sigh got away from me, like those yawns you can't swallow. Outside, the train hooted gently and set off. Not many people get out here. They go further, to Windermere or to Oxenholme, back into the world where I never want to go. 'People can't hear, on the platform, when they're waiting?'

'No,' she said. I stared at my hands. 'No, this is private.' I looked at the lines criss-crossing my palms. Would fortune-tellers know the gender of a hand? Do the lifelines change if your gender changes? Private was about to be public. This was completely different from telling Ruth. 'Is there anything else you'd like to say?' Her voice stayed soft, quiet.

'No.' I closed my eyes, as I strained after the fresh green smell of the canal. 'When I look in the mirror, it doesn't match. How I look doesn't match.'

'Doesn't match?' I stared at her orange and yellow shoes, at my stained trainers and the black skirt sticking to the lycras underneath. The clock hadn't given up tick-tocking. I could not find the words. 'What are you hoping for, now you've come to talk this over?'

A great swell of heat. 'I don't know.'

'Maybe you could tell me what made you decide to consult me today. You say you've had this – something – in your mind for a very long time.'

I thrashed about before I remembered. 'It was Ruth. Ruth is my Ma's best friend. She's the only person I've told. She said it might be good for me to come.' The doctor waited, waited, till I blurted into the space, 'Ruth's known me ever since I was a baby. She stays every summer. She wants me to talk to my parents.'

'You haven't talked to them?'

I was breathing fast now. 'I don't know what to say.'

'It might be helpful to talk to somebody close.'

'I've known Ruth all my life.'

'You're nearly eighteen. You decide.' The decisive tone was so different that I was startled into looking directly into her face again. She looked as if she believed what she said. My heart beat painfully as ideas crowded into my head, so many that they kept flitting away, seeds on the wind. *I was born this way.*

'I want to be me.' She shifted in the chair. 'I go online.'

'What does that mean?'

'There are websites for people like me and we talk.'

'People like you?'

'Some people are trans, some people are crossing over, not everybody. We talk about stuff.'

'Could you help me out with that?'

'Some people think they're going mad.'

'Does it feel like that?'

'Not me. It feels more like people don't see other people straight.' My knees jerked at the skirt. I wanted to pace the room, peer through the venetian blinds at the station outside, the sunlight on the fields. 'People don't look properly. They see what they expect to see.'

'I guess that's true.'

'And I hate periods.'

'Your periods hurt?' She tugged at the collar of her yellow shirt. The buttons were pearly, different colours. She unbuttoned one, fastened it again. She wore colourless nail varnish. I was tapping my fingers together.

'Inside me. It doesn't belong.' I jabbed at my belly. 'People I talk to online have hormone treatment. Testosterone. I could live like a man.'

She tucked her hair behind her ears. 'Like a man.' I nodded. 'Is that what you feel?'

'I feel I got the wrong gender when I was born.' She opened her mouth and then I found myself saying, 'Maybe.'

For a moment her face was blank and then suddenly purposeful. 'You know that women as well as men have testosterone, and men have oestrogen.' She smiled, showing white, slightly uneven teeth. One of the front teeth was chipped. 'I came across some interesting research not so long ago. I wonder if you've seen it if you go online. It's about male scientists. Apparently they have the same levels of oestrogen as testosterone in their bodies.' She pulled a notepad towards her, looked up at the screen, scrolled with the mouse and scribbled something on the pad. 'Something to do with the way the scientists think and work. This generates hormonal changes, apparently.'

'Work?'

'The research – this bit of research, anyway – the conclusion is that the way you work can change your hormones. I suppose it depends on the work you do.' She handed me the slip of paper, web address, something medical. 'You might like to look it up.'

I gripped the paper hard. 'People online, they don't judge.'

'I hope I'm not going to judge either. But I do need to know what you would like to happen next.' I stared at the paper, at the whitening patches in my fingernails. 'Joey?'

'I don't know.'

'Ok. Well. You spoke about testosterone treatment. I guess you've looked up what happens with that. We don't start people on powerful hormones without lots of preparation.'

The chair creaked as I shifted. 'I wondered, maybe I've got other organs inside too.'

'You mean testes? Do you want to find out?'

'I can?'

'It would be straightforward to book some scans, tests, if that's what you want.'

'Who would know?'

'That would be up to you.' We were level, eye to eye. 'It's my job to help you with what you want, if I can.' I was remembering what I knew, a rush of things to say. 'I will have to understand what you want to happen and make sure it's within my brief as your GP.'

'I've read, some kids, they get operated on, to make them either girl or boy, and they grow up miserable.'

'That's possible.' She stretched her tanned legs, showing the swell of muscle in the calf. Perhaps she was a runner too. 'Any intervention will bring changes. That's why in this country there are strict guidelines. You have options, Joey. It depends whether you want to think about yourself in a medical way. Do you? Are you bringing a medical condition to this consultation? Is that what you mean? I can't promise counselling if that's what you want.'

'Counselling.'

'It's not an idea that appeals?'

'Like therapy.' My socks were rucked up inside my trainers.

She looked into the palms of her hands as if the answers were written there. 'If you want me to arrange hormone tests, scans, I can do that.'

My chair rocked on its legs. 'I don't have a condition.'

'Maybe not.' Her face was smilingly neutral. 'Can your family help?'

'My family has nothing to do with it.'

'You started with something that involved your brother, you said.'

'But I can decide.'

'Absolutely.'

As I got up she threw another grenade. 'You said you want to live like a man. The question you have to ask is, like a man or becoming a man? Different answers?'

The baby had fallen asleep in the girl's arms and she was nodding over its head.

Halfway through the afternoon, I leaned against the counter and watched two girls not buying a strappy green dress. Dr Hallgrave had given me a present. *Like a man. Becoming.*

At home, I rebooted the laptop from its endless updates and suddenly got a mental picture of myself walking across the sports field into school. I wore dark grey trousers, slung low, a polo shirt, thick-treaded black shoes. My hair was slicked flat at the sides. *Important updates have been installed. To see them, click here.*

Boys' toilets are disgusting, though. Everybody says. Why?

Zef's Blog

To enter a running club you have to choose Male, Female. The Borrowdale Fell Race has Mixed races. I could enter as Mixed.

I looked at videos of bodies coming off the top of Scafell Pike, running down the screes towards the Corridor Route. They come down like dancers only their arms are awkward. I don't think Carlos Acosta could run down a fell side any better than the best fell runners. His body looks super-male. They make men dancers do specific moves. Perhaps it's only men with certain physiques who get to be professional ballet dancers. I looked it up.

Fell runners in the mist on the videos could be any gender, not just either/or. When you look hard sometimes the only differences are in the thighs or whether the larynx is big. Everyone is skinny-hips.

Chat

Bex   Thanks.

Joey   Bastard troll.

Bex   Come to school for results?

Joey   I'd like to kill him.

Bex   His mum came round tonight. Mr Jolly rang her.
           She looked awful.

Joey   My driving test tomorrow.

Bex   You could have changed the date.

Thursday August 17

I went to the shop. The thought of going to school made me feel sick. Matt would be with his mates, blagging. His jeans would be flying low because it wasn't a school day, no uniform code, and his hair would be all long blond curls and fancying himself and knowing I'd run away from him. I pictured him leaning against the white corridor wall, dragging his trainers across the ridges of the green carpet, sneaking sideways looks under his lashes to see if a girl was watching. I wanted him to feel like shit. His mum obviously did. I hoped Mr Jolly had done something but maybe he couldn't. Bex wanted me to go to school with her, but I didn't want to see her in the same hall as Matt, chalk-white, black holes for eyes.

You don't even have to go to school for the results, you can get them online. And these results don't really count for uni, but our school makes us do the exams anyway. It's supposed to be good for us. My year group seems to like everyone suffering together, like waiting to get into a gig when you don't know the act.

I started straightening the stuff on a rack, until Shirley shoved her way out of the stockroom with more of it draped across her arms. 'What you doing here? I didn't expect you this morning. Don't you get some sort of exam results today?'

'Later.' I slid the straps of a lace-bodiced red and pink dress, with several layers of skirt, into the holders of the hanger that kept the whole thing together.

'Don't be daft,' said Shirley, slinging her armful on the counter. 'You want to get them now, don't you? Don't you want to tell your parents?'

'I'm off at lunch time, don't forget. It's my driving test.'

'Yeah, yeah, but exams are important.'

'The results will be the same tonight.'

'Stubborn bugger.' She was smiling, though.

My phone gave its feeble beep. It was another of those pictures. From Bex's number.

'You look as if you're going to throw up.'

'Maybe I'll go to school.'

'Well, cut along then. Something wrong?'

'No.'

'You look like somebody walked on your grave.'

'I'm getting burned not buried,' I said, buckling my bag around my waist.

'Well, you make sure there's none of that leaping in the river to celebrate sort of thing.' Her voice followed me down the street. 'Don't come back till after your test. It's going to rain. There won't be any punters to speak of.' There was a word for never giving up. Indefatigable. I tried not to run but I couldn't help it. The skirt tangled itself round my knees.

The photographer was already setting up his camera outside the front entrance of school. Every year they set up this pose, for the final year kids who think getting their photo into the *Gazette* is a good idea. They practise leaping about for the camera. I hadn't been near school since the end of July and it was just as if the buildings were wearing the burka too. Scaffolding covered the front of the main block, and the heavy glass doors that had been added last year to extend the entrance were hidden under long strips of canvas. The notice that was usually posted on a door was now attached to a freestanding easel:

STAFF AND VISITORS ONLY
MAY USE THIS ENTRANCE

Today, however, us nobodies were to be let through. On the other side of the easel was:

EXAM RESULTS IN HALL
ENTRY THROUGH FIRE EXIT ⬆

At the side of the main entrance, the fire door was wedged open. Rule-breaking was ok for today. Staff always find ways of breaking the rules. School teachers jump the lunch queue in front of you however long you've been waiting. It must be wonderful to know how important your work is so you can't wait like everybody else.

A few people were standing about waving slips of paper or looking at their phones. I slid past, pretending I was invisible. In the old days there'd have been separate entrances for boys, for girls. even separate schools. Whatever did people like me do in those days? Another noticeboard was propped against the reception desk, as if the one outside was not clear.

RESULTS IN SCHOOL HALL ➡

I guessed it was so people didn't badger Mrs Patten, the receptionist. She wasn't there, anyway. Half a dozen people from my year leaned against the long dark curve of the Reception desk, texting and chatting. The air felt electric, acrid. They noticed me.

'Woo-hoo, Josephine.'

'Fancy dress.'

'Who's gonna fancy ya today?'

'Who're ya kidding in that outfit?'

I couldn't be bothered to blank them. Matt must be already in school. He'd never stay away today. Maybe he was already outside Mr Jolly's door, ready for gutting. People said Mr Jolly was nice enough till you did something properly offensive.

The new olive-green paint on the doors and window frames irritated my eyes and nose, and a beige mist from new carpets made the air feel sticky. Masks at the door would have been good, like they wear in some places for flu. I'd have liked to clap Hallowe'en pumpkin eye-slots and grins across the faces of everybody standing round.

One of the doors behind Reception banged open and Mr Jolly walked slowly out of his room, examining a sheet of paper. He stared around, seeing no-one. The deputy head appeared in the doorway and suddenly Mr Jolly swivelled on the balls of his feet, like an old-style dancer, only he wore no jacket or tie and his collar was unbuttoned. 'I agree your stats. Ok. Publish.' He wasn't seeing anything except *his* results.

I'd seen him like this before, last year at results' time. He didn't look quite dressed then, either. Ma went to work in uniform and so did Mr Jolly for the rest of the year. In mufti, he looked like a normal human being. Like Ma at home. He rubbed his face with both hands, smothering a yawn, fingertips dragging at the grey-brown bags of skin beneath his eyes. Ma looked exhausted this morning, too, after spending all day yesterday at school – as if they both were patients who'd been told they didn't have a terminal illness after all. Mr Jolly caught my eye and leaned across the desk, displacing the morning's post and a heap of papers.

'Have you picked up your results yet, Joey? I'll be ringing your mother. If you don't mind. After you've spoken to her, of course.' He strode back into his room, where he could be heard talking loudly to the deputy head.

Mrs Patten made to clear the chaos on her desk, but the phone began to ring. She clucked, flipped both hands. 'Get along with you. If you've got your results, go outside.' Nobody moved. 'Good morning, would you hold the line, please?' clapping her hand over the mouthpiece. 'Go, go and tell your parents, God help them. Get along with you. Sorry to keep you.' She tried to produce a smile for the person at the other end of the phone.

They shuffled towards the door and I waited for them to pass, trying not to breathe in. The taint in the air was sickening – somebody's favourite cologne, unwashed clothes, overheated photocopier. Mrs Patten caught my eye. 'Don't stand here like a cardboard cut-out, Joey. If you're on your way to the hall, take a message.'

Everybody knows who they think I am. I took the slip of paper, went into the corridor and stared down its length. Some of last year's notices were still pinned up, curling where they weren't attached properly. The walls were like patchwork – notices, blank spaces covered by glass, empty display case. A Bex textile masterpiece, two years old, was still on show because Spikey Todd, her art teacher, had asked to keep it. She had made a textile forest, like a tapestry but lots of different stuff, not whatever it is you normally use for a tapestry, with strange creatures peering out between trees or wading into a pool. Bex said her latest work was much better, but this one still made you want to run your fingers over its surface. There's a saying, "She wears her heart on her sleeve". Bex sews her heart into her textiles. Something in my guts twisted at what was happening to her now.

My phone beeped again but I wasn't going to look. One of our English teachers rushed into the corridor, talking loudly into her phone as she ran towards the hall. I crumpled the sheet of paper in my hand. TO SIXTH FORM TUTORS. My tutor would have to do, if I could find her. Now that I was close to where Bex was likely to be, I didn't want to arrive.

The hall echoed with shouts, laughing, phone-tones. The walls here had been newly painted, too – off-white, hint of something – and the new carpet had been glued in place. The fishy aroma was almost overpowering. Long tables were set up against the right-hand wall. They must have been carried from the dining room, cleaned up a bit. Somebody had already left a grey mark in the paintwork. The smell of disinfectant competed with the odour of carpet glue, and bodies, and shampoo, and coffee. Several of the staff clutched mugs.

At the end of each table was a laminated label, A–E, F–K and so on. Envelopes had been lined up, but many had been shuffled out of order. Some schools pin up exam results so everyone can look at them. At least our school keeps them private. It is up to you to show and tell. I headed through the crowd in the direction of U–Z, thinking that Bex might be there, but it was hard to get past all the texting and crying and air-kissing.

Somebody grabbed my shoulders and dragged me aside. Spikey Todd was a stout, bearded guy with green eyes and the smell of white spirit on his hands. You could get addicted to it. White bristles had begun sprouting in his eyebrows. He was Bex's best teacher, her friend, her mentor. He'd been watching out for her since we were twelve.

'She's over there!' He had to shout. 'In the corner under the fire notices. Something's wrong. Have you got your results?' I shook my head. 'Go and talk to Bex, will you? I'll find your results and bring them across. Ok? Bex has done brilliantly so it's not that.'

182

I screwed my eyes tight, staring around the pale walls till I glimpsed several people from Bex's art group leaning together like mannequin dummies. No sign of Matt. At least Spikey Todd knew something was up.

'Are you supposed to do something with that?' I reared back as he bellowed, snatched the paper from my hand. Quickly he scanned the words. 'I'll deal with it, Joey, you get to Bex.' His beard was flecked with green paint, and so was his blue denim shirt, as if the sparkling anxiety of his bright green eyes had overflowed.

I zig-zagged through the crowd till I found Bex, slumped to the floor in a corner, hair behind her ears in that scraped-bare expression I was beginning to get used to. I squashed beside her, cringing at the tacky surface of the carpet. 'Spikey Todd says you've done brilliantly.' I could smell my trainers now, sweat and mud and something from a pavement.

'Yeah.' Her eyes flicked sideways and away again. Black holes in a white face, as I had imagined. Still, she was warm. I thought zombies would be cold from lying in the earth.

A voice above said, 'Matt pinched her results and her phone. Where were you?'

'Thought he might have your phone,' I said, wanting to touch the back of Bex's hand.

'Sophie got the results off him.' The speaker dropped to her knees, her blue gaze resting on Bex. 'He's a wanker.'

Sophie squatted on her heels alongside Bella, flicking her streaky blond plait into place. She shared my Critical Thinking classes. 'He dropped them when he ran off, stupid fuck. Bella nearly got hold of the phone.'

Bella tapped Bex's knees, which were hunched up under her chin. 'Let it go, forget him. You were right to give him the shove.'

'Bex thought you were meeting her.' Sophie spoke without

looking at me, her voice flat. 'We'd have met her. If we'd known you weren't going to be here for her.'

Bex said under her breath, 'Joey got rid of all the hate stuff online, Soph.'

'Yeah yeah, but what about today?'

Bex put her hands across her eyes. 'I could've handled Matt better.'

I realised that I was shaking. 'Didn't any of the staff see, try to stop him?'

'Too busy yadda-yaddering. Anyway, I got her results slip.' Sophie had taken up position on the other side of Bex, her arm laid casually across Bex's shoulders.

The hall began to empty, as if there had been a signal. I thought of the tide going out at Morecambe Bay. The bay could be deadly when the tide was out. Quicksands everywhere, shifting with the tides. I was going to have to tell Bex about the new image.

A couple of people still hung around Spikey Todd. Maybe he had my results envelope in his hand. I hoped he had delivered Mrs Patten's message or she would have a go at me. She has a long, curved nose, beaky, sits like a hawk on a fencepost, seeing everything when you think she's dozing. I watched as Spikey Todd gestured, tugged at his beard, clapped a member of staff on the shoulder, caught my eye, waved an envelope in my direction. I wrapped my skirt closely around my knees, staring at the rolling ridges in the carpet. Already it was snagging bits of white cotton, black threads from unravelling hems. Pity the cleaners, for once. Bex, beside me, seemed scarcely to breathe.

'Get your results, Joey.' She sounded as if she were sitting at the bottom of a trench. 'They won't hand them out unless you sign for them.' Her gaze was fixed somewhere. 'I tried.' She felt boneless beside me, a rag doll.

'Bex got brill results.' Sophie spoke as if Bex were a pet. 'Where is he?'

Bex tipped her head against the wall. Her hair smelt stale. 'I didn't see him. I waited outside for a bit.' One of those sighs that makes you wonder if she will ever breathe in again. 'I was one of the first in, there was hardly anyone in the hall.' She tipped her head back so sharply that it banged on the wall. 'I went to the atrium. He must have been on the lookout. He came up behind, grabbed me. I dropped my phone.'

'He was like stalking her.' Sophie chewed the end of her plait, baring her teeth. 'I hope his results are fucked.'

'Matt doesn't get dumped.' Bella's hands shaped Matt's ego into a balloon. She lives on a farm and is addicted to Cumberland wrestling. 'He thinks he's the man.'

'You're well rid. We just need to get your phone back.'

'Sophie. Let it go.' Bex lifted a hand, dropped it heavily into her lap.

I couldn't wait any longer. I leapt up, ran across the hall, past Spikey Todd and Mr Jolly, past a couple of lads still whooping at each other, and through to the atrium that linked the hall to the science labs and the arts block.

This huge glass building had been added last year, part of a big development scheme for the school. Mr Jolly had written to all the parents and some of them were buying more bricks for the new music studios, yet to get beyond a set of plans. This summer's scaffolding must be Phase 3. Ma said it was another of Mr Jolly's marketing efforts, said she would buy a couple of bricks, it would be hard-going for him. He told everybody the atrium would become the marketplace of the school. Lots of people did go there at lunchtimes to chuck money into the fountain. You could see the sky through the vaulted roof, and long glass windows opened on to the playing field. The Friends of the school had donated indoor plants

– a couple of yuccas, fig trees, heart-leaf philodendrons supposed to keep the air pure. They were still alive. The brown-tiled floor was wet. Someone had been splashing.

Matt posed on the coping stones that edged the fountain. He had tied back his hair, and two or three dreadlocks dangled across his face. Half a dozen lads nearby were laughing, shaking the water out of their sleeves. They were in the rugby squad, bluster and testosterone Matt's disciples. Once upon a time they were small, awkward, anxious new kids like the rest of us. Nobody's born with huge shoulders and bent noses.

If Mr Jolly had tackled him about the porn, Matt didn't seem bothered. He was holding a phone in each hand, staring from one screen to another. I burned for him to be forty, balding, getting fat and full of regret. Suddenly one of the others waved his phone. 'Nice one!' Half-hidden behind a philodendron, I ignored the vibration of my phone.

Matt began to juggle his phones, leaping into the middle of the group, whilst the others were engrossed by their messages. 'Skill, man!' 'Pussy!'

I've learned to be fast. Running's taught me to skip and dodge where I thought I might lose my balance or skid on tumbling scree. I slid past the leaves, between the bobbing figures, under Matt's arm, and snatched both phones from the air before anyone realised what had happened. I could have drowned in the silence.

'Slag.'

It wasn't Matt who spoke.

'Maybe,' I said, bouncing on the balls of my feet, stepping lightly back. I was acutely aware of the doors nearby.

'Leave it, Matt,' said another voice as Matt's face reddened and swelled.

I did not take my eyes from his face. I recognised Bex's phone, tucked it in my pocket and tossed the other towards

Matt's left hand. 'Watch it.' He had to dive and roll, fumbling. The phone cracked against the edging stones of the fountain.

'Dyke.'

I shrugged. Matt yelled, 'Fuck yourself, nobody else will.'

'Lezzie Wilcox.'

'Want a mouthful? She needs a mouthful.'

I backed to the doors and slipped into the hall, pressing Bex's little phone with its identifying purple cord against my throat. Seconds later, somebody burst through the doors and reached my elbow. 'Wait, wait.' It was another wide-shouldered figure, narrow in the hip – probably the perfect Greek athlete. Oliver. I had managed not to see him for almost a year. School's large enough for that. I suddenly remembered the feel of his skin, his warm breath in my neck. He had gentle hands. 'Joey, please, wait.' His face was pink. I felt hot too. 'Tell Bex, will you? It's not right. Matt's out of order. We're not all up for it. It's not right. I don't know how to stop him.'

'What?' I tried to look away, but his expression made me nervous. 'What?'

'He's a bastard. Tell Bex we don't all think like him.'

'I don't – what?'

He gestured at the phone. 'I'm so sorry. I wish I knew how to have stopped him. If it gets really nasty, tell Bex I'll be a witness, will you? I'm up for that, anyway.' Then he turned bright red, headed for the far doors and the exit. Tight brown curls clustered at the nape of his neck. Despite the bouncy walk, the neat jeans, the crisp shirt, his head was bowed. His twin was Bella. Maybe Bella had been the link Matt used to post online.

I looked at the screen of Bex's phone and opened the message – an image that could only have been made by superimposing Bex's head on another truly pornographic photo that Matt had found online. Bex would never in a million years have done anything like that, have got involved with anything like it. There were two men in the image, as well as the naked female figure. I saw the handcuffs, the swollen penises, the truncheon, the spread legs and then almost dropped the phone as Mr Todd called out, waving my results envelope. Bex was with him. The others had gone. In a flash I erased the picture. There was no time to get rid of the other messages sent by Matt when he stole the phone. At least she would not see this one. How many other phones had he sent it to? My throat closed up. I wanted to kick him in the balls. I'd find my winter boots, polish them, plan.

Bex mouthed *Thank you*, taking the phone before I could hide it. My hand trembled. I should have dropped the phone in the fountain. Mr Todd gave me the envelope, his eyes bright. 'Go on. Read them.' I turned away. He would know the results anyway, but I needed to straighten my face. The printout said I'd done ok. Bex said something about the summer art exhibition and Mr Todd said it was a great opportunity for her. 'See you at the Town Hall. Well done, Joey.' He ambled off.

'It's half-past ten. Can we go out over the playing fields?'

'If you like.' I folded and refolded my results slip into a hard, tiny lump of paper that I could shove into my shoe. Bex shook her head with a tight half-smile, eyes that flicked right and left around the near-empty hall, so plainly checking to see that it was safe that I had to look over my shoulder.

As I followed her to the main corridor I hoped Matt was still in the atrium, swearing at his broken phone, that somebody – Oliver, Bella, Sophie – would do something. Whatever Ma had said to Mr Jolly two nights ago, nothing had changed Matt. Like that old saying about the wind changing and your expression forever being stuck in the face you were pulling at the time. But it was a stupid saying and I didn't believe it. I had to know that everyone could change, even the most surprising people. It was the only way to make sense of what was happening to me. Even Matt. I pictured his huge body squeezed and reshaped like wet clay. Caroline could remould him into a jug, or a sheepdog. Bex could sew him into a tapestry and nail him to a corridor wall. We'd have to catch him first.

We found our way through a classroom that was being repainted, its fire doors wedged open. The workmen ignored us. A fine mist drifted over the field, two dogs chased each other in a wild dance and a man wrestled with a kite, a small child and a push-chair. From beneath its rain-shield came the yowls of a trapped baby. The kite fluttered to the grass. We sheltered against the wall beside the new bike sheds, lined up like empty peapods in a row. Driving test. I tried not to look at my watch. The man tried to roll up the kite.

'My father was hanging round on the main road when I got here.'

'I didn't see him.'

'You didn't come.' There was nothing to say. After a moment, Bex said, 'Sorry. Enough has gone wrong in the past few days for the next million years.' She bit her lip, teased hair across her cheek and tugged at her cuffs. 'It's like harassment,' she said after a while. 'I don't have to see him just because he's here. It's not in the agreement.' Her voice sounded thin in the open air. There were shouts from the far side of the field, where students from our year were kicking a ball. It bounced over the wall into the road beyond.

'What agreement?'

'I told you. You've stopped listening. My father.'

'Your father?'

'Who did you think?'

'Well, Matt?'

'Matt? Matt's just a jerk.'

She'd got him so wrong but she didn't know yet, didn't know about the porn. Her father was a creep but that was no big deal. 'Can't Jack help?'

'No.'

'Why can't he? Being a policeman. And he'll be your stepdad.' I pressed my skull into the gritty bricks of the wall. 'Why can't he help?' Mist was becoming rain.

Bex's fingers worked up and down her inner arm as if she were trying to find a pulse. 'I can't ask him, not with the wedding.'

'You said Jack would kill Matt.'

Her sleeve fluttered as she shrugged. 'I'm not getting Jack involved in my crap.' I didn't know what to tell her. How many messages were flying from phone to phone? Pornographic images move like Himalayan Balsam, seeding worldwide and pestilential. 'Anyway, Mum would be miserable. She'll do anything to avoid a fight.'

'A fight.'

'I don't want Jack dragged into something from our past.'

I remembered Caroline balanced on top of a ladder with paintbrush in one hand and paint pot in the other, whitewashing their little terraced house – Bex and me leaning on the ladder to steady it but trying to kick one another's ankles – Caroline shouting at us to stop messing about. She had fought for years. Yet Caroline had once been married to that man. Bex used to be Rebecca Ainsley. The image on the phone was like a burn in my brain. 'What sort of policeman was Jack?' Surely Jack would want to do something.

Bex took the pulse of the other wrist. 'Custody sergeant. That was his last job. He was in charge of anybody locked up in the station. If they were arrested.'

'He knows all about coping with thugs then.'

Bex looked across the field, not meeting my eyes. 'I'm not getting Jack involved.'

In a couple of hours I would have finished my driving test. Either I would have passed or I would not. Some things are cut and dried. 'I just wondered.'

'Show me your results.' I fished the wad of paper out of my shoe, surreptitiously glancing at the screen of my phone. The message icon flickered. I opened, erased. But the tinkling sound of Message Received was unmistakable. Bex sighed. 'Your test, I bet.'

A spatter of rain flung against the wall. 'Just a reminder.'

'You are so well organised. No wonder your Ma thinks you'll end up Prime Minister.'

The shock of it made me shout with laughter, excessive. 'She's got that wrong.'

'Well, you could go into the police. Jack says it's all about being clever these days.'

'Clever how?' The man with the pushchair was trying to get the child to walk faster. A gust of wind threw rain into my eyes.

'Oh, like being custody sergeant. Jack's clever. He says all the time his work was making the right judgement-call. He had to measure risk.'

'What's risky about locking up thugs and drunks?' The child began to cry as the man dragged a waterproof cape over its head. How did Ma cope with Noah and me together? It must be like prison, being tied by the ankle to little children, dragging them or being dragged. The girl with the baby in the surgery yesterday was practically a child herself. Risk sprouted up everywhere. Risk was sitting behind Noah when he was driving. Risk was waiting for some proxy to send the image again, again, seed on the wind and almost

191

indestructible. Risk was showing Bex the image. Caroline would go wild if she knew. I pictured Jack in his warm red pullover, his golden house, and the sheer nasty unkindness of Matt's attack. He'd been in the house whilst Jack was converting it. He used to adore Bex. He said he did. Bex was unaware, still talking. The man was trying to wedge the kite in the storage area beneath the pushchair. Anguished yells from baby and child together.

'Thugs can be mad, or ill. Jack had to decide whether locking them up was necessary.' Bex heaved herself away from the wall, rain-drops on her face like beads of sweat. 'Something about the principle of necessity. You'd like it, critical thinking stuff.'

'Yeah, sure, my principle would be lock up Matt before he does any more damage.' The man with the kite had stuffed it under his arm.

Bex gave a strange, barking laugh. 'Anybody under eighteen, the sergeant has to get an adult in. He wouldn't lock up Matt without.' Another gust of rain.

'But you can't tell by looking. Matt looks eighteen – twenty – how do you tell?'

'Yeah.' Bex started walking. 'That's the risk too. Come on.'

She increased her stride. 'Bex, why are we running? Matt's in school, he's not following us.' The pushchair lurched over the clumps of wet, newly-cut grass.

Suddenly Bex's phone and mine beeped together. We halted, opened the messages.

11:21 Sophie

Scrub messages, don't read

192

'What does she mean? Have you got a message from Sophie too?'

'Don't look,' I said. 'Don't look.'

'What does she mean – why – oh.' Bex swayed. I grabbed the phone by its purple cord and saw the image again. Again, I deleted it.

'You really have got to tell Jack.' Bex shook her head, and retched into the grass, throwing up slimy gobbets. 'For God's sake,' I said, 'he must be able to do something.'

'It's not important,' wiping her mouth on her sleeve.

'Bex.' I caught at her elbow.

'It's nothing.' She dragged herself free, sweeping wet hair from her face.

'Well, tell your real dad then.' I don't know what made me say it.

'Dominic.' Her tone turned the rain to ice. 'His name is Dominic. Not dad. He has nothing to do with me. I have nothing to do with him.' Then she said, in the same frozen voice, 'Text me when you've passed your test.' Her arms were tightly clasped across her chest and despite the chill of rain her cheeks were pink.

'You can't keep this inside you.'

'Watch me.'

Zef's Blog

I am cyborg. I drove like the machine and I were melded. I drove as if Matt were in the middle of my route, whichever way I turned. I flattened him thoroughly under the wheels. I three-point-turned him into a dinner-plate. Mr XL Drive-to-Success watched me reversing round a corner at the end of the test, was impressed.

Sophie forwarded texts from her friends, Bex's friends, saying they were never talking to Matt again, striking him off their list. I showed Bex, in the shop. I said, change your number, the companies will do it. They'll have seen the messages. Why won't phone companies ban people who text abuse?

It feels like I'm living in a different universe from everyone else. I can't make anyone pay attention. We're in parallel worlds, shouting. Shirley went on about being a model again, it was great PR, I can earn my way through university.

I could almost think it was funny. She has no idea when she asks me to be her clothes horse that I'm a Trojan horse. She wants me in her world and I could blow it up.

Bex's parallel universe has rules that I can't understand. She won't do anything to stop Matt. It's nothing to do with me, I keep telling myself. I said, 'Let me fix him. I'll sort him out.' But she kept walking away. Ma texted me about the results and then she rang. Mr Jolly had been on at her about my personal statement, getting it in early.

Research Sheets (Private)

<u>Risk assessment</u> means assessing the risk and potential risk that each detainee presents to themselves, staff, other detainees, and to others coming into the custody suite.

Every detainee is an individual. Changing events and circumstances for the detainee, and within the custody suite, may affect the detainee's mood or behaviour and the risk that they pose to themselves and others.

Jack must have been mind-reader to do this

Risk assessments should be as objective as possible and assumptions should never be made when assessing risk. Police custody is stressful for most detainees and for some it is particularly traumatic. Simply being placed in a police cell may immediately raise the category of risk for a detainee.

emotional minefield – what does Jack remember?

mindfield??

Zef's Blog

I've been watching the videos again, Noah and Simon at the Bowder Stone. Noah moves like a lobster, all claws and shoulders, and Simon's an elegant fish, flicking and arcing up the rock. I practise talking deep. It's easier than I thought. You open up your diaphragm and let the air sort of rumble at the bottom of your ribcage. People expect men to have deep voices. Sometimes on the radio I can't tell whether it's M or F.

I asked Ma, roundabout, how she copes in her school with bad stuff online, abuse. She said girls are the worst. Some nice girls send wicked messages. She makes them read the messages out loud. She says they don't realise half the time what they're posting. When they stand in her official headmistressy office and have to say their texts aloud they can't bear it. Ma wanted to know why I was asking. Pa says she's worse than any bloke as an employer. She's so interested you don't escape.

Surfing, I found the clips from the fashion show. I guess we signed some sort of consent form but I didn't realise it meant seeing me onscreen. I didn't notice the clothes they put me in but it's me in that big room, wooden panels, me in narrow trousers, shirts with high collars like from another century, waistcoats, a cloak thing. I really don't remember the shorts or the big boots laced to the knee. I never saw myself walk before, not from behind. My hips don't sway from side to side like the other models.

Here it is, the bloody pink blob tucked in between bladder and coccyx.

U= uterus, such a little organ, such a huge effect.

Thank you gutenburg.org.

If Matt was a woman he'd still be gross. It's not his dick that makes him gross, it's his mind.

Wonder if Jack was/is any good as a mind-reader.

Friday August 18

Bex did not come to the shop all day, again. She rang in, Shirley said, bad headache, something. Bex never has headaches. I knew she wouldn't be able to bear it. I hoped she had told Caroline. The sun shone all day long and after the drizzle of yesterday, the racks of clothing seemed to radiate heat, thickening the air. On the way home I felt almost sick for the cool of my room, the window open to let in the evening, birdsong, Marmalade on my knee. He hadn't come in all night and I needed his sharp claws.

Voices clanged in the kitchen. I stood in the hall, suddenly filled with dread.

Noah: Did somebody move my wet-suit?

Ruth: Moll, I think I'll be ready to serve in about five minutes. Don't disappear, Noah, will you? Oh thanks, Simon. The plates are in the bottom oven. I'll want the small ones for the starter.

Pa: Hey sweetheart, there you are. Am I laying a place for Bex tonight?

Me: No.

Pa: Is she poorly again? She's looking a bit peaky. You girls need a holiday.

Ruth: I'm sorry she isn't coming. Do you know what's wrong with her, Joey?

Me: No.

Ma: Is it me or is it getting hot in here? Andrew, when you've finished with the table could you open the window? I must be getting hormonal.

Noah: Si, did you see my wet-suit? I swear it's walked.

Pa: Nothing wrong with your hormones.

Ruth: I'll dish out here, I think. How hot are the big plates, Simon? I wonder if we need glasses for water, too.

Ma: Noah, please. The doorframe won't take your pull-ups indefinitely. Is your hand steady enough for carving? It's no good scowling. I didn't move your wet-suit.

Simon: Something smells wonderful.

Pa: Prosciutto and asparagus for starters? Leg of Rough Fell lamb. Knife sharpener?

Simon: I've read about Rough Fell Lamb. And isn't there another local breed, sheep that graze on saltmarshes?

Noah: Mutton dressed as lamb.

Ma: Knife sharpener third drawer along. Saltmarsh lamb is different, Simon.

Pa: Your wet-suit's in the garage.

Ma: Caroline rang this morning, She's asked Ruth to help out at the reception, too. Someone's let her down. That's nice, isn't it? Not being let down I don't mean. We'll practically all be there. We can see the house at last. You don't mind do you, darling? If Ruth and I are there too?

Noah: What's it doing in the garage?

Simon: Maybe I could cook for you one evening.

Ma: Thank you, that's a very kind offer, but aren't you busy most nights? Noah said it was difficult getting you both off shift together for tonight.

Ruth: I'll enjoy helping for Jack and Caroline's reception, seeing Caroline happy. Those little girls seem to think Jack's the king. I hope Bex is going to be completely well. Would you sit down now, please? The prosciutto is perfect, crispy.

Pa: So it went ok at school today?

Ma: Only two or three going through clearing. One girl completely changed her mind. Peter Jolly's extremely pleased with himself. I guess he's done well by Joey.

Noah: Who's a clever girl then.

Ruth: When does your university application form have to be ready?

Ma: We try to get them off next month. Hit the admissions tutors as soon as we can, before they get jaded. That lamb smells delectable, you've done it again, Ruth.

Simon: Is it appropriate to ask about your results, Joey?

Ruth: Watch out, the plates are red hot.

Ma: Politics, History, English, Psychology, Critical Thinking. Five top grades. They don't count for universities, but the school reference will be really good. Better had be.

Simon: You must be delighted, Joey.

Noah: They're all wordy subjects.

Simon: What is the exam in Critical Thinking?

Pa: Where did you buy the lamb?

Noah: Maths without numbers. Passes as logic.

Simon: It's amazing, Joey, I didn't realise you were so – I thought you were the outdoor type – running, dry stone wall sort of thing. I didn't know – I'm digging myself a hole.

Pa: She takes after her father.

Noah: Oh God, another competition.

Ma: I caught sight of Bex with Caroline in town this afternoon when I was driving through. I thought

Bex looked wonderful, like having a flower painted on her hair.

Noah: What? What's she had done? What happened to my portion, Ruth?

Ma: I've told you about wolfing food. You know where Bex had the streaks of red and white? She's had a sort of flower tinted right across where the streaks used to be. Shades of deep pink – almost purple. Like a Chinese screen, almost. I could fancy it myself.

Pa: I thought you said she was ill, Joey.

Ruth: She'll be thinking about the wedding, won't she? Talking of walls, are we having another go tomorrow?

Ma: Have you decided what to wear? That reminds me, did you see that that woman about more fashion photos?

Noah: We found a video of you, Jay-Babe. The hotel's got the fashion show on its website. Jay-Babe could make all our fortunes if she could be bothered.

Me: I'm entering the mountain marathon.

Pa: You can't, lovey.

Noah: You have to enter as a pair.

Simon: What is the mountain marathon, please?

Ma: Noah, can you carve? Let's get this party back on track. Joey, I know you don't like a fuss but we are so very proud of you. I knew you'd be brilliant. Your driving test too.

Noah: Bugger.

Pa: Noah.

Ruth: Use the hand-towel, it's just behind you. Is it deep?

Simon: Actually, perhaps I could carve?

Ma: Your mother would be proud of you.

Simon: Do you like it carved from the middle or the end?

Ma: Plasters in the second drawer along. Stop dripping blood on the table.

Ruth: Where did you learn to carve like that?

Simon: My father taught me. He's a chef.

Ruth: In London? Your own place? I must look you up when I'm back.

Simon: It's in the family. My grandfather started it.

Pa: Where did you learn to climb, Si?

Simon: At school. I went to boarding school. We had a climbing wall. But we didn't often climb on real cliffs. That's why I joined the climbing club in Leeds.

Ma: You're doing a great job there. You can come again.

Simon: Is your application for university ready, Joey?

Me: No.

Pa: We don't want her to go too far away, do we, Moll? But we're just sentimental.

Ma: She's full of ideas, aren't you, darling? She's been to several open days. And there are hordes of websites. She doesn't need advice from me. It's really hard to stay out of it, Simon, when it's half my life, getting pupils on the right route.

Ruth: Hard work circumnavigating parents, I should think.

Ma: Anyway, she can drive now. Andrew, watch what you're doing.

Ruth: How do you get pupils on the right route? I can't see anyone getting Joey to do something she hasn't decided on. Look at Noah.

Pa: Toast to Joey.

Ma: Wait a bit, Andrew, let's dish out the rest before it gets stone cold. Could you pass round the veg whilst you're on your feet? Noah, are you joining us?

Simon: We could run up Coniston early tomorrow, if you want. You could come, Joey.

Pa: Shit.

Ma: Oh Andrew – that was a really lovely Rioja.

Noah: Seriously, Pa, white wine works. Let me –

Ma: Don't you dare. That's Ruth's Sancerre. This meal feels doomed.

Pa: There's too much testosterone in this room. I'll change.

Ruth: I've heard about the white wine trick.

Ma: I wonder if my elderflower champagne would count.

Simon: Would you think of London for university, Joey? I wanted to get away from the south. I guess people in the north might want to get away from here.

Me: No.

Ma: Money's changed everything. It all costs so much now.

Noah: So what're you going to do, Jay-Babe?

Ma: I know I should stop making suggestions. It's the job. It deludes me into thinking my opinions matter. Mind you, it's all my school parents think about, where their kids are going to university. It's infectious. I didn't mean to catch it myself.

Simon: Did I carve enough, do you think?

Noah: I know what it is, you don't know what you think, you're fannying about, wondering about a gap year, not going to uni at all, putting it off.

Me: No.

Noah: People who haven't a clue what to do with themselves do gap years. If you don't get it by eighteen, when are you ever? Waste of time.

Ruth: You carve like a professional.

Noah: Are we going to eat this meal or just look at it?

Ma: We all talk too much.

Ruth: I wonder what too much is.

Pa: What have I missed? What are you saying?

Ma: Whatever Joey decides to do when she leaves school we'll support her, won't we?

204

Pa: You're very tense, lovey. You'll sail into university.

Ruth: I'll put the veg back in the oven for a bit.

Noah: Dish up, Si. Shame Bex isn't here. There's a girl knows just what she wants.

Ruth: You seem very sure.

Simon: She told us about her exhibition the other night. When we walked her home.

Ma: She has a remarkable talent. And so has Caroline. They're such a lovely family.

Me: I got the wrong gender when I was born.

Noah: Oh for God's sake.

Ruth: Noah. Please.

Pa: What? Did I miss something? What did she say?

Me: I'm not hungry. I'm going for a run.

Simon: Wait, Joey. Please wait.

Pa: Where are you going, Joey? What's happened? I leave the room for two minutes.

Noah: Joey's gay or something. She says. It's ok. For fuck's sake, Joey, don't run off, nobody thinks twice about it these days. Tell her, Si.

22.43 Ruth

> Where are you? Ruth
> xxx

22.56: Noah

> What was all that about.

> Sulk then.

> Where ru?

Ma's in a right state.

Si says 3rd sex in Thailand.

no big deal 2 b gay

ru in luv with Bex?

sorry, none of my biz.

Research Sheets (Private)

"Oh, what ARE you going to do, Laura?" cried Pin, in anxiety.

"I'm going to have a good run," said Laura; and tightened her hair-ribbon.

"Oh, but you can't run in the street! You're too big. People'll see you."

"Think I care? If you'd been years only doing what you were allowed to, I guess you'd want to do something you weren't allowed to, too. Good-bye!"

She was off, had darted away into the leaden heat of the December morning, like an arrow from its bow, her head bent, her arms close to her sides, fleet-footed as a spaniel; Pin was faced by the swift and rhythmic upturning of her heels. There were not many people abroad at this early hour, but the few there were, stood still and looked in amazement after the half-grown girl in white, whose thick black plait of hair sawed up and down as she ran; and a man with mop and bucket, who was washing statues, stopped his work and whistled, and winked at Pin as she passed.

Cross and confused Pin trudged after her sister, Laura's hat and gloves in one hand, the leather bag in the other.

wisdom = running or running away?   AM I in love with Bex?
                                      What??

Zef's Blog

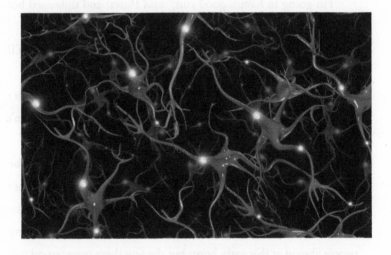

my exploding brain or picture of wisdom?
Normal neural pathways look a muddle in this pic
You aren't wise if you think you are, you're BLIND
when nobody's telling you who you are you have a chance
of finding out
am I in love with Bex?
noah's on about sex he's obsessed with fi

FOUR
ROCK

Zef's Blog

Nobody tried to talk to me last night, nobody knocked on my door. Can't find Marmalade. Can't get hold of Bex. Wouldn't know what to say to her anyway.

The person who wrote *The Getting of Wisdom* is called Henry Handel Richardson but really it's Ethel Florence Lindsey Richardson. One day I'm going to write a book about all the people playing hide and seek.

I skipped breakfast, shower, everything this morning, went straight to the shop. At lunchtime I bought a toothbrush and toothpaste, washed in the shop's toilet.

Bex came back to work, mouth zipped. Her new hair flower is another work of art. This afternoon Julia turned up, talking at Shirley. She wants to buy 'something special' for Bex, for the wedding. I hid in the stockroom, Bex sneaked in, said it was a ploy to make Caroline feel awkward. It was almost old times, hugger-mugger. She talked to me, proper talk.

I can't find the proper words to say how I feel. Except I feel for Bex, not about her, I think. Not sorry for – it's too close. Shirley came to get us, said she understood Bex's dad being a bit funny, now there's going to be a stepdad. Another man around all the time, Shirley said, you can understand a father getting anxious. Bex turned into zombie again. We had to go back in the shop, and the woman, Julia, kept picking things off racks, trying to drape them on Bex. I said, 'Bex's got a dress already.' Shirley tried to smooth things over. 'Bex might want something for the autumn, new stock.' Not from Girly-Shirl.

Ma knocked on the door and said would I like to borrow the car tomorrow. She looked kind of crumpled. I want her to hug me. They've gone out to the pictures. But I will take the car. Amazing.

Research Sheets (Private)

Yossarian looked at him soberly and tried another approach. "Is Orr crazy?"

"He sure is," Doc Daneeka said.

"Can you ground him?"

"I sure can. But first he has to ask me to. That's part of the rule."

"Then why doesn't he ask you to?"

"Because he's crazy," Doc Daneeka said. "He has to be crazy to keep flying combat missions after all the close calls he's had. Sure, I can ground Orr. But first he has to ask me to."

"That's all he has to do to be grounded?"

"That's all. Let him ask me."

"And then you can ground him?" Yossarian asked.

"No. Then I can't ground him."

"You mean there's a catch?"

"Sure there's a catch," Doc Daneeka replied. "Catch-22. Anyone who wants to get out of combat duty isn't really crazy."

If you do what guys do, look like a guy, why wouldn't everyone assume you were M?

is what I do the same as being me?

CHANGE what I DO = change ME?

if your parents think you're a girl they assume what you do is what girls do, but if you do things that other people think are boys' things, why don't they assume you're a boy?

does being M/F get decided by what you do? or you act M/F because your life gets shaped by what your parents expect? and your brother?

what happens to wild children?
children on the streets?

Sunday August 20

Ma has packed a proper picnic and I might even eat some of it. Her face is shiny this morning. I haven't seen Pa since Friday night. Ruth and I have talked about food, the washing, Marmalade being off on a bender. She asked about Bex, but I don't know what's happening with Bex, I can't understand her. I pretended I didn't hear.

Ma gets the car out of the garage and hands me the keys. Then she pats my shoulder and goes back in the house. I've never driven this car, her pride and joy.

I sit in the driver's seat and have to change the mirrors. Ma and I are about the same height but we obviously don't like the same angle of view. I sit farther back from the steering wheel than Ma. The seat fits her rather than me.

As I take the corners of the A591, heading for Keswick and Borrowdale, I work out that Ma must have insured me to drive her car and I have to pull over into a lay-by. I bet it cost a bomb. She must have done it yesterday, while I was at work.

I get out of the car to look at the rising fells. It's nine o'clock, just after, and the road is quiet. Sunlight on the shoulders of the Kentmere fells warms my shoulders too. I might be looking at Wansfell, maybe Fairfield. I'm not certain. Everything is achingly familiar though I can't label everything I see. There are smaller fells I don't have names for. They're on the ordnance survey maps. You see things differently from the driving seat.

I look west, towards Windermere. Sometimes I think this is the most beautiful view in the world. The Way There. *There*. I imagine myself an archer, arms straining as I pull back the string from the bow, my body poised against the growing tension, gripping the arrow, then releasing it into a soaring, rising arc to the heart of *there*. The sky is that pale blue you get when no cloud will form. The elements are balanced – earth, air, fire, water. Today I will drive to the Bowder Stone and keep my balance on the Stone, get the grip right.

I've told Ma I'm running in Borrowdale. I promise to keep my phone in my pocket and switched on. I don't tell her the signal is patchy/non-existent. I say that I mean to be home by five. Noah's inflatable crash mat is in the boot and I expect to spend half an hour blowing it up because the pump has vanished into one of Noah's black holes.

This morning, early, before Ma, even, Simon knocked on my door. Not that I had slept. I read the rest of *The Getting of Wisdom*, looking for clues about Bex. She reads books nobody else would touch so maybe they're important. Simon had some of his clothes tucked under his arm, and a frowning, shy expression as he held them out. 'Try them,' he said, 'walk about the town in men's clothes. See how you feel.' Everything was clean. I can't process it but his yellow tee shirt has found its way into my rucksack. Wearing it, I might be like him on rock. I've pinched the bag of chalk, too. The shoes are mine. The beat of my heart skips whenever I picture climbing, and my hands stick to the steering wheel but I'm going to do it. I'm climbing that Bowder Stone.

This car is sweet on corners. My body wants to lean as I steer. Me + car = I am Cyborg. All of a sudden I get what the bikers love, the closeness to the road, the machine's power, the tilt, the swooning speed, o god. I could be a biker.

O god the car swerves and I brake, grabbing the wheel. I'd like to get safely into Borrowdale. So that's what Jack does when he thinks about Risk, or insurers. Am I the sort of driver to crash into walls for the joy of cornering on two wheels? The rush of adrenalin has brightened my concentration. Maybe I'd do better with a microchip in my brain. I could volunteer for an experiment as soon as I'm eighteen. November.

The road from Windermere to Ambleside to Rydal curves like a snake through undergrowth, under the summer-green branches. The road has muscle and sinew, adjusts to the landscape, flows. Is water muscular? It's strong. I think about 'spineless'. The snake has no spine but the python can crush a pig to death if it wants to. We're always being told how good it is to have 'backbone'. Brave, a proper human being. The climbers I looked at on videos seemed incredibly bendy to me. Snakes, lizards, fish, we all come from the sea.

I pull down the sun visor to look at my reflection, unclamp the jaw. Driving is meant to be liberating, not to make me sweat. I'd like to switch on the radio, but my left hand won't leave the steering wheel unless to grab the gear lever or handbrake. It has a life of its own.

I stop at Thirlmere, by the viewpoint over the reservoir. Campervans stack up in front of the viewpoint, people eating sausage rolls. I swig the orange juice Ma has packed. Hot day, great for tourists. I gaze at the far side of the lake, dark and heavy with conifers, a green that seems to soak up light instead of giving it back. Beside me someone takes a photo. 'It's wonderful,' she says. 'I can't believe we're here.' I realise with a shock that she's talking to me. Here I am, Public.

'We're from Wolverhampton,' she says as if I were about to be interested. 'What about you? Have you come far?'

I say, 'I live down the road. I live here.' I realise it's not very exact but she doesn't seem bothered. Her face crinkles with genuine envy.

'We'd love to buy somewhere round here,' she says, turning to the man who approaches. 'We'd love to live here wouldn't we, Jeff?'

He hefts his binoculars to his eyes, smiles at the view, isn't getting involved. I say goodbye and get back into the car. I feel better. I'm so lucky that Ma and Pa both wanted to live here. For what I have received I am truly thankful amen. It's a long time since I was anywhere for grace to be said but amen feels great today. We learned it in RE. It means "So Be It". "So Be It" sounds good for today.

I stop in Keswick to find a loo and that's instantly a problem. I slide into the Disabled, feeling cross and guilty at the same time. Still, that I can park the car between others – look over my shoulder, assess the width, reverse neatly, brake – makes me Cyborg. Machinery kills, but I won't, I am Cyborg with my posthuman brain. I am Enabled.

Matt is big bug or Himalayan Balsam.

When I take the road to Borrowdale I have to focus on the road instead of gawping at the lake and its reflected fells. Borrowdale is the most beautiful of all. Maybe. I glimpse early canoes and kayaks, somebody standing knee-deep, white-backed, a new arrival. He'll probably go home white, too. In a flash I know that I'm free to stop the car anywhere. I park like a sight-seer at places I used to despise – the falls at Lodore, the bridge at Grange – get out, stride around the car, lean against it like an owner, drive on. I wave at the trees, royalty.

It's well past eleven by the time I switch off the engine in the Bowder Stone car park. I feel giddy. If somebody x-rayed me now, they'd find my arteries and veins sparkling, all rich minerals through quartz. I have said out loud to Ma and Pa, are you sure you labelled me correctly? Has it occurred to you that you might have got it wrong, that day when you stared at me in Ma's arms in the hospital, my face still screwed tight and smeary? Have you thought that you've been kidding yourselves, all these years? That what you want is another version of you? I inhale so deeply that I'm dizzy on the smell of bracken in full growth. I'm going to explode, lungs, guts, brain. I could shout at Bowderstone Crag and King's How, rearing up behind their cladding of trees to the skyline above, waiting to toss another boulder into the valley. I am who I am.

A walker crunches through the car park, gives me a sideways look. How long have I have been leaning on the bonnet, with the car door wide open, keys in the ignition? What if Ma's car were stolen? I snatch my phone from the car seat where it's been lying in full view.

When I reach the Bowder Stone I am dismayed to find two other people already there, experts, it's plain. One of them is teasing excessive chalk from handholds. He has brought a brush for the purpose. It seems bizarrely housewifely to dust a rock before climbing.

I decide to begin with what the girl has already completed – the girl who is about to start climbing at an impossible angle. She limbers up by going hand over hand up the underside of the wooden staircase. I will do that except that I want to use my feet too. I have to work out how to swing my legs above my shoulders, defying gravity as the others seem to.

Despite recent rainfall, the wood is dry, flaky. I launch myself, clinging like a slug to the underside of a bucket. I am unprepared for the sheer downward weight of my legs, dangling and flailing. A voice says calmly, 'This your first time?'

and cool hands lift my legs so that I can jam my feet into the steps. I feel a total clown. 'Go on,' he says, 'you're doing fine, you've got the right idea.' He wouldn't help a lad but I can't resent it. Somehow I scrabble up half a dozen steps until I lose my grip. I ought to have brought the crash mat from the car. In videos, climbers seem to land on their feet. Probably all their falling over is cut.

'Your grip's good,' says the man, extending a hand. He has a pleasing, ordinary face. I say that I've been practising with a spring-loaded grip to strengthen my fingers. The girl calls him, impatient, and he backs away with an apologetic spreading gesture. 'It's upper body strength you need for overhangs,' he tells me. 'Maybe a few more press-ups?'

I watch them for a while. The girl has launched herself again, and needs his help to reach the first foothold, which seems to be well above her head. It's incredible that she's so happy to be almost upside down. There's a cleft in the rock that runs parallel to the diamond edge of the boulder, leading to the top, and she's trying to use it for her ascent. The rock bulges like a swollen cheek. Suddenly she swings free, gripping by the tiniest of finger-holds, and throws herself up at the rock. And one foot is locked into place above the bulge. Maybe she's got cyborg hips. Now she twists her hips insanely, bringing the other leg into position, ready for its move. In seconds, she has swarmed above the rocky cheek and practically runs to the top of the Stone. She isn't ant or bee, yet she runs across the rock like someone who lives on it, then bounds down the wooden steps, spitting on her hands, wiping them on her shorts. The man turns to me. 'Do you want some help? We can help, can't we, Jane?'

I say I came alone so I wouldn't make a fool of myself. 'Fair enough,' he comments, and the girl says, 'But Fred can give you a leg up if you want. We've got to go in a minute.'

I want to refuse. My thighs tremble. I've strapped on the chalk bag and dip my hands into the fine powder. 'Not too much,' he warns. 'You slip if you have too much. You have to be able to sense the rock, feel all the little cracks, so's you can get a good grip.' Jane steps forward with the brush, dusts off the excess. She's built a bit like me, I realise – flat-chested, narrow-hipped, with long, muscled thighs. 'We've got to get back to Brum.' She wrinkles her nose as she smiles. 'It's been a fab weekend. I'd stay till late but Fred's got the early shift, three o'clock.' She has a lean, brown face, rather like his and their voices have a similar twang. I think of Dr Hallgrave and wonder if she's truly paired as these seem to be. Is this Yin and Yang?

They ease me into place beneath an overhang, in the boulder's shadow, where white blobs extend sideways, and I recognise them. It's where the beginners start. You go sideways like a crab, not up. If you fall, you won't break. The route is only a couple of feet above ground level, in the dark niche between the upward jut of rock and the flattened soil beneath.

I lay my hand on the rock and lean into it. The rock smells warm, old, surprisingly of vegetation. Rock digs into the palms of my hands like someone waiting to be noticed. Like Marmalade when he is determined to get my attention, bony-headed. Rock is the earth's skeleton. I reach sideways, my fingers almost stroking the rock to find the finger-holds that others before me have used. 'Keep close to the rock,' says the man. 'Don't let your body weight become a drag. Find your balance before you start. Anticipate where you'll be, how your body will feel.' *Picture it, talk about it, name it, do it, become what you dream.* This is what it means. 'Ok?'

His question is the starting gun. I swing one leg high to the right, wedge the foot into a gap. Gravity wants to suck me down but my back arches. The hardest part is working out what to do with the dangling leg. I thought I was supple but I'm scissor-stiff by comparison with this pair. He doesn't mean balance the same way I do. He means I've got to find a way of breathing smoothly even when my diaphragm is screaming. Now I've to move my centre of gravity to the side, and I feel the whole weight of myself through my fingers, wrists, forearms, shoulders. The jammed foot has to extract itself.

'Isn't it easier to go up?' I squeeze out the words, fall off. He's placed their crash mat under me, so the bounce is ok.

'You'll get better,' says the girl. 'Keep at it. You have to practise. You'll be fine.'

I watch them pack their bags. Once they've gone, I decide to try the staircase again. This time I'm going to swing my legs above my head, same as she did. On my own. Same as she did. I will have to inflate the crash mat, in case.

After half of hour of struggle I run up the Stone the easy way, not the wooden staircase but the rocky steps smoothed out by toddlers and grandmas. The hills are watching. I lose patience with bouldering. The very act of leaping up the rock is such a release that I think I will give in, run the route where I fell asleep and complete the round instead of retracing my steps. I'll wade across the Derwent, I know where to go, through the woods, up the quarry path. I'll jog up High Spy, I know it so well, then over Maiden Moor to the end of the ridge, to Catbells, down towards Hause End, back along the track above the Derwent, back to the crossing point. The track is easy, easy running. I'll probably have to dodge past a playgroup coming down from Catbells. I won't even bother to move the car. Then I truly can say to Ma that I've been running.

Yet I can't avoid this great slab of rock. I wish I could feel that it threatens me, but it doesn't. Here it balances, spattered with chalk and human perspiration, lichens marking its surface, and rampant, insistent vegetation sprouting where you least expect. Rock is ok with me. I am building a wall from baby rocks.

I dawdle back to the bottom of the steps and glower at the overhang. There's something about this rock, about laying my hands on it, that won't go away. It stares me in the face, every weathered crevice. Thousands and millions of years have gone into its making and it won't back off.

Zef's Blog

I tore such a chunk out of my knee that Ma took me to casualty. Only 2 hours waiting. And I did something to the gastrocnemius that I might live to regret. Driving home from Borrowdale was agony. Every time I pressed the accelerator, calf muscles screamed. There's blood on the upholstery.

I ruined Sunday night. The things Ma has not said:

1. *Tell the truth.*
2. *Take somebody with you in case you get hurt.*
3. *I trusted you.*
4. *I lent you my car.*
5. *I expect you to be more sensible than Noah.*

I replay the commentary as if it was directed at Noah:

1. *You're a terrible communicator*
2. *You're always doing something daft to yourself*

3.   *For goodness sake, take more care next time*
4.   *At least you didn't run the car off the road*
5.   *Will you try setting a better example?*

Pa knocked on the door to say he felt I'd taken advantage and it wasn't like me.

He didn't look like Pa, his face all smoothed out.
I wanted to punch him in the mouth. I don't like the feeling of being angry.

Maybe I do. Girls don't shout and scream unless they're off their faces.

Zef's Blog

Pa's been back, sitting on the end of my bed. He said, 'I am sorry. I haven't looked at you properly for years. Maybe I kept on seeing you as if you were still a little girl.'

We both got emotional. I wonder if he and Noah hug each other like this, privately.

Marmalade's still not home. Hunting nights, just what he loves.

I can't get rid of the sense that Pa was putting it on, he didn't really mean it. I bet Ruth has been talking to both of them. She probably still is, right now.

Give me cats not people. Cats knead your thighs with their paws. I cut Marmalade's front claws for sheer preservation but still he purrs like crazy. He calls it grooming and pats my face to tell me I'm doing ok. I don't know exactly when I last saw him. Where the hell is he? I try telling myself about the time of year, his time, summer time, dawn, when his strange song yowls up the stairs. He's bringing home booty. He streaks straight under my bed to crunch, unless he's so full of rabbit or mouse that he makes for my pillow and sprinkles it with thorn, grass seeds, moulted hair. Ma's given me fresh bedding but I don't need it, everything's seedless.

I can't sleep. I'd really like it if Marmalade would lie with all his weight across my neck.

I don't know what to think about Bex. It's like she's cutting me out. It's like, where's Bex, where's my father? He doesn't want me, just his idea of me. Bex is better off with a stepdad. Jack has chosen Caroline, Bex, Susie, Tess. He knows what he's getting and it's what he wants.

Pa doesn't like what he's got. That's what I think. I wish I could forget it.

Tuesday August 22

Monday was a day for sleep. Ma made me stay home so she could have me under her eye and for some reason I let it happen, like a kid with a temperature who couldn't go out to play. A wad of bandage sat on my knee and from time to time I replaced the cold compress around my calf, to reduce the swelling. I could have worked in the shop, but it was such a relief to stay away. I did not have to see Bex's zombie face. I could watch out for Marmalade.

Three of us added to the wall – Ruth, Ma and me – and we finished the second layer of stones. They worked on either side of me but not like on guard duty. Pa was away in Ennerdale on the new project, Ma said, and Noah and Simon were on long shifts. She must have said something to Noah because he only screwed up his face at me, and Simon smiled as usual and said he was looking forward to another session of wall-building.

Every now and then Ma would touch my shoulders as she stepped behind me, or she'd take one of my hands to look at broken finger-nails. Once, she tipped my head by the chin and stared into my face for a long, unblinking minute, oddly reminding me of Marmalade. Ruth kept on picking up stones, trying to make them fit. Ma talked about soil, stones, birds, herbs, washing on the line, picnic lunch, fish soup for supper.

Ruth sat late in the garden as the sun went down behind the fells, her notebook on her lap. Ma came out from clearing away, and I sat between them on the rough bench. We listened to sheep bleating, a twilight tractor, a distant quad bike, a dog, and the birds, of course, the house-martins soaring and twittering and swooping till the curves of their flight were like arcs of song. Swifts, keening. Ma said Marmalade would be in his killing fields. He'd come in eventually, and probably sick up all over the house. I lay in bed for hours, turning over, rubbing my eyes to get rid of the tears. They had been so kind, Ma and Ruth. They had spent all day on the wall with me, building it up. I heard Pa's car on the drive, the slamming of the front door, a low murmur. He did not come to say goodnight.

Next day, I strapped up my leg to keep the dressing in place under the skirt and went back to the shop. The first shock was that Bex was not there. It was even more gross having to put my hands on all the floppy clothes again. I kept thinking of snakes sloughing their skins. Pa had brought home a casing last week. It was still on a windowsill in the hall. Even the new autumn range of female stuff dangling on the racks was repellent. I tried not to think about Marmalade. What would Pa think if I parked an unwanted uterus on the hall table?

The sky was overcast and the shop filled up with bored tourists. Just after ten o'clock Bex appeared. Shirley seemed to know where she had been, but I did not ask. I was not going to ask. Bex had carefully painted not only her eyes but her lips and cheeks. She looked more than ever like an Oriental portrait, behind glass. I was almost glad when Shirley waved me over to say Daphne was on the phone again about a photo shoot for the shop. I said yes. Curiously, it didn't seem so bad to be a clothes horse. At least I knew I was dressing up. Shirley said she'd fix the meeting for tomorrow, maybe.

Tomorrow and tomorrow and tomorrow. We did Macbeth at school when we were younger. He didn't understand his own feelings. He got more and more violent, more angry. It was totally engrossing. And Lady Macbeth was played by a boy. A boy with an unbroken voice went storming round the stage in long skirts and everybody believed he was a woman as long as he was onstage. It's odd how you get to believe something even when you know it's not real, not unreal, but a different kind of real. There was Lady Macduff too. I used to wonder who acted the children's parts. Were they younger, smaller boys, learning to act?

The shop got so busy that Shirley sent me for lunch separately from Bex. I went to the library. Our teacher told us Shakespeare wrote parts where characters who are girls dress as boys to get what they want – layer upon layer of staging, image-making. Shakespeare must have had an intuition. I had to read his boy/girl lines. But I couldn't find his plays on the shelves. I wondered if I could surf boy-actors playing girl roles but all the computers were taken. Tomorrow and tomorrow and tomorrow. Shakespeare knew about the waste of time.

There was one easy-chair free, next to the coffee-machine in the Teen section. I sat down heavily, feeling the drag of my skirt against stitches. Shakespeare imagined a boy actor who's freed from the skirts of the play's character and puts on the real boy's clothing only it's part of the deception. The boys must have got used to it. Perhaps they loved being on stage, so they did whatever the playwright wanted. And the audience expected it. They looked at a boy and saw a girl – or they saw a girl pretending to be a boy and it was a boy all along, but they played the game that it was a girl. Astounding. Who decides what's real?

The Teen section was full of books about vampires, boy spies, fantasy worlds, broken homes, how to pull at school.

I day-dreamed going into school as a boy and nobody looking twice. It was ok onstage so why not in school? I could feel the ridges of Simon's boxers under the droopy black skirt. I had told myself they would be more comfortable than lycras over my wounded knee and that was true. But they made me feel bold, too. Daphne might swear if she knew – or laugh. She was the one who said I had the androgynous look. I saw myself walking along a corridor and the girls sizing me up as a guy, not as competition. I pictured the fashion show videos of me on the catwalk, striding along in narrow black trousers. How different it must be to have cock and balls slung before you, gently wobbling. Girls' tits wobble but not mine. Men walk with their legs slightly apart. I watched an old guy riffling through books. His belly hung over a tight canvas belt and his thighs seemed ludicrously skinny.

Halfway through the afternoon Bex's face suddenly appeared around the end of a rack. 'You've forgotten.' She disappeared again. What? It wasn't till closing time that she swept a vacuum in my direction as if she'd like to see me vanish up the hose. Black eyeliner emphasised the fullness of her eyes. 'You promised. The exhibition.' The dress slithered off the hanger to the floor and I scrabbled at it, ham-fisted. 'I knew you'd forgotten.' Bex dropped the vacuum head, leaving the machine still whining, and grasped my wrist. 'I'm relying on you to come.' I tried to step back but her grip was strong. 'I need you to come.'

'It's ok, I want to see my life-mask.' I gestured toward the hanger. The hook had caught in another dress's straps.

She relaxed. 'There's more than that.'

'I really do want to come,' I said.

While she finished vacuum duty, I fetched my rucksack, texted Ma and met Bex outside the shop. At least Bex wanted me to be with her. We walked slowly towards the Town Hall, and after a bit she flashed me a smile. Something unclenched and I breathed in the scent of her rose perfume as if it were a secret message.

The little girls were outside the entrance, swinging from Caroline's arms. Susie danced to make her trainers flash and Tess hung on her mother's hand, letting go for the fun of it, and then reattaching herself. It must have been hard on the wrists, trying to keep the children clear of passers-by crowding to cross at the traffic lights. Cars, lorries and queuing buses belched out clouds of exhaust fumes and cyclists pushed in.

Caroline's dark, straight hair was newly trimmed, curving heavily into the nape of her neck, and she wore her favourite velvet. The rich orangey-brown enhanced the glow of her skin and the neat bones of her face. Tess had the same birdlike movements. Suddenly I saw a likeness to Julia in the angle of her jaw. But Julia was fierce. Maybe she needed to be.

As soon as she saw Bex, Caroline's face relaxed and I realised she had been anxious. Across the road, Jack shouted, hopping between the stationary cars to join us. He picked up Tess as if she were a toddler. Her face went pink. She gave him a gentle kiss on the top of his ear and patted his rough red jacket before he set her down on the pavement.

Bex said, 'Ruth's on her way. She texted,' and I was instantly on guard. We filed into the Town Hall and I tried to concentrate. It was a huge event for Bex. She said she was relying on me. The goblin in my brain whispered, *why is Ruth coming?*

Earlier in the year, someone from the arts centre had visited our school, had seen one of Bex's works on display in the entrance hall and asked to see more. She was invited1 to show her work in the town's summer exhibition, an artist among artists. He liked her forest, too. Bex kept saying, 'But I'm a textiles person, I'm not an artist,' and then Caroline would say it was in the blood.

The piece that had drawn the guy's attention was a textile mask. I'd been the model, putting my head into the frame so Bex could adjust and pin and mark. She said it was my life mask. It wasn't a life that I knew. Over the willowy frame she had laid a face with feathers that morphed into wool and fur that seemed to spread out like the whorls on fingerprints into waves. The mask flowed down from the head across my shoulders and chest. It became quite heavy, in the end, hot from the weight of fabrics and feathers and threads.

Bex made three more other-worldly masks, all like creatures from fairy-tale. I guess they were beautiful. For one she chose textures and colours you find in the mountains. It made you think of how a mountain would be if it were alive. In the old days, Blencathra was called Saddleback. People must have saddled up then as a matter of course. Bex saw the mountain differently and asked Caroline to drive her into the northern fells so that she could research on the spot. I went too. Bex took photos, collected samples of everything that grew, made sketches and recordings. Caroline drew in charcoal and Susie and Tess ran around picking up small stones of many colours, chirping to one another like nestlings. I was in charge of the stone collection. Bex said she was developing an idea about how the shoulders of a mountain support its summit. Then she made Blencathra into Stingray.

She made gauntlets, too, long fingered, with every knuckle a miniature world – like spreading out your fingers and holding planets and stars. She built a breastplate, with ribs on the outside looking like precious metals, only she got the effects by lots of gold and silver thread. And she put the heart behind the ribs, bronze and oddly dark. Something got drafted for the exhibition programme, saying her work "transformed the human body, fusing it with the physical and metaphorical material of the universe."

The town hall's a bit small, really, lot of dark wood and pale walls, corridors and closed doors. There was a reception for the artists, and the woman at the door said TV cameras were coming. Bex didn't say much when we went in, but her gaze went everywhere.

Susie ran straight to the refreshments. She had her eye on the crisps. Bex said she was going to the loo and disappeared. In a flash I decided that I was never going to a LADIES again. I'd rather go into the Disabled and risk a fight with a guy in a wheelchair.

Caroline asked me to fetch orange juice for the girls whilst Jack went to collect wine and it was a relief to be towed along by his rusty-red jacket. His hair looked as if he had made an effort at brushing. I passed a number of large canvasses that were splashy bright colours – somebody's ideas of landscape, though I couldn't be sure. Jack said he liked the water-colours and got close to a vast, shadowy painting of the view along Wastwater, towards Great Gable. He read aloud from the programme. '*Cloud, mountain and water exist in the same spectrum of colour and substance.*' This view was once voted the Best in England, but the artist made it look sinister. Clouds swirled down from the summit like fingers reaching and squeezing, using a palette of greys, dead greens, murky browns. Somebody didn't see the fells the way I did. Bex had taught me a lot about colour.

'I like that,' said Jack, squinting at the price in the catalogue.

I said, 'What's the red dot for?'

'Hah. Damn. It's sold.'

'It's awfully expensive,' I said, peering past his shoulder at the catalogue.

Caroline appeared with Tess still attached. 'Could you come, please.' Her voice sounded unusually flat. Jack looked over the top of her head and made a clicking sound.

Bex was standing beneath her display, back half-turned from her father. Julia stood beside him, wearing white trousers and a heavy-looking white sweater. Her clothes seemed exotic, different from anything Caroline ever wore. A large black leather bag curved over her ribs like a wet crab-shell, and her head was tilted.

Jack and Caroline steered between people clutching plastic wine glasses, talking holidays. I followed, eerily aware that I needed Ruth to hurry up. Tess held her mother's hand in a tight squeeze. Caroline tried to loosen it but Tess would not let go.

'You ought to have priced it,' her father said to the back of Bex's head. 'I want to buy it.' Today he wore a black roll-necked sweater, the same sort of heavy knit as Julia's, narrow grey jeans and shiny black pointed shoes. I couldn't imagine the world in which he had been married to Caroline. Jack was Borrowdale volcanic to this man's heat-moulded resin. I ought to think of him as Dominic. It made him somehow smaller to name him.

Bex had tucked her hair into a black comb behind her right ear. The delicate flower-pattern rippled over her left cheek as she lowered her head. Slowly she pulled from her bag a long, thin, stretchy pink scarf, which she wound around her neck, over her chin, across her mouth. Her eyes flashed at me, at Caroline. Susie hopped from foot to foot, the wink of her trainers like traffic warning cones.

After a moment, Caroline said, 'Jack, you remember Dominic. I didn't know you were in town, Dominic.'

Bex's dad put one arm round Bex's shoulders like he owned her and stuck out his right hand to Jack. 'My business focus has largely been abroad, but I've shifted my interests back home, now. Good to see you, Jack. We'll be like family, I guess.' He smiled down at Bex. Her face was shut behind pink gauze. 'As soon as you let me know you were getting married, Caro, I knew I had to come back, get to know my girls again.' He smiled broadly, his even teeth whiter in contrast with his tan, his beard-beneath-the-skin.

The way he looked didn't square with the way he sounded. His accent was like Jack's, but he didn't deserve to sound like a local. I took a couple of small sideways steps. He shouldn't be anywhere near the life mask. My fists itched. The mask had me in it somewhere. Jack accepted the handshake though you could see he really didn't want to, but Dominic's snaky long fingers must have had a wicked grip because Jack winced. 'I've bought a place just out of town on the road to Windermere so I'll be able to keep in touch, much more.'

Caroline cleared her throat, tugging at a strand of hair. 'I'm sure we can work something out.' Her voice was hoarse. A small hand crept into mine. Tess. I hadn't noticed her leaving Caroline's side.

Julia said stiffly, 'I'd like to get to know them too.' She took a position on the far side of Bex, pushing her hand through the rigid crook of Bex's elbow. She looked anxious.

Susie grabbed Jack's wrist, tucking her hand into his as she planted herself in front of Dominic. Even her profile looked fierce. 'You're not my daddy.' Her clear, thin voice cut through other people's talk and heads turned. 'Jack's my daddy. And he's daddy for Bex and Tess.' I glimpsed the tough teenager she could become, and my eyes prickled.

The man stooped, opening his eyes wide. Green and

black flecks in the pale eyes glittered. 'Well, aren't you just like your father?' He tapped his chest. 'I think we'll get along fine.' He flashed a smile in the direction of Caroline and Jack. I felt, rather than heard, the rough intake of breath from Jack.

Susie's lip quivered and she leaned into Jack. Her eyelids fluttered. She still had delicate baby skin, and her father's profile.

His arm tightened around Bex as he turned to Julia. She was his wife. I had to remind myself. 'We'll have a chat to Nigel about access. You remember Nigel, Caro. He's handled my stuff for years. Now, this amazing piece of yours, Rebecca. I want it on the wall of my new office. I'm going to show my business colleagues what a talented daughter I have.'

The pink scarf still smothered Bex's mouth. Jack said gently, as usual, 'I'm afraid it isn't for sale, Dominic – at least, not for a while. Bex needs it at school, for her portfolio.' He raised his free hand towards her. 'Have I got that right, Bex?' Susie flung herself away from Jack and into Bex, knocking her free. Bex's glance skittered this way and that. Last month, Marmalade brought a bird into the house and let it go. The bird flew into the bathroom and perched on the shower rail, trembling, shedding feathers. I hated that my cat was a hunter.

The new voice made me jump. 'Hello everyone. Bex.' It was Spikey Todd, bouncing on the soles of his feet, ready to take off, a yellowed vest straining through the buttons of his shirt and his beard wagging with his smile. Caroline opened her mouth but he barged ahead. 'Bex, Figgie's here to see your work. The Scottish artist, the one with the studio in Fife? You remember?' Bex unwound the scarf, produced a faint smile. 'Come and talk. Is that ok, Miss Woods?' Susie stood like a sentry as close to Bex as she could get. In another year or so she would be as tall as Bex. 'Hi Joey, come to see your mask? Remarkable, isn't it?' Mr Todd didn't notice anyone else. Bex put out her hands for the little girls, nodded to me and followed him. Caroline stared blankly at Dominic. Incredible that my friend's mum had ever been married to this man. She'd had sex with him at least three times. Three girls.

Jack and I caught one another's eye and my heart juddered. Jack's face wore an expression I had never seen before.

'I don't get it,' said Julia, rustling into her bag. 'Why does he say it's your mask?' I watched Jack's face immobilise.

'I was the model.'

'Is it meant to be a likeness?' Dominic sounded more Cumbrian than ever.

I wanted to punch him in the gut but kept my face straight. He had the air of someone who always smoothly gets what he wants. Against my will my heart fluttered. I couldn't escape the musky, warm smell of him, the sense of developed shoulder muscles and strong hands. His eyes were dark and deep. Bex's eyes. He shifted, and the mask glowered over his shoulder. Its cavernous eyes glittered.

'Dominic.' Julia put her hand on his arm. 'That sounds a bit rude.' She tried to laugh. 'Joey, I'm sure you know he doesn't mean to be rude. It's a wonderful mask. I love it.'

Jack's face was thunderous. I said, 'Bex doesn't do her stuff so only private people see it.' It came out louder than I meant. 'She loves having her things on show, like in here. And she's got to have the mask. For the grade. Like Jack says.'

I saw Dominic's knuckles whiten and held my breath. Julia said, 'Would you mind getting me a drink, Dominic darling? Not the white, it'll be warm.' Very deliberately he pressed his lips to her pale cheek, his mouth fixed in its half-smile, before pushing away through the crowd towards the makeshift bar.

Jack stood stiff as a shield beside me. I thought Julia was trying not to cry but I was not going to sympathise. 'He wants his daughters. He's very fixed on it.' Her large blue eyes glanced from me to Jack and, for a second, I thought that she would burst into tears but she slid into the crowd. It would have been satisfying to loathe her, but I had seen the glint of panic in her eyes when Dominic gripped her arm. Caroline had lived with him. And Bex.

Jack's hand cupped my elbow. The waves of his body heat braced me. 'That man,' he muttered, deep in his throat. My spine tingled.

'Joey, here you are,' said Ruth and I flinched again. 'Hi Jack. Sorry the Ainsleys turned up for this. They must have read the bit in the *Gazette* about Bex.'

Bex in the local paper? I was going to ask but Spikey Todd marched back with the others. A new woman talked to Bex, gesturing rapidly. She had a wide smile. Bex's hands twisted the flimsy pink scarf into knots and her eyes were bright. Tess swung on Susie's arm, careering into Jack as Caroline introduced Figgie. They shrieked when Jack captured them. Caroline's face was pink. Bex went from one piece to another, explaining her techniques, her feelings, what she saw, and Caroline threw in comments, too. Bex brushed her cheeks with the ends of the scarf, removing some of the blusher. She seemed not to notice or care.

Figgie's deep, soft voice carried through the babble. 'This is wonderful, Bex. You have such a tactile sensibility. You were right to get me here, Spikey.' I saw bystanders smiling, somebody pointing out Bex. 'And I'd forgotten that your mother's an artist in her own right.' Bex nudged Caroline and their eyes sparkled.

The masks were fixed to the wall on a sort of brown cloth, scratchy to the touch. They reminded me of totems.

Gauntlets and the breastplate were pinned up too. I went from one to another, seeing them afresh, remembering where we were, Bex and I, when she was getting the ideas. We wandered along the twisting trails of the woods above the town, we sprawled by the tarn on Blencathra, staring up at cautious walkers silhouetted against the sky on the high, narrow ridge of Sharp Edge that led to the summit. Caroline said she'd gone up it once, never again, she wasn't going to add to the casualties. On my runs I gathered fir cones, fronds of dead bracken, frost-marked stones, curious-shaped twigs, anything I thought might be interesting. It was like magic, what Bex did with the bits and pieces, making them seem as if they always were a part of what she created.

One step further, and my stomach suddenly churned. There was a new mask. I stared at it stupidly. The mask stared back. Bex had given the mask huge round eyes with sets of lids that seemed to open from every angle – like the cat's third eyelid, only this creature had any number. It made me think of insects and beetles and creatures with too many scuttling legs rustling under leaves. Bex was talking but I couldn't bear to look round. 'I made the feelers from fine wire, and I found this stuff, it's wool round a core of stainless steel so it holds the shape.' Figgie sounded as if she knew what the stuff was.

Behind the woollen feelers were other, sticky-looking strands – tentacles – formed from thin green rubbery strips that looked like gelatine. My toes wriggled in my shoes. It was like those dreams where you are swimming through deep water and something clutches at your feet, the dream where you have to wake up, find your knees snatched against your chest.

Figgie's voice said, 'But this is haunting. Fabulous textures, not intricate for the sake of it. What was your inspiration?' I turned away, unable to look any longer at the mask.

Bex actually smiled. 'It was something I read.' She shook her hair forward and the artist exclaimed at the pink flower sprayed into her hair.

I felt as if I was looking at the scene through the wrong end of binoculars.

Ruth said, 'I could write the back story for this mask,' reaching up to touch the quivering tentacles, and Bex said, 'Kafka beat you to it.' They got talking about *Metamorphosis* and Ruth said she could supply a reading list of horror stories to make Bex's imagination work overtime. I wished I had not finished Kafka's story. Gregor Samsa's father threw apples at him and one stuck in his back, where it rotted away. In the end, his family pushed him into a little room where they chucked their rubbish. Gregor starved to death without anybody paying attention or caring about him as long as he was out of sight. They only saw how thin he had become when he was dead. I snatched glances at Bex, whose face was full of movement as she listened to Figgie and Spikey Todd, telling one another what Bex should do next. Bex must have been making this mask in the last few days.

We went for a pizza. Figgie told stories in the Scottish accent that I couldn't always follow. Bex's face was almost as pink as Caroline's. She sat opposite me, between Caroline and Jack, with Figgie and Mr Todd at opposite ends of the table. The stretchy pink scarf was now around her wrist, a slinky bracelet, and her hands moved just like Caroline's, fingers pressing, twisting, shaping, under the long, floppy sleeves of her thin white shirt. The restaurant was full of families, at least two with birthday parties, and there was singing. Jack caught my eye across the table, winked. I must have completely misread him earlier. He mouthed, 'Thank you,' raising his glass. I wondered if he would thank me if the next time we met I wore Simon's gear. He might not know anything was different, of course. Practically all my stuff was unisex. Tonight I was in drag, of course, the uniform I had not been able to change out of. Shakespearean.

Tess's eyes were slits of fatigue. She had eaten the dough balls, a sliver of pizza, and chocolate ice cream, leaning so tightly against her mother that Caroline had to eat one-handed. Susie pressed into my shoulder like Marmalade when he wants to sit on my knee and I haven't yet made space. Marmalade asleep on my lap is a drug. It was Pa's idea, giving them the same name. My Marmalade is a queen. Question – when a cat is speyed or neutered is the behaviour less gender-specific, or the same as before? What does the cat remember?

Suddenly I wasn't hungry and there was too much pizza in my mouth. Ruth quietly slid the glass of water across to my left hand, catching my eye, flicking her gaze at Bex as if trying to tell me something. But the waiter brought another bottle of wine and fresh glasses.

Caroline raised a toast, 'To Bex. I am so proud of you, my love. I am proud of everybody. I could not be happier. Well, apart from on Saturday, of course.' Jack laughed, reached across, stroked the back of her hand with his rough forefinger. 'To Bex.'

Bex lifted the glass. I'd been poured some white wine, too. Jack said, 'To Joey.' Figgie asked about Saturday and there were more toasts. A pang of misery tightened my gut.

Ruth tucked her arm into mine as we walked home but I could not warm up. I was afraid to ask why she was at the exhibition. I asked, 'Why do they keep turning up? He must know Bex can't stand him. Why does he try to spoil things?'

'Maybe he loves her.'

'You don't think that.'

Ruth went quiet. 'I'm trying out an idea, Joey.' We had reached the track leading up to home. 'He seems very, very focussed on her, don't you think?'

Behind the house, long feelers of cloud strung themselves across a faint moon. Shadows were filling the garden and darkening the shrubs. Ruth pointed at the folding poppies in the hedge.

I felt afraid.

Zef's Blog

Marmalade has been missing since Thursday night or Friday morning. That's 5 or 6 days. Ma says it's ok, Marmalade's poaching, the weather's fine, stop agitating, it's the time of his life.

Pa won't look at me straight.

Marmalade's living his secret life. Except he doesn't hide it. He's just doing what he does. Unless he's trapped somewhere, locked in a deserted cattle shed. OR he's been caught by a combine harvester.

I have to think about what Dr Hallgrave suggested but my mind is fuzzy with emotion about a cat. And Bex. And Ruth. And the man I should think of as Dominic but it makes me think of mastering, of dominating, because that's what he does, I can feel it.

Is this me aged 7?   or this?

Wikipedia has a heading, disambiguation. It's supposed to sort things out, separate things that look or sound the same but aren't.

There's lots of different kinds of love. How are you supposed to know which is which?

I love Ma and Ruth, and I sort of love Noah, and definitely Pa and Bex, but Marmalade? What's the love-label for how I feel about my cat?

Research Sheets (Private)

> **Disambiguation** in Wikipedia is the process of resolving conflicts that arise when a potential article title is ambiguous, most often because it refers to more than one subject covered by Wikipedia, either as the main topic of an article, or as a subtopic covered by an article in addition to the article's main topic. For example, the word "Mercury" can refer to a chemical element, a planet, a Roman god, and many other things.

if you want to post on Wikipedia you've got to make sure if you're talking about the element or the planet or a god and weblinks connecting your article to other articles about elements or planets or gods or whatever and you've got to say right up front that your article has the heading **'disambiguation'** at the top.

You're supposed to know what you're thinking before you ever get started.

Zef's Blog

I woke up with everything clear.

No Marmalade, but my body knew this all night long.

We used to get our cats from the refuge in London. They must have had our phone number pinned up in their office. Pa used to bury the corpses on the common because there was no room in our yard for a cemetery. Marmalade had several reincarnations – roads, urban foxes etc, and soon after we moved here, Marmalade was killed on the road. Noah couldn't speak for rage. Cars aren't supposed to drive faster in the country than in London but they do.

And then my Marmalade appeared in the long grass along the track only two days later, before we found the local animal refuge. He was just a kitten when he sat on my neck. He knows all the farmers. The farmer across the valley understands him. He will be across the valley in the old barns, stalking with the sheep. He has to be.

Today I have to tell Bex. No editing

Wednesday August 23

The work skirt made a pool of shadow on the floor. I stared at the blank white wall, tapping out the rhythm of the folk song against the end of the bed, using my big toes.

> *I listed in the army in uniform quite new*
> *And if they let me have a drum I'll be a drummer too*
> *To rush into the battlefield with a broadsword in my hand*
> *To hear the cannon rattle and the music play so grand*
> *And the music play so grand, and the music play so grand*
> *To hear the cannon rattle and the music play so grand*

She ran away to be a drummer boy and I love that she escaped.

I needed to forget the night, forget the dreams, get up, get moving.

The floor boards were cool on my bare feet, and my shirt flapped in the breeze from the open window. All night long I had rolled about under the surface of sleep, straining to hear Marmalade's yowl. I kept seeing him hiding under the hedge, his amber eyes challenging me. Inside the dream was another, the same one, over and over. I was tracking a faint figure across fields, past trees that twisted to follow my movements. The lines and curves in the bark turned into faces behind my back.

I leaned out of the window, taking in the half-finished wall below, the path, and next door's garden where they had begun to dig a pond. It was going to be hot again. You could smell it on the air, you could hear buzzing insects in the clematis around the porch. Bees dived in and out of the beds of sage and thyme that Ma planted last year, and the sunflowers tracked the sun like gorgeous solar panels. I should be climbing through the hedge at the top of the back garden and lapping the field, flushing Marmalade out of his hiding place. I should be heading west to Wasdale to run over Yewbarrow and Scoat Fell.

I pulled back into the room and rubbed my face, removing a tiny spider that had drifted on to my cheek. Today I would make the space and the occasion to tell Bex.

Somebody scratched at the door. My family bangs on doors.

'I am so sorry,' said Simon, frowning at the sight of me in a towel, I guess.

'It's ok.' He scrubbed his thin brown hands across the top of his head. The black hair sprang back and forth like wires. 'Really, it's ok. What?'

'I wondered how you were getting on.' He looked, as always, gently interested. For the past two nights I had washed out his boxers by hand (Machine Wash 40° C) and dried them on the window ledge. Last night the bizarre image of him wearing my pants under his jeans jostled into my head and made me smile until another thought dislodged it. Simon described men in Thailand who, dressed immaculately as women, wait at table or serve in department stores. Customers do not look twice. There must be men all over the world wearing women's clothing, hidden or obvious. Deciding which garment was for men or for women was a lottery, a game. Only it was more than a game. My skin crawled at the thought of dragging myself again into the shop's black skirt, with its embroidered hem and tiny black beads. I must have winced. 'I do apologise,' Simon said again, pressing his hands together. It's a Thai salute, Noah says, a statement of respect. 'It's too early in the morning. But you will be off to work shortly. I'm on late shift tonight. I heard you moving.'

The spice of his body odour was utterly different from the sweaty rawness of Noah or Pa in the early morning. Perhaps the small attic room where he slept, next to Ruth's room, smelt of cinnamon, of lemons. His slight, wiry figure was comforting. 'I wear your boxers.'

'Is that ok for you?'

'Do you know about doppelgängers?'

'I'm sorry?'

Ma's voice sounded downstairs. 'Cup of tea, Joey?'

'I'll be down in a minute.'

'Do I know what a doppelgänger is?'

'I keep feeling that there's another version of me, like a doppelgänger.'

'Isn't it bad luck to see your doppelgänger?'

'Maybe. Maybe it is.' I pulled the towel tight.

'I expect most people feel there are other versions of themselves.' He shifted awkwardly from foot to foot. 'I'm a UK citizen, I was born here, same as you. But everything's Thai at home. I get used to it.' I digested the idea. 'Look, it's obviously a bad time. Glad you're ok.' He bowed again before running silently downstairs. He must find our house very loud.

In the shower I scrubbed furiously. People change their body shapes all the time, especially women. My reflection glowered from the steamy surface of the mirror. Back in my room, I picked up the tiny photo of a child self that was probably me. I suppose it could be Noah. When I had scanned it, saved it black and white and then reversed the image it was curious to see how neutral it became, how easy to manipulate. Matt knew about digital manipulation but probably I did too. I'd played online at being M not F often enough, though I'd never been an elf or a wizard. I couldn't take them seriously.

I directed my glare at the small mirror on the wall. Who is the fairest of them all? This mirror displayed a hollowed-out face on which the black eyebrows and full upper lip drew attention. Maybe everyone has a second self, a ghost self, a second life never lived to the full, or life spent in secret, or online. Or you could pass your life under strange lights – infra-red or ultra-violet – seeing everything differently, x-rays and CAT scans, ultra-sound, magnetic resonance imaging.

You could not trust any online image to be truthful.

Dr Hallgrave didn't say what sort of scans I could have.

I knotted the towel under my arms, flipped the lid of the laptop, looked up CAT. Computerised Axial Tomography. I looked up Axial and Tomography. The x-ray machine is a ring. You lie in the middle. The scan is called a tomogram and you get a virtual 3-D image of whatever's inside you. Clever. The MRI scanner sends out radio waves to all the protons inside your body and they ping back. It's like pixels, millions of them. And you get this kind of computerised photograph of your inner self. They can do this to your brain, too.

I sent to print, closed the lid, fretting as I thought about the structure of my brain changing under the influence of testosterone. I'd found that out, online. If I did hormone therapy, my brain would change. Maybe it would take out all my confusion. I'd know what to do every day. I wondered if the scans came out black and white, grayscale or coloured.

Today I would talk to Bex. I tried to picture us together in a quiet moment. Perhaps at lunchtime I might get her to Maude's Meadow again. But even Bex the shop girl had changed. She used to be quite interested in what people were buying, would make helpful suggestions. In the last few days she stood back. She could offer to be a clothes horse too.

A whack at the door. 'Tea outside,' called Ma. 'I thought I'd better bring it up, it was getting cold. It's late, my – Joey. It's quarter past eight.' Only last week she would have knocked and opened the door, waiting for me to invite her inside. She hesitated before calling me her love, her darling. I hated the way she sounded uncertain.

'You self-regarding – queen – tom – make your mind up.' I stuck out my tongue at the image in the mirror and towelled my hair dry. At least it was easy to make the bed with no cat-shaped patch of mud in the middle of the plain white duvet. Marmalade had to be cushioned on long grass under a hawthorn hedge, his stomach full of mouse, his ears twitching in the excitement of dream-hunting. The farmer had let the land go back to meadow this year, and summer wild flowers stippled it like a painting. Pa was keeping a list on the whiteboard by the utility room door: rosebay willow herb, blue scabious, red campion, pink Herb Robert, Ragged Robin, great blowsy red field poppies that I love, huge white plates of yarrow and cow parsley.

No, the painting was like the field. I'd got it the wrong way round. Life comes before art. I went back to the window to gaze at the brilliant meadow, sick at heart in case Marmalade was not out there. I craved Pa's detachment, his curiosity about every living creature, even when it was dead. Maybe that was his brain structure. M/F? I climbed into the F clothing. The skirt was looser than ever. An old leather belt, fastened tight would have to keep it in place. Shirley would make me wear something glittery if she caught sight of it.

In the kitchen I poured the cold tea quietly away and opened the back door. At first I didn't see Ruth at the kitchen table, head bowed over a notebook. She looked up, glazed. Then her eyes met mine and she closed the book.

'I'm telling Bex today.' I steadied myself against the door jamb.

'Take care, for both of you.'

'You told me I ought to.' I wanted to lean my head on her shoulder but she was still behind the table, one finger tracing the golden-brown arc of an eyebrow.

'Bex is under a lot of pressure. Her father turning up, the wedding.'

'You mean I'll balls it up.' This brought her round the table and hurrying towards me, but I reversed into the garden. 'You don't have to tell me what to say, Ruth. I'm sure you've more important things on your mind.'

I ran to the front gate and out to the track so that I did not have to listen to whatever she was calling. I can drive, climb, run. I don't need breakfast. Could a CAT scan interpret the pixels of my mood? I ran down the hill like a cat, light on my pads over paving stones, past the gardens that were more densely scented, more sugary than the fields – pink and yellow roses, blue hydrangeas, tall red flowers I didn't know the name of, flowers like trumpets, pots brimming over with tiny bouncing rainbow-shades. I picked up pace past shiny front doors, and paths humped with mosses, and clipped green hedges and woven brown fencing tangy with creosote. The folk song made me feel great. Gender games aren't new.

They led me to my office, they led me off to bed
And lying by a soldier's side I never was afraid
And taking off my old red coat I oftimes used to smile
To think myself a drummer, yet a female all the while

Padding like a cat seemed to protect my torn calf muscle. Maybe I could run home at the end of the day. Running up-hill is great practice. At the bottom of the hill I stopped to inspect a wall. Tiny plants grew in the mortar. It was staggering that they could grow so well in such places. Earlier in the year every crevice had been smothered in miniscule pink flowers. Now there were little egg-shaped fruits, so small the Borrowers would have made a meal of them. I asked Pa what they were called but couldn't remember it. He was surprised I found it there. Sometimes you can look all over the place for a plant and not see it.

Bex sent a text. I punched the air. By the time I got to the usual place, my skipping had flattened to a slouch. The tables were slightly damp but somebody had tipped the water off the chairs. Bex wore yesterday's filmy pink scarf around her neck and her hair was still wet from the shower. The purple flower lay in separate strands across her cheek. I remembered the way she laid out strands of wool and silk when she was making the life mask.

'I ordered already.' She flicked a glance across the top of the mug as she took a careful sip. 'I ate too much last night.' Today her face was bare of make-up.

'Figgie?'

'She says I can stay in her studio if I want, learn a bit. Before I go to art school.' She wound the ends of the scarf around each hand and tugged. 'It's an option. Mum and Jack think it's too good to miss and I should do it straight after sixth form. Figgie says I can go now if I want, but I won't. Don't think so.' The sudden idea of Bex going away gave my coffee a bitter taste. 'My new mask, spooky, yeah?' Bex gave a tight laugh. 'My best, Figgie says. It kind of invented itself.

I just supplied the hands.' I had nothing to say. 'Sorting out the tendrils, the eyelids, took forever. Couldn't get the silver and gold cloth to lie down, curves, like over the eyeball.' Her fingers recreated the gestures. 'Mum helped, sort of. My apprentice, she said.'

Her words were oddly disconnected. Maybe it was the way her head seemed severed from her body by the scarf, and the deathly white pallor of her face, with huge dark holes where the eyes should be. Maybe she was wearing makeup after all, a whitener. She tended to play with face paints, like a kid. We learned in history that there was lead in the white paint women used to make themselves fashionably pale. It killed them. At least the female drummer would have got killed in action.

Shirley had already jammed the doors open and turned on a fan. The hangers clattered as garments rose and fell on eddies of air. Two serious customers turned up by mid-morning. One guy bought a floppy blue dress for his girlfriend's birthday. I said she could exchange it, but he was anxious about letting her know how much he had spent, even with a gift receipt. A middle-aged woman bought the outfit from the new collection that Shirley favoured, 'Autumn Glory, Harvest Gold and Berry Red'. But where Shirley's hair was the colour of Morecambe Bay mud, this woman's hair flamed in short curls all over her head. She had narrow, bright green eyes, and was almost six feet tall, reckoned by how she stood in the doorway, square-shouldered and lean. 'She's going to a Do, the Lord Lieutenant of the Shire's going to be there.' Shirley's whisper was too loud.

After the woman had gone Shirley went along one of the racks, rehanging every garment, restlessly shaking out and inspecting it against the light. We were instructed by a nod of the head to do the same. When we had finished, Shirley stood in the shop entrance for so long I was afraid one of us would be pushed into the high street with a placard. Then she tried to explain her business development plan. She was so excited that the long-legged woman would be at the same function as the Lord Lieutenant, had bought an outfit. Well-off women like his wife would see the new outfit and ask where she'd got it.

I said, 'She might be the Lord Lieutenant.'

Shirley tugged at her ponytail, curling it over her fingers. 'You're both being very peculiar this morning.' She gave me a long, pouting stare. There were still only the three of us in the shop. Her face rearranged itself. 'Daphne's been on the phone. You can go and see her if you like. It's dead here. Go on. If you want to.' I scowled. Bex wandered behind the counter to rearrange bracelets on a stand. Today Bex had no book with her. She was not reading Two Worlds and Their Ways at work and she had to be as bored as I was. Shirley was fed up, definitely. 'I've negotiated a fee for you, Joey.' Shirley's teeth looked whiter than normal. Last week she had been reading a magazine article about signs of ageing. Yellowing teeth are right up at the top with bags under the eyes. 'Go on, half an hour.'

Daphne's studio was tucked at the far end of one of the Yards, not my sort of place. Café for middle-aged live music, expensive kitchen shop, boarded-up windows that you can't see from the high street, and Daphne's studio. Here I was, anyway, doing what I was told.

The waiting room was lined with life-sized photographs of men in dress suits or so-called farming gear or design-er sweaters, just like Dominic's, and children in frills and women almost identical to one another. I was the only living person there. It was like sitting at the doctor's but with cardboard cut-outs. The women were mostly skinny, like me, but with glossy cheekbones and big lips and lots of jewellery and cleavage. Lots of that.

Dominic Ainsley. Maybe I should think of him as a cardboard cut-out.

I counted twenty photos. The room felt crowded. I sat in one of two deep green leather chairs and it was hard not to be impressed. The floor was tiled with small wooden blocks, freshly polished. White bowls of lavender were carefully placed on a couple of small tables, highly polished too. Hidden wealth. I know there are wealthy people in Cumbria. There's a show room full of Porsches in town. I wanted to picture instead a room full of scans. They could be beautiful. The ones I'd seen online were spectacular.

Daphne's voice on the phone from an inner office rose and fell. Then I was in her gleaming little office – solid black desk, black leather chair, black filing cabinets, long mirrors. She offered to sign me up, to be my agent. I wanted to laugh out loud. I stared out of the window at the disused building on the other side of the Yard, with its blanked windows and peeling blue paint. I could strut my stuff as girl and boy alike, be paid for it. Maybe with testosterone I could even produce designer stubble to order. She described my face as 'usefully androgynous'. I might meet half a dozen others all exactly like me.

Who's like you? Ruth's question.

I agreed to let Daphne shoot photos – well, not her, but the man with electronic gear who had been outside school the other day. I didn't let on. He said he worked on commission for national magazines. He was ordinary. Ordinary is ok. Probably, ordinary is just what you want. You want to be like everybody else so nobody tries to change you. You can get on with becoming yourself if nobody pays attention.

Shirley had gone for lunch by the time I got back to the shop. Bex sat on a high stool behind the counter, looking at nothing. She glanced up as I approached, her face slightly more alive. The pupils of her eyes had adjusted so that she was less like an animal yanked into daylight from the bottom of its burrow. 'Three more paying customers since you left. Business booming. Three kids from school buying cheap.' She even sounded like herself.

I leaned on the counter beside her and we played at stringing bracelets as if we'd never grown older than eleven. Outside, the air grew hotter still and long blocks of light trembled across the racks of clothes, transforming them into slivers of rainbow.

It was too good to last. Julia came, slipping between the racks. 'Your father has arranged to take Tessa out for the afternoon. He thought you might like to come too.'

Bracelets rattled on the surface of the counter. 'He can't do that.'

Julia behaved as though nothing had been said. 'We'll be meeting for tea. He really wants to have time alone with each of you.' She flicked at a bracelet. Deep pink nail-varnish drew attention to the perfect scimitar curve at the end of each finger. 'They're going to Sizergh Castle grounds. This is his phone number if you want to come.' She looked at me sideways. Black mascara, scrupulously applied, every lash given its due weight. She should have been negotiating with Daphne as a model, not me.

Bex's voice was tight. 'What about Susie?' She bit her lip so hard I thought the skin would break. Julia folded her arms. The white silk shirt was sleeveless and unflattering, I decided. No muscle tone in her upper arms.

'Your dad wants to see you individually.' She raised a straight black eyebrow, visibly lifted the edge of her upper lip. The pale fingers with their carnation nails grew agitated. 'Take the phone number.' She placed a white card on the counter. 'Please. Your father's business card. His mobile,' pointing it out with a single tap. 'You're his daughter forever, you know. He wants you to feel it. We've been together for five years, and – and I hope you'll get used to – feel better about it.' She picked up the white card, took the pen that customers use who have to sign instead of chip-and-pin, and scrawled large numerals on the back. 'My number. I'm meeting them for tea, I could drive you too, if you like, I mean, it's your choice.' Her hand shook but I didn't want to know. The way she said 'tch' sent a fine spray across the counter that I had to wipe off after she left. Bex disappeared into the office. Once, a host of small birds mobbed Marmalade and he scooted for cover. 'Tch tch tch.'

More customers drifted in, bringing with them the scorched smells of traffic fumes, blistering cobbles, their own fiery skins. Two buses panted in front of the shopping centre, opening and closing doors with wheezes of pneumatic air. I leapt. 'I didn't hear you.'

'I have to find Tess. I rang Mum. Can we meet later?'

'Shirley's going to have a fit.'

'I can't help that. Will you meet me later?'

'Ok. Where?'

'Walk. Meet you?'

'What do I say to Shirley?'

'I'll explain.' I worried away at the meaning of this, afterwards, as I stared at the business card Bex had left behind. Julia's writing was strangely childish. She'd had to rewrite the 'u' of her name. What could Bex explain? She was the reliable one, not me. I was only the Saturday stand-in.

Bex sent me a text as I was struggling with the vacuum. The last shopper of the day dithered over a turquoise silk scarf from the bargain rack. Shirley smiled fiercely, hand on door, ready to shoot the bolts, turn the key, set the burglar alarm. Several pigeons danced up and down on the cobbles, as if they were hot coals.

I rang Ma to say I would be late. 'I'm going out for a bit with Bex.'

'Is she ok? Ruth said she thought something was up.'

I chewed the inside of my cheek. 'What time's supper?'

'Don't worry, it'll wait. Don't get lost, will you?' She tried to laugh.

'It's only Scout Scar.'

'You're a big girl now.' We both listened to her embarrassment until I laughed.

Bex was waiting by the wall at the bottom of Beast Banks. At my approach she leapt across the road in front of a laden cyclist. She swerved, recovered her balance, tightened the strap of her red helmet, checked her panniers and freewheeled down the hill without looking back. She must be used to it.

I wanted to ask about Tess, tea, happy families but Bex set a brisk pace up the hill. I overtook, and the late afternoon ramble turned into a sprint until we reached the bypass. Bex had to lean on the bridge. Beneath us, cars and lorries headed for the motorway or Windermere. Her face was, relaxed. 'God you're fit. I suppose you could keep on for ever.'

'Not forever.'

We wandered towards the stile, where, as usual, several cars were parked on the verge. The sky was intensely blue. A heavy, muscular woman hovered over the gap in the wall, the stitching of her green linen trousers pulled taut by the swell of her bum. 'Up you come!' The black dog leapt with a clatter to the top of the wall beside her. She made a fuss, gathering his lead into loops around her wrist. 'Always a bit of a tussle to get back,' she said, smiling broadly at the sky as she jumped down into the long grass on the verge. 'He needs to lose weight, the vet says. I tell him I'll have to rename him RolyPoly instead of Roland.' She batted her eyelids and shouted. 'The dog, not the vet, obviously!' Bex and I did not catch one another's eye. 'But I can't, he'd be so embarrassed. The dog, not the vet, I mean.' She nuzzled into the dog's large head, tugging him off the wall.

Bex watched as they crammed themselves into the smart red sports car at the back of the row. 'Do cats get embarrassed?'

I had not told her that Marmalade was missing and just shook my head. There was nobody else in sight as we slid over the stile and sauntered across the short, dense turf of the racecourse. Cows looked glassily in our direction, then got back to chewing the cud. Twice I bumped into Bex. I seemed unable to walk in a straight line.

On the Access land, the path zig-zagged between small trees, springing bushes, shattered limestone and patches of bracken. Hawthorn berries were turning red and already there were blackberries ripe enough to pick. Black and orange Painted Ladies and Red Admirals quivered in the afternoon sun and I sighted the pale yellow and brown wings of Meadow Browns spiralling through the branches of a rowan. Brilliant yellow gorse jostled against purple heather. I swept a few flowers of gorse into the palm of my hand and stuck out my hand towards Bex. 'Pa says gorse smells of coconut, but I don't get it. I can't find a word to describe the smell. Somewhere between honey and pee? What do you think?'

With a quick movement, Bex batted my hand upwards, scattering the gorse over my shoulders and suddenly we were careering up the path like kids playing tag. Bex swerved into a narrower trail and I threw myself past her, shrieking as the black skirt billowed out and snagged on a blackthorn. I wrenched at it, barely hesitating as the skirt tore free. A ragged flap of cotton swung at my ankle, Bex gave me a hearty shove in the small of the back and again we were off, hurling ourselves up the narrow path that ran under a rising ridge of ground. My gastrocnemius muscle twanged. I felt the plaster stitches on my knee giving way.

Bex darted away from the path and plunged up the bank through tussocks of spiny blue grass towards a small tree shaped like an umbrella. By the time I caught up she had collapsed on to the bony turf beneath its branches. 'It's a parasol,' she said, pulling at a low-growing twig. 'What sort of tree's this?'

I patted the coarse trunk and pressed my nose into the bark. 'Juniper, it's juniper, see?' I clipped a couple of hard black berries from a branch. 'Ma puts these into stew.'

'I could take some home for Mum and Jack,' thrusting her arm deeper into the tight-growing mass, not caring as claw-like branches scored streaks of green and brown along her tight sleeve. She balanced juniper berries one by one on a flat fragment of pale limestone near her feet, before unfastening the rainbow-buttoned bag and throwing the berries inside. 'Nine, ten. That's enough. Come on.' She scrabbled clear of the tree on hands and feet and stood with hands on hips, staring around. 'What's that?' Ahead of us at the top of the rise was what appeared to be a wall. We made our way between bracken and anthills to the foot of a stony rampart and, magically, it was the old ruin from the night I got lost.

We worked our way from end to end, idly chatting about who built the walls. It was uncannily like being with my best friend, Rebecca Woods.

There was no obvious entrance, no connection between three collapsed rooms. It didn't look like a sheepfold or shelter, though sheep graze on the Scar. Welsh Black cattle were more recent comers, according to Pa, so this would never have been constructed for them. No obvious path led to the ruin. The only inhabitants in this area were ground-nesting birds, voles and shrews. But the ruin still looked like a would-be house. There were even shards of glass among the stones. Here was the ledge that I had called an altar. In daylight it was more of a shelf or seat. There was no sign of fireplace or chimney.

Bex balanced on one of the walls, shading her face and staring out across the valley towards the far hills and the town below. 'It's beautiful. It's so peaceful. No wonder you come up here.' Her eyes were bright and excited.

'You could have brought a book.'

She sat down, resting her feet on the rampart and plaiting her fingers. 'I've given up reading for the moment.'

It was my turn to stand on the wall, one-legged. 'How was tea at Sizergh?'

The plaiting stopped for a second. 'Not doing it again, not if I can stop him.'

A stone slithered underfoot, and I slipped with it, tearing the skirt still further. 'What about Tess?'

'I'll talk to Mum. It mustn't happen again.'

'Julia?'

'Skinny bitch. Poor cow, probably.' Bex looked at me sideways through her purple-flowering hair and laughed softly. I waited. 'You're luckier than you know.' A small brown and white bird flew quietly down to a boulder below us, chirruped, cocked its head on one side, and preened a wing. Stonechat, maybe? 'Tess and Susie, they're so, I dunno, little. They're so little, still.'

'You've got Jack.'

'Yeah, Jack's a good guy. He is.'

The bird chirruped again, hopped off its rock and up the slope towards us. I held my breath. A dog barked in the distance and at once the bird swooped effortlessly away across the Bradleyfield Allotment, disappearing against the shrubs and grasses and outcrops of rock. I fiddled with the long strip of frayed black cotton that had once been part of my skirt. 'Suppose I'll have to pay.'

'Never. You're the golden girl.'

'That's ridiculous.'

'She thinks you'll make money for her. You will, won't you? That woman, Daphne, she's offering you a contract, you said.'

'But I might rather be a golden boy. A boy.' I was breathless.

Bex lifted the hair clear of her face with a look of intense concentration. 'What does that mean?'

'Apparently I have a wonderful androgynous look.' My heart doubled its beat.

'Yeah. You've been working on it for years.'

'Is it that obvious?' Inadvertently I had gripped her wrist. She raised her arm but did not break away.

'What?' The purple flower in her hair rippled as a warm wind bent the grasses, whitening the heavy seed-pods. The hairs stood up on the back of my arms.

'I – maybe – I got the wrong gender.'

She pulled away. 'The *wrong* gender.' I tried to look at her straight, but she was taking her pulse again. 'The wrong *gender*,' looking skyward. 'Have you talked to Ruth?'

'I always talk to Ruth.' I tried to swallow.

'You're still coming to the wedding, are you?'

Somebody else was writing the script. 'Yes.'

'Ok then.' She tipped back her head to stare up at the sky and I followed her gaze. High above, two hawks wheeled on a thermal, dark wings effortlessly spread against the thin blue sky. They turned in majestic, masterful curves, shaping their territory. *'The sun is behind me. Nothing has changed since I began. My eye has permitted no change.'*

'What?'

'That poem we did, about the hawk? Ted Hughes. I love that poem.'

My throat tightened. 'Mrs Tully. *It took the whole of Creation to produce my foot, my each feather.'* I had forgotten what I knew. The teacher, Mrs Tully, didn't stay long in our school. She was young and excitable and her lessons kept on going well past the bell. We had all thought she was bizarre, exotic, from another world.

'I could live here. Do you think anyone ever lived here? I could die here.' Bex picked up a flint-shaped shard, spun it into the sea of stones, and leaned back on her elbows, staring up at the circling hawks. I shifted, caught sight of a plant that seemed to float in stone, slid down to the floor of the ruin. It was the same little flower that clung to the town wall. 'What is it?' asked Bex.

'Nothing. It's perfect. It grows on nothing at all. I can't remember the name.' The little flowers leapt to view everywhere. I hadn't seen them, but they were under my feet and hands and probably I was sitting on them. 'Rue-leaved saxifrage.' It was a small triumph and I fingered the firm, red, succulent leaves. 'I saw lots of it this morning on a wall in town. I didn't look for it here so I didn't see it. But here it is.' The white flowers swung at my touch. I wanted to plant flowers like these in my wall, when it was finished. If ever it was finished.

Bex spoke over my head. 'I won't be in the shop tomorrow.' Slowly I stood up, adjusting to the stab of pain in my calf, the tight feeling in my chest. 'I fixed it with Shirley. Mum needs a bit of help. Keep an eye on the girls. That sort of thing.' That sort of thing.

She gestured for me to go first, not meeting my eyes. I followed the line of the wall, listening for the clatter of her step behind me on broken limestone or the swish of her skirt against heather. The air was so still that I heard someone say, 'Not tonight,' from a car parked below. I wanted to smash my fists into a wall.

Please look out for Marmalade

Classic grey tabby, weighs c. 3.5 kilos

Usually wears red collar + bell but may have discarded these. Friendly and talkative. Favourite places: fields at top of hill, garden walls, watching out for people/other cats. Microchipped, regularly wormed, no fleas. Went hunting Thursday August 17th; has not been home since.

Please ring, text Zef 07992113100

Zef's Blog

Every lamp-post, fence, tree has a poster on it. I've been in the field, pushed open every door that isn't actually locked, yelled at sheds and garages. I ran round the town, stuffed posters through letterboxes, especially the vets'. I'd have stayed longer but I didn't want to meet the yobs coming out of the pubs or anyone else for that matter. One black cat followed me all the way back up the hill, howling.

I don't want to go to bed except it might be a magic token to get Marmalade back. If I sleep the hours will pass and he might turn up as usual, sitting on my face.

How I would love to be woken by wet cat sitting on my face.
www.lostyourcat.org
www.homeforlostcats.co.uk
www.findyourfeline.net – lots more no use at all.

Zef's Blog

Pa came to the shop at lunchtime and insisted on taking me out for lunch.

Town was half-empty, everybody sane on the fells, so Pa escorted me to a sofa in some coffee corner so that we could sit squashed up. He was terribly polite. I had water and a bowl of soup. Pea and ham, too many bits. Pa had a cheese sandwich. He made even more crumbs than me. He said, this idea I'd got, he wanted to understand it but he was having a bit of a struggle. Ruth had talked to him. Noah's friend was freaking him out about the third sex. I wanted to say, third sex isn't it, Pa.

I thought he might work out the gender/sex difference but he couldn't fit it with me. He wanted me to say how I know what men feel like. Like he was setting me an exam, like he knows how all the men in the world feel. I tried to say we aren't exactly definite when we're born, we find out and we sort of invent ourselves too. Pa said he's spent his life observing nature and I've got it wrong. I said, 'Pa, it's still me. I'm just working out the details, I've got my brain, my feelings.' He got up in a hurry, bread pellets all over the sofa. He said, 'You can't call it detail, what you're saying.' I could give him the weblink about morphs of gender. I don't think he'd take it in.

Simon and I built a bit more wall before he went to the pub for his evening shift. Ma and Ruth cooked stuff for the wedding. I think Ma's had a row with Pa. No Marmalade and the black cat keeps turning up in the garden. I don't want to think. I just want Marmalade back. Now I know what sick at heart means.

Zef's Blog

Pa left a note on the kitchen table. I'm obviously taken up with more important things so he's asked Harry to come and sort out the new wall. To make sure it gets finished in time for autumn planting.

I showed the note to Ma. Her face went completely flat.

I am not going to think about it. Today Caroline and Jack get married and I am going to spend time with Bex.

He's so full of his Ennerdale wilderness.

My leg hurts.

Friday August 25

The carrier bag of clothes that Bex had given me to look at for the wedding was under my bed. I supposed I ought to investigate. Bex had worked out what I might have chosen myself – narrow black trousers with a fine grey stripe, a jacket with sleeve buttons like a man's and a stiff white shirt. I don't know how she found these in Shirley's stock but as I inserted my foot into the trouser leg, I knew I'd worn these before, or their twin, at the fashion show. Bex had folded them carefully, interleaved with plastic wrapping from the shop store-room. My eyes smarted.

In the depths of the mirror a hologram tilted – now you see me, now you don't – doppelgänger, male/female in the blink of an eye. I'm running along a high, knife-like ridge with plunging depths on either side. People fall off Sharp Edge, Striding Edge, kill themselves, every year. There are much easier ways to the top of Blencathra or Helvellyn yet people queue to get up the hard way. The shirt collar tried to meet under my chin but I didn't want the tightness of the top button. The jacket lapels lay flat across my chest. Perfect.

Ruth whistled and Simon said, setting down a buttery knife, 'Hold on. I've something for that.'

From the kitchen sink, Ma looked over her shoulder. 'What's that about?' she said in wondering tones. 'We'll see you at Caroline's. Did you know there'd been a problem?'

'What sort of problem?'

'One of the girls, maybe? I didn't like to ask. I hope it's ok at the County Offices.'

Simon reappeared with a thin yellow scarf. 'Don't look so anxious, Joey, I think this will do the trick.' He tucked the scarf round my neck and over the stiff collar of the shirt. 'Now you're ready.' Carefully his eyes surveyed the jacket, the trousers, my hair, the scarf, as if I were about to walk out on to the stage of a huge auditorium. 'I wonder. I hope you don't mind.' With a courteous gesture he pointed at my feet. 'I don't think you can wear those, can you? What do you think, Mollie?'

Ma spun round, laughed, sighed. 'She won't collaborate, Simon. She's thrown out practically everything that isn't trainers or running shoes or heavy winter boots. I can't make her.' She turned back to the coffee grinder, spooning the beans with a rattle into the metal cup. The nutty scent of fresh ground coffee lifted on a breeze from the open door. 'It's a lovely day. You could always stop in town and get some new trainers. Could you? I'll buy them. If you like.' She was doing her best to sound uninvolved.

Simon tucked his fine white shirt into belted cotton trousers. 'If you please, just wait till I've eaten my toast. I'd like to be your clothing consultant. I'd enjoy it.'

Noah thumped into the kitchen, pulling on a crumpled but sweet-smelling sweatshirt, fresh from the washing line. 'What do you mean, clothing consultant? Fi's coming back tonight. She texted me, changing planes in the middle of the night, nightmare. You don't look bad considering. Somebody ill in the family, I think. I'm going to Manchester to meet her.'

'What about your shift?' said Ma, turning round with hands that dripped soapsuds.

'Simon can sort it out, can't you? I'll have to go back to Fi's, see what's happening.' His face looked strangely piebald from the clean shave. 'What do you want to do, Si?'

'I'll ask if I can move into the pub, there's a spare room.'

'Simon, please stay – we'd like you to stay. I expect Noah will turn up here with Fi in another day or so. We'd really like you to stay, wouldn't we Joey?'

'Would you say at the pub it's a family crisis, mate. They don't need the details.' Noah had gone within ten minutes, his rucksack crammed.

I checked my phone for news about Marmalade. Nothing.

Time went in a series of overlapping loops – wedding at midday in the Register Office/ shoe shop/walk back to Caroline and Jack's after the photos/gallery/kitchen/garden. I was still trembling at midnight when I reached Scout Scar.

GUESTS FORBIDDEN TO ENTER in Ma's neat

capitals was posted on Caroline and Jack's kitchen door but I decided to be family. When I'd come to visit we hadn't eaten in the kitchen and I had barely glimpsed it during Bex's guided tour.

Ma eyed me with a frown. 'If you're coming in you have to work.' She was wearing her oldest jeans and a pale green cotton shirt, which must be her concession to the party. Ruth's trousers were in better condition, but her feet still wore the favourite yellow-striped trainers. 'Take off that jacket and scarf.' Ma retied the black and white striped butcher's apron. 'Did you get photographed for Shirley?'

I scowled back. In a while, I might tell her about Dominic Ainsley. The words ran round and round my head – domination, dominance, dominion.

'Nice shoes,' said Ruth, sliding past the laden table to sling her arm around my neck. 'You look fab. So – what's the word?'

'Skinny,' said Ma, with half a grimace.

'Ignore your mother. You look comfortable. Photogenic. Svelte might be the word. We'd better get the photos sorted. Maybe we just have to buy you the jacket and trousers and never mind the photos, what do you think, Moll?'

Ma was carefully balancing olives and pancetta on fingers of toast. 'Nearly done here. It's her choice. Sorry.'

I hung the jacket over the back of a chair as instructed and surveyed the kitchen. It was a large, airy room, with sealed cork tiles on the floor and the familiar amber and terracotta tiles forming a dado around the walls. You could see the garden through two long windows. At right angles to the sink was a great black range, set into an alcove, with terracotta tiles to frame it and an old-fashioned drying rack hanging from the ceiling. Bex said Jack had made the kitchen table himself from a slab of yew that he had polished and varnished so that small girls' paints would not damage the surface. The upright chairs had been gathered from junk shops in town, and Caroline had upholstered the seats. She'd gone for all the colours of the rainbow. The cupboards were, I remembered, painted white but as virtually every door was open the room was at risk of a crockery explosion.

'So those are the shoes you bought with Simon,' said Ma, handing me a cloth and indicating glasses for me to polish. 'They'll all be in here eventually. Jack's got a chum serving champagne on arrival. We have to create a sort of servery.

What's the time, Ruth? He's got good taste, Simon. We'll need at least two serving points. How many guests did Caroline say?'

In the shoe shop, Simon had stared closely at the ranks of boys' and women's shoes, and then shepherded me towards the shelves. 'Do you see? These are identical, just stacked with different labels on different shelves. Shoes for women that are almost the same as shoes for kids. Boys. You need shoes that fit. I think you won't get into boys' sizes, will you? And anyway, you don't want to look like a child on an outing.'

He picked out two pairs of narrow black shoes with pointed toes, shiny leather soles, tiny square heels. One pair was patent leather and the other a matt black with stitched whorls like fingerprints across the toes. I would never have noticed them. I glanced at his feet in highly polished light brown shoes.

For someone so correct, so polite, he was very determined. A slice of my savings vanished in buying my fingerprinted shoes, but Ma would insist on paying. She was always ludicrously excited at the notion of buying clothes for me. These she would never have predicted. I wondered if Ma would buy me a man's suit. Before today, I could never have imagined myself in anything tailored.

Simon said goodbye in the County Offices car park amidst clouds of exhaust fumes, with a shake of the hand – again, that dry, warm skin and the faintly cinnamon smell of his coarse, shining black hair. 'Haircut next time,' he added. 'It doesn't need much to give it a slightly more masculine feel.' I did not know how to thank him. He walked away with a fast, gliding stride, confident and easy about inserting me into his familiar world. Noah was in that world too. Was

Fi? They were all there together, in Leeds. I could get out of a train in Leeds and be somebody else. Then I remembered that Marmalade was missing.

'You're doing fine with those,' said Ruth, taking the cloth. 'Can't we get Joey to do something more creative and less menial?' She placed a cool hand at the back of my neck and frowned, shaking her head slightly. Under her breath she muttered, 'Have faith.'

Ma poured wine into a glass and gulped it. 'I needed that.'

'Did anybody ring, before you left?' My voice sounded stupidly pleading.

Ma looked up sharply, set down the glass and ran to grasp my shoulders. 'I'm sorry, my darling, but no.' Her square face was flushed, and I saw for the first time the fine lines around her mouth and eyes. 'We have to brace ourselves. He's never stayed away so long.'

Sometimes she could be psychic. I was haunted by the image of Marmalade lying up somewhere with a broken back, licking the dew off grass to stay alive. Ma kissed my cheek. She smelt of the limes she had been slicing as well as the wine. 'Don't torment yourself,' she said, breathing warmly into my ear. 'Keep busy. You've done everything you possibly could.' Then she choked on a laugh.

I began to ferry glasses into the galleried sitting room. Everybody was making for the garden, and the full gaze of the sun. The French windows stood open, and the sweet smells of roses and lavender and something honeyed strayed into the room. Marmalade. I'd never bothered to find out if queens behave differently from toms, especially if they're spayed. Does spaying or neutering save cats from longings? Not in Marmalade's case, for sure.

The front door banged and more people streamed through the mellow wooden tunnel of the hall towards the garden. Jack's police colleagues cracked jokes as they came, inspecting door frames and the way the floor had been laid, shedding uniform jackets like nuts bursting out of shells. Then Caroline's artist friends came leisurely up the garden path, stopping to sniff lavender or stroke the stained glass, making a rainbow of discarded soft scarves and coats in riotous contrast to the solemn blue-black fabric heaped around the coatrack. I suppressed the Shirley instinct to pick them up, find the hooks. At the end of the hall was a rectangle of brilliant light, framing the energetic, quirky figures in the garden – a series of film clips to be cut, spliced, uploaded. Somebody would be videoing. Touching the void.

There had been a great deal of excitable snapping outside the Register Office earlier, when I had been hanging around in the car park, too early and stuck on my own. It was all because of buying shoes. Still, they were ok. I'd been working out a different pattern for the laces when a fleet of long black cars with darkened windows eased into the car park. Men in official-looking peaked hats climbed out of the drivers' seats and flung open doors as if it mattered. The wedding guests were obviously relatives, larking about. I began to feel alarmed. Most of the women wore flimsy dresses that they could have bought from Shirley. They didn't seem like friends of Caroline's or Jack's. I would be wildly out of place. Of course, they could be aunts or sisters. Caroline must have cousins.

They tottered to the steps with the forced arch of the back that goes with high-heeled shoes, all grooming one another. Peck, peck, peck – this strand of hair, that ear-ring, a slippery strap, a neckline to be hitched up or down. Then the men followed, all grey and black suits with flashes of red and pink by way of waistcoat, cravats, buttonholes. *I'm in the wrong place*, I thought. *I'm going home to look for Marmalade.* A smartly-dressed woman appeared at the top of the entrance steps, and instantly they all seemed to know what to do, picking their way up the steps.

Get out of here, I thought, but suddenly more people appeared on foot, some in police uniform. Jack's colleagues, I realised, stepping round the corner from the central police station. I had been watching the wedding party before Caroline's. It was like when cramp grabs your calves if you don't warm-down after a run, and then the pain lets go and your muscles tremble with relief.

A man in a striped suit slid out of a car I hadn't noticed, neatly balancing a box full of blue and white flowers in one mighty hand. He greeted the others with ringing confidence, handing out one flower apiece for the people in uniform. Drawing level with me, he said, 'Hello young'un, are you an usher?' I shook my head. 'But you're going to Jack's wedding?' He gave me a flower anyway, a buttonhole. The pin pricked my finger. I dandled it like a fool, having nowhere to put it. Bex pinned it on for me, later.

The flower was shedding petals all over the kitchen floor, right now, where I'd slung the jacket over the back of a chair. Caroline's voice called me to attention. 'Hi Joey. I'm so glad you're here.' She was on her way from the garden to the kitchen. 'I only caught a glimpse of you at the Register Office. You look very smart – different, somehow. Have you done something different to your hair? You look very fit. It's very sweet of you to help.'

After Simon's comment about a haircut, I had thrust my fingers up and through my hair to form a crest. 'That's ok,' I said, balancing the tray of glasses. 'I'd better get on. Ma's got a timetable.' I saw myself in the long mirror, a thin figure in black trousers and white shirt, bearing a tray of empty glasses. The figure in the mirror shifted weight from one foot to the other and Joey stared back. Joey>Zef. Josephine Wilcox on the school register, on my birth certificate. Earlier I had stuffed old pants into the crotch of the boxers to see the profile of trousers with a fake dick and balls.

The man in the pin-striped suit stood at the door into the garden and announced in his loudest voice that food was served. Ma took charge, issuing instructions, sending Ruth and me plunging to and fro with bowls and bottles, squeezing between guests to pour wine or juice, or to 'save me the hassle' of collecting a plate with 'just a couple of those little grilled lamb chops' and 'some more of that delicious salmon trout'.

I recognised faces after a while, and not just from the Register Office. Two of Caroline's artist friends looked at me twice, trying to work out if they knew me. They had come sometimes to her tiny terraced house to practise new techniques, and a couple with a studio in Wasdale made it into town for a concert. Bex and I had half-listened to conversations or been called to admire new onscreen designs. A middle-aged man with a vast beard stopped me for a top-up of red wine. 'I seem to know you,' he said, indicating with his finger how far up the glass I should pour. 'But you're not Matt, are you. I met Matt.'

My heart performed an acrobatic loop. Excusing myself, I pushed back to the kitchen. Jack was talking to Ruth. 'If you come on Monday afternoon that would be terrific.' He had stripped off the rich brown jacket he'd been wearing and hung it alongside mine on the back of a kitchen chair. The shoulders were huge in comparison with mine. I saw myself dwarfed, ridiculous, in a standard masculine jacket. 'Pray for the weather to hold. We aren't going far. I couldn't get a flight at such short notice so we're going over the border and up to Glen Coe. Hi Joey. You're doing great work here.' He linked his arm through mine, the warmth and sweat of his body like a great fiery engine. I reached out to stroke his jacket, rough as bark.

When they arrived at the Register Office, Jack and Caroline, in the stupendous car they had been lent for the occasion, their faces shone. A huge white ribbon bow perched on the bonnet like a seagull giving its blessing. Bex and the little girls sat opposite, smiling hard. Caroline stepped out to applause and cheers for a blazing orange outfit and Jack emerged afterwards in the nut-brown jacket. His police friends wolf-whistled. The little girls were wearing brilliant, full-skirted dresses with orange and blue flowers splashed around the hemlines. And Bex wore the close-fitting, wonderful bluebell dress I'd seen before. They looked like summer. Even Jack's friend, the driver, boasted an orange waistcoat. He closed the doors with a tremendous flourish and stuck his thumbs into the waistcoat so that everyone could admire it.

I lifted the sleeve of Jack's coat to sniff the fabric. It smelt new. He hadn't yet given it the odour of wood polish, sawdust and oil that usually wafted from him.

Bex looked amazing. The purple and white flower-pattern in her hair gleamed as if it were spray-painted, and from the right temple her hair was swept back by a shining silver comb. She stopped to say hello before the formal procession up the steps and into the Register Office. 'It's real,' she had said, lightly touching the comb with a fingertip. 'It's real old silver. Jack gave it me. It's my bridesmaid present.' Her skin looked polished white, like a statue, and for once, the eye-shadow was a muted grey. But her eyes looked through me. Tess held her hand, her small mouth firmly shut, as usual. Her glances shot everywhere.

'Are you a bit nervous, Tess, being bridesmaid?' I dropped down on one knee. She put out a finger to touch the yellow silk scarf.

'That's nice,' she said in her fluting, precise little voice. 'It's the same yellow as my flowers, look,' thrusting out her bridesmaid bunch. I admired them.

Bex looked me up and down. 'Neat clothes.'

I wanted to touch her cheek. 'Thanks.'

She glanced at my feet and raised her eyebrows. 'Have you done a smash-and-grab?' Her face wore an expression of genuine astonishment. 'They're cool, Joey.'

'Simon.'

She nodded. 'See you at the house. I'm glad you're here.' That's when she had seen the buttonhole wilting in my hand, taken it from me, neatly pinned it to the black lapel, given me a straight, distant look. 'I'm glad you're here. You look different. I thought you would.' For a second she focussed, saw me. Then she led Tess up the steps.

Jack squeezed my arm again. 'Did you enjoy it?' Ma was giving him a glass of something fizzy.

'Yes,' I said. 'Yeah.'

The Register Office was a large hall. I had expected something like our school office but of course it was wood-panelled and a bit like a stately home. In fact, most of what happened I had not expected. Music, for instance – Jack and Caroline had chosen a recording of brass band music for their entry, and all the friends had cheered and applauded. It was a police band from somewhere. A woman friend of Jack's read a poem that started, *Yes, yours, my love, is the right human face*, and my eyes filled up. I was tired from not sleeping.

'The brass band was good,' I said. 'And you guys looked great.'

As Caroline and Jack began to exchange their promises, a shadow cast itself along my bench. From the corner of my eye I glimpsed a dark grey suit that flickered like silk. Bex's father. I stopped breathing, willing him to move on, but he decided to settle by me. His strong musky scent had filled the space, and his tanned hand rested on the back of the seat in front, golden thumb ring tapping on wood. His designer stubble was pronounced. A shimmer beyond him was Julia, on the edge of her seat like an exotic bird in stripes of black, grey and white, shot through with purple. I suppose they were free to walk in. Nobody had told the people on reception to get out their AK74s and fire.

Dominic insisted on talking in a low monotone. 'My girls look gorgeous. I'll catch them for a photo. Julia has the camera.' I guessed he would not spoil the line of his suit by an object that was thicker than a credit card. 'We wish them well, Caro and Jack. Don't we, darling?' Julia wore a tiny feather clipped against her dark hair. 'I'm still negotiating with Bex for that mask – that glorious death mask. I think it's a death mask really, don't you?'

I stared ahead. They were breathing my air and the only way not to notice was to think about Marmalade.

I broke from Jack. 'Better get on,' I muttered, picking up some forks and spoons at random.

'Caroline says that the girls' father turned up at the Register Office,' said Jack abruptly, rubbing his eyes. 'With his wife. I didn't see them.'

'No,' I said, dropping cutlery into a sink full of soapy water. 'They didn't stay long.'

They hovered outside when the photos were taken, as the steps filled up with jostling, happy friends. One guest wore a green and red checked shirt like a lumberjack's and hugged everybody he could grab. He didn't seem bothered about whether he knew people or not. Jack and Caroline shook hands with all their guests as they left the Register Office, but Dominic and Julia Ainsley strolled out early, stationing themselves by the railings. When Jack invited me for a photo with the family, Julia's face stiffened.

Ma was stacking dishes in the dishwasher. 'I'm sure it was beautiful. Are you getting more photos taken? I haven't seen Susie or Tess in their dresses yet.'

I had seen Tess slide her hand out of her mother's and hop down the County Offices steps towards her father. I saw him bend to whisper something in her ear, and her small, secret smile. I saw Julia fix the purple feather in Tess's hair.

'They're around,' said Jack, running his thumb across the rim of the glass to produce a piercing note. 'I'll send them in to you. Or Joey could, you wouldn't mind?'

'You look as if you've been sucking lemons,' said Ma, giving me a push. 'Go and find those girls.'

I went back into the butter-yellow hall and slid my hand across the silky, smooth surface of the curving cupboard, visualising Susie and Tess scampering past and stroking the cupboard as they ran. It ought to be that sort of home, where kids played games and clambered over furniture. Noah and I used to play the game of getting around the edges of the sitting room without our feet touching the floor. Pa was amazingly good at it but he didn't often play. Ma would tell him off. One night we had been woken by shrieks and had crept downstairs to find Ma playing the round-the-room game too, even better at it than Pa.

Perhaps the little girls had gone upstairs to change. Slowly I mounted the staircase and on impulse wandered into the gallery where Caroline's materials stood neatly in a corner.

I peered down on to the bobbing heads below and saw at once that Susie was twirling in front of a stocky policeman, holding out her skirts, pirouetting, pointing the new shoes – first position, third position. I wondered if she would regret asking to have her hair cut short.

At the Register Office, when the wedding car came to a standstill in the middle of the car park, Susie leapt out, face pink with excitement, dragging impatiently at her full-skirted dress and staring at the waiting crowd. As soon as she caught sight of me, she launched herself. 'Joey's here!' She swung on my arm, pushing her bouquet to my nose. 'Don't they smell lush? Smell my wrist. I've got perfume. I've got nail varnish, look.' Her fingernails gleamed. Somebody had lovingly painted them with a pale pink gloss. White and yellow petals escaped from the tight little bunch of flowers in her hot clasp.

Now she was showing the policeman her newly-varnished nails, raising her hand like a queen. Tess was nowhere in sight and neither was Bex. I turned to look through the round window at the fells across the valley, where sunlight created deep shadows between hump-backed hills. Jack built this house with space for dreaming. Up here, the air was thick with the smells of fresh bread, mayonnaise, mint, strawberries, cold meats, smoked fish, meringue, whipped cream. Fragments of conversation and laughter wreathed upwards, and someone began to strum on a guitar. A soft tenor voice sang.

> *I sow'd the Seeds of Love*
> *And I sow'd them in the spring,*
> *I gather'd them up in the morning so soon,*
> *While the small birds so sweetly sing.*
> *While the small birds so sweetly sing.*

Still no sign of Bex. I couldn't believe she wasn't in the garden, but I knew she was not. From the gallery window there was an excellent view. Most people had come inside to collect their food before drifting out to sit cross-legged on the grass. The guitarist set herself up by a sundial at the far end and someone wearing blue-black trousers had produced a flute. They were tuning up.

There would be an even better view from Bex's room. I guessed she would be there, peaceful in her tower, and with reluctance went up the stairs rather than Rapunzel's ladder of handholds. It wouldn't be right to use them unless she invited me. In the old days, of course, I would have gone up by the holds, banged on the navy-blue door, shouted the best friend's catcalls. She was my best friend.

I stood at the door with a sick feeling in my stomach that perhaps I was no longer hers. Here at the top of the house sounds echoed and were magnified. I couldn't hear any movement on the other side of the door. Maybe in my room, behind a closed door, Marmalade had crept home and was deeply asleep on my pillow. I closed my eyes and pictured it. Wish it, see it, make it. Only the mantra didn't always work. I ached from not having his tough, furry body wedged into my back in the middle of the night and his persistent claws in my nostrils before dawn. There were hours to crawl through till I would know the worst. It would be the worst.

I knocked gently on the wooden panel with a knuckle, feeling more and more uneasy. Why couldn't I hear Bex? I would talk to Bex about Marmalade and she would understand. I tapped again, two knuckles' worth.

The room was empty. Her bluebell dress lay on the floor. The new mask, its huge eyes veiled by many eyelids and gleaming, sinister feelers, was propped against the pillow. My knees trembled as I ran down the stairs, my new leather shoes clip-clopping on the wood. I ran into Ruth and forgot all that I had just seen.

'I was looking for you.' She took my hand. 'Can you come into the kitchen?' Several stray hairs lay in damp strands across one cheek.

'More dishes?' I tried to sound light-hearted but my voice cracked.

Pa leaned against the black range. He looked yellow around the eyes and Ma had linked her arm through his. As

288

soon as I walked in, he straightened, avoided looking into my face. I saw his expression change as his glance fell on my shoes and knew he'd suddenly worked out how I wanted to be. He scowled. I was almost ready for the fight. But Ma's elbow dug into his ribs and he looked up with a different kind of frown. Something in my chest squeezed tight. 'We had a call from someone about a cat that might be Marmalade.' I thought I would fall over. 'You'd better come and check it out with me. I brought the car.'

'What did they say?

'They found a cat in the ditch by their house,' he said flatly.

'Is – is he alive?'

'He was when they rang.'

We drove away from the party at six o'clock. I know that was the right time. Pa was listening to the car radio, and it was news time. At least he had come for me.

Voicemail

Bex, why don't you answer? I've been looking for Marmalade, we went to the vet, we got a report, but it wasn't him. I came back to the party but you weren't there. I've got to talk to you. Please. I'm by the Birdcage in town. It's heaving tonight, everybody's out partying.

Voicemail

Hi Ma, why aren't you answering? Ma? Bex went off somewhere. I know Caroline rang you at home, I went back to the party twice but she's still not there, Bex isn't anywhere. I got an idea, I'm going to the Scar, I think she'll be there. Jack said he was going round town with some of his mates, I mean, police mates, in case she's gone clubbing but Bex doesn't do clubs, he knows that, I tried telling him but he wouldn't listen. Well, that's it. I've got my headtorch, I'll be back soon. Bye. I got my compass too, you don't have to worry, I know the Scar really well. Bye. Has your battery gone flat again? We both need new phones. Bye. Oh shit are you out looking for Bex too? Stupid reception

FIVE
WILDERNESS

Saturday August 26

It's dark. It's the middle of the night, of course it's dark, star-less. The moon appears, scowls, drags the huge swathe of grey cloud across herself and disappears, woman in a sulk. The cloud is fretful yellow at the fringes till the dark rushes back.

I can't work out if it's better or worse with the headtorch. At my last eye check the optician kept asking if the black circle was clearer on red or green and I really couldn't be ar-sed. I suppose it matters. Seeing shades of difference matters now. At least I've stopped shaking. This is my ground.

There's such a pain around my heart. Pa told me I was freaking him out. The young tabby from the ditch is just hanging on. We took her to the vet and she hasn't a micro-chip so nobody knows where she belongs. One of her legs is broken. Pa said we'd pay anyway, till the owner comes. A stray black cat sat under our half-wall and howled.

Getting across the racecourse is easier without the head-torch. My eyes adjust and I see the worn trail across the grass as far as the hedge and the gate to the Allotment. That's when I switch on again. The torch shows a tangle of thorns and scrub and within seconds I've lost all sense of direction. When I turn my head it's like a sabre, cutting the summer night into slivers of greenery that won't stay whole. In the total dark, after a few seconds, there's a spectrum of shade and I sense the solidity of things.

The path vaguely shows itself.

This is a fool's errand. I've heard the saying. Now I understand it. I'm here on a hunch. I couldn't bear another minute of watching Caroline's face crumple and smooth out and tense until a sob tore out of her throat like something breaking. I couldn't bear Jack's begging face, wanting to take the strain but she won't let him, she can't. I can't bear how they sit close but the air between them is jagged. The girls are asleep, thank God. They won't know anything about it. Only Tess might. Tess had the secret smile. Susie thought it was a wonderful day, I'm sure of it. I tried to be useful all day so I wouldn't have to think. I stare down at the dirty white of my trainers and think of Ruth's yellow-striped trainers, yellow shoes. A yellow brick road. I'm not going over the rainbow.

I know Bex is here somewhere, I just know she's gone to the ruins. I keep seeing her face the other day when we sat up here and watched the sun setting.

I don't want to think about why she would be here.

I should never have told her. I should have kept it to myself till I went away.

I don't know how she would find the way in the dark. Only she's been gone for hours so perhaps it wouldn't have been crashing through the dark like this. Perhaps she came straight here to watch the sun painting shadows across the hills. It's funny that you can't have shadow without light. I would never have thought of the sun as the bringer of darkness.

I keep sensing something out of the corner of my eye, but I don't waste time swivelling round to catch it. It, whatever It is, knows exactly how to keep out of sight.

At least I can get my bearings. I know more or less where to go, even if I can't see how to get there. The needle of the compass flutters in the light of the headtorch, swirls round like a drunk, finds true north. I close my eyes, switch off the headtorch. Slowly the shades reassemble themselves into suggestions of scrub, a huddle of bushes, maybe a tree or two, the faint glimmer of a path. Limestone. My footsteps are cautious. There's no point in trying to be fast. I have to find her, can't be chancy about the route.

I am so LOUD. Limestone clitter scuttles underfoot like stone ants on the run. My ankles remember the twists and turns and how to miss them, this time. Accidental memories flare – Bex laying a gauzy purple dress against her face – standing with arms outstretched at the edge of her room – flinging a book into the air as she runs away from Matt. I remember her today in the bluebell dress, her face too full of expressions for me to make sense of them.

Brambles and thorns snatch at my ankles. *Atishoo atishoo we all fall down.* I trip, grab at the nearest plant and I'm down, my head slamming into a stone. Lights flash inside my eyes and the pictures tear me up. The lamp slides off my head like it's got a will of its own. This is stupid. This is ridiculous, actually. What's the time? Get a grip.

I squat on the path, methodically pat the ground all around. The headtorch can't have rolled far. And I picture someone with a night-time video, animal-watching, falling about with silent laughter at what they've caught in their view-finder. Maybe badgers and foxes feel as ridiculous as this. The ground is warmer than I expected. I could lie here and wait for the dawn. Maybe if I stopped breathing I would catch the sounds of Bex.

Suddenly the moon sashays into sight – huge, yellow, lop-sided, with tatters of cloud like torn cloth drifting across a wild face and I get the meaning of *lunatic. Lunatic.*

The torch slips under my fingers, stays still.

Lunatic. I wind the strap of the headtorch round my wrist and teeter forward almost into a run. The narrow trousers drag at my thighs, at the stitches across my knee and I wince at the jab of pain. My toe stubs itself against a boulder-in-waiting, perfectly obstructive.

Shrubs are more disturbing in this pretend light, black and silver as the breeze shifts, sticking out their roots, grabbing for my sleeves. I wriggle, infuriated by the delay. So what, if the wedding shirt tears too? In nightmares, the faster you run the more slowly the ground unrolls. The air stiffens, I bend double, clutch the knife in my side.

Gobs of sweat run into my eyes and I dash them away with the back of my hand. I'm not even out of breath and yet I'm panting. There are too many bushes, too close. The Bradleyfield Allotment clenches its walls around me, making a fist. Beyond is the wide-open expanse of the Scar, where the paths run straight and the shadows thin. The knife twitches under my ribs but I will ignore it.

Breathe in, breathe out. Where is Bex?

I snap on the lamp to check the compass, but I've lost my bearings. If you don't know where you've come from and you can't see the lie of the land, you can't work out where to go. Half past midnight. No one has seen Bex for six hours – not unless she's with someone now. The very idea of 'someone' makes my fingers tremble.

This is the void. You are thrown into the dark and there's nothing but you. And inside you there's nothing but the dark.

Leaves rustle. A bird twitters, a piercing, sweet sound that sends a thrill through my nervous system. If a bird can sit in a bush and get along with its own business, so can I.

The moon disappears. I stand still, listening to the patter of my heart and the nervous rasp of breath in my nostrils. The bird calls again. All I have to do is wait till daylight. Daylight will come. If Bex is here I will bring her home. Today I will have brought her home. Future perfect. Name it, do it. I sit on a boulder, imagine the spatter of lichen on its surface, the bird on its branch. I wonder if its nest is close by. The quiet of the night begins to seep through my defences. Silence, soil, stone. I lift my head, hearing something different.

There it is again – a rattle of stones, a surge of wind that might be a sigh. I won't move, won't lose the sound by so much as the twitch of the hand. So I'm ready when the moon yanks her cloud aside. I'm at the bottom of the rampart of stones, where Bex and I sat on Tuesday. I have known how to find it again, after all. I take a moment to thank the instincts I do not control, and then I clamber hand over hand to the top as fast as I can.

At first it's hard to be sure what's there, for the pits overflow with shadow, but my hackles have risen regardless and my heart hammers against my ribs. I can't swallow, I can't breathe, her hand lies limp at the edge of the shadow, she's drowning in shadow and dark, ragged lines criss-cross her wrist. A new and unmistakeable metallic odour sharpens the air. I reach towards her hand. It's deadly cold and sticky. The sticky darkness has spread over stones. I ease myself over the edge of the rampart to where she lies across the inner ledge.

Take a First Aid Course on the Careers noticeboard, *Give Blood* on the cloakroom walls, *Carry a Donor Card* in the loos – my mind clams up with pictures – until the hand in mine twitches and I grip the fingers.

There's blood everywhere but I am not going to panic. She's so cold. I have to know she's alive, that it wasn't my twitch. I bend to her face, hoping for the fan of breath but the breeze is playing games and I can't be sure. I lean into her breast, into the sodden fabric of her shirt, where blood has also found its way. How not to hear my own heartbeat?

299

Blood on my cheek – I brush it off – it's in my mouth, raw meat, Bex, gross, o god.

I wrestle off my shirt and use the rent in a sleeve to tear strips of fabric for bandages. Round and round her wrists, tight, not too tight, don't know about her circulation. Is it better to strip off my trousers to use as a blanket, or warm her with my body? I waste precious time, almost drop my phone. There's no signal but they say that 999 works wherever you are.

I slide my arms beneath her, straining not to judder so that I can move her gently, gently to the ground. My vision swims. She's little and light but not a child. A fingernail breaks as I scoop stones out of the way. The ground is rock hard, naturally. Bone of my bone. Now she lies on her side and I become her double, her outer body, curved like a comma tight against her spine. I breathe slow and hot between her shoulders, sending surges of warmth from me to her. The heat fans back to my face, but her hands are still too cold. The faintest scent of rose arises from her skin and I bury my nose in her neck, inhaling, exhaling.

Ringing 999 is not straightforward. I jab again at the phone, can't explain where we are, keep repeating that mountain rescue will know. She's kind, the operator, a bit slow, won't stop asking for details I have already given.

Time yawns. I am so cold. I want to think it isn't my fault but here she lies and here I brought her. She came *here* where I told her I was not a golden girl but maybe a golden boy. She must have thought I was gross but she kept it inside. Everything is so dark. I can't see the stars. I can't let go. I have to keep pushing out long hot breaths into her body. But I am so cold, only my face is warm from the endless breathing into her back and I feel sick and blackness yawns and —

— a wet nose in my face, a bark, dense looming figures.

They say she's alive. The paramedics wrap her in foil, set up a drip, lift her to the stretcher with tenderness that makes my eyes water. The dogs snuffle. Loud patting and mutters. 'Good girl Sheba, good girl Betty.' Somebody wraps me in foil too and I'm half-carried by a huge man in a fleece to the road where the ambulance is waiting. There's a car behind it and I'm astounded to see Ma and Pa leaning against the bonnet. Their faces are green by flashlight.

'How did you know?' I say, my lips muffled against Ma's hair where she has me in so tight a hold I can hardly breathe.

Another voice says, 'Oh Joey, oh Joey,' and I feel Jack's hand between my shoulders.

Ma says, 'Caroline's in the ambulance. Ruth's gone to babysit the little girls. I can't tell you what it's been like.' My ear is wet. She's crying into my ear.

We follow the ambulance to the hospital. I have no sense of time. Pa drives, Ma sits in the back seat alongside me. She won't let go. I'm ravenous and then I feel sick and hot and cold, shivering with feelings I can't name. Ma says, 'She's very shocked, I guess they'll know what to do for the best.'

I want to ask about Bex but my mouth won't work. Why did she quote the hawk poem when we went the Allotment on Wednesday? The hawk's a killer. In the poem, the hawk says *I am going to keep everything like this*. Nothing stays the same unless it's dead. Even the rocks change.

You really do get hot, sweet tea. I hate sugar in tea but it's wonderful. We wait for a while in the reception area on stiff, fierce chairs, and then for a long, long time in a cubicle where I lie under a thin blanket and Ma and Pa take it in turns to sit with me or go to the drinks machine. Pa has insisted on giving me his sweater that smells of cow. I could be lying in a field. I try to explain what I did, how I knew where to go. Ma's face has a white, scrubbed look, like a little girl's.

Pa rasps his hand over his face, flicks the pages of *Good Housekeeping, What Car, Cumbria Life,* tosses them on the floor, picks them up again, flicks through. At one point Ma collects them up and takes them back to the waiting area but ten minutes later Pa has found them again. He starts to read the Small Ads aloud. It makes me laugh. Suddenly he drops them, grabs my hands and his face is scarlet. 'I got it all wrong.' Ma puts her arms around him and we shudder together as if the earth has shivered too.

A man in a white coat with a swinging stethoscope and tired eyes say he'll be along shortly. Ma asks why he can't stay now but she's talking to his back. Was that his ghost, then?

Pa wipes his eyes, takes my hands again. 'I'll find out about Bex.' It's almost too painful to smile. There's a grim set to Pa's smile that I have hardly ever seen. He releases me, strokes my forehead, and pushes himself up from the chair with a stiff, mechanical movement. 'I'll find out.' He disappears through the gap in the curtains.

Ma says, 'I don't suppose you could sleep. You could close your eyes, though. This is a horrid light.'

'What's the time?' My voice comes out cracked and squeaky.

Ma slips her hand across my eyes and instinctively I shut them. 'Nearly five o'clock. Soon be breakfast.' I wonder if Ruth gets story lines from real life or if she just makes things up. I wonder if Bex told her the secret story that I don't know. I wouldn't blame her.

Text

14:12 Noah

God, kid. Noah ( )

14:12 Joey

Feel like shit ☹

14:13 Noah

Home 2day?

14:13 Joey

Waiting for dr

14:14 Noah

Pa's lsot it ☹

14:14 Joey

Yep

Sunday August 27

'I was the friend who let her fall. I cut the rope. I wish I hadn't seen that film.'

Ruth grasped my fingers. 'Explain to me how you cut the rope.'

'She kept telling me she needed help. She didn't say so, words out loud, but I wasn't paying attention.'

Ruth had dragged me out into the garden, to the wall. She was choosing the pieces for the stone jigsaw. I half-saw the curve of her backbone, a ridged but flexible hoop bent over the heap of stones on the moist brown earth. Her pale blue shirt lifted in the light wind that blew over the house and up the fellside, carrying a spray of rain. 'Come on, Joey, it's your design, tell me if I'm selecting the best stones. We need to get this finished, plants in.'

I wiped my face with the familiar striped jersey. Figure in landscape, faded rugby shirt and black jeans, short dark hair and straight black eyebrows. Everything felt dreamlike, distant. Then Ruth put a rock into my hand. 'Come on, Joey. Time to build. Let's get a yard done by lunch.' She grasped my hand again, pressing my fingers over the stone until the sharp edges cut into the palm of my hand. It felt good, the solid weight and rough texture, smelling of wet earth and fine green moss. I wedged another stone into place. *Ruth says it's not my fault.* The loop of the last two weeks was replaying uncontrollably.

Ma woke me first thing with tea and toast in bed. She said she couldn't help it. If she thought I'd eat boiled egg and soldiers she'd have appeared with those. I was a hundred years old when I woke up. My knees creaked. Very old people get treated like babies.

I slept with the curtains open, and early light painted the air pink. By the time I had finally struggled into clothes the sunshine had been wiped clean out of the sky by a wet grey sponge of cloud. All morning long, an invisible hand occasionally squeezed the cloud. No sooner had we dried out than another squeeze left us sodden again.

Ruth crushed a forefinger trying to make two stones fit. I said, 'Ease them. I'll look for a different one.' She arched her back, smiled, rubbing the aching muscles.

I said, 'What if —?'

'—You can't be responsible for her life.' I thought of all the time we'd spent together, Bex and I – all the texts and messages, the summer days in the field behind our house, the evenings when she read and I studied maps of Cumberland and Westmorland, looked up old fell races, did squats-sit-ups-press-ups in my bedroom or hers. I tried recapturing the sense of how it felt inside the framework of the life mask, its weight and slipperiness, the smells of willow and wool and crinkling paper, a hot smell of something metallic when she soldered, the burn on her finger, the yelp. But it was fading. You can't make sensations come again. I remembered sitting flat on a slab in the yard of their old little house, playing spit-cherry-stones. That was easier to recreate – stone, moss, damp earth – they were all around me now.

Ruth said, as if her last remark had only been made seconds ago rather than half an hour, 'You're not the only influence in her life, are you? What about Matt?' I dug into the pile of stones, threw several aside in search of a match. Another torn fingernail. Blood.

Simon came to the open door, leaned out, disappeared. Five minutes later he strode into the garden in neat jeans and a clean denim shirt, swinging a couple of water bottles in each hand. Noah wandered out later still, wearing ragged brown shorts and a climbing top that used to be green. His face was scrubby with black stubble. If Fi were here, she would tell him off, rub her hand across his stubble and mutter into his chin. He would grin and pull her against him. The muscles of his tanned forearm would swell as they tightened around her body. Where was Fi now?

Noah took long strides down the garden in my direction, arms half-raised as if to hug me, stumbled, dug into his pockets with a puzzled scowl. The weight on my chest lifted for a moment and I punched him lightly in the arm. 'You're up early.'

'Can't see my sibling struggle.'

'What happened with Fi?'

Simon half-turned from the wall, opened his mouth, thought better of whatever he might have said. Noah shrugged, spread his hands, pointed at the wall. 'Instructions?'

We lifted and checked, placed stones in position, repositioned, stood back to wipe the damp from our faces. Time was marked in inches.

Ma called us for lunch. She had made vegetable soup and almost visibly stopped herself from sitting beside me. Instead, she sat across the table, watching through her lashes as I lifted the spoon. Her mouth opened as I opened mine. Eventually, I said, 'Ma, would you like to regurgitate it for me?' Even Pa smiled. He still had the shocked look of somebody whose clothes stand away from the skin, whose features are trying to recall how they fit. He saw my glance and stretched his arm along the table in my direction, barely giving Ruth time to whisk her bowl of soup out of the way.

'We nearly lost you,' he said, mouth twitching. 'I nearly lost you.'

'No, no. I was ok.' He gripped my hand so hard that my knuckles cracked. *It's Bex who was nearly lost.* I was glad of the pain.

'I nearly lost you,' he repeated. Around the table everyone fell silent. Finches twittered in the bushes by an open window and water from a saucepan lid over the soup hissed upon the stove.

When the phone rang, I jumped.

It was Caroline, telling Ma that Bex had just been discharged. She wanted to see me. My stomach tightened and I didn't want the soup anymore.

'Surely it's too soon for her to be discharged,' Ruth said, frowning, pushing her bowl away too. 'I thought she had a transfusion or something. They can't just kick her out.'

Ma said slowly, 'I rather think from what Caroline said that Bex discharged herself.'

'Can you do that? Surely you can't do that, not after something like trying —.' Noah stuffed a hunk of bread into his mouth, looked as if this had been a mistake, and groped for his glass of water. He had an odd, closed look.

Ma said, 'I think you can if you're of age. If the doctors think you understand what you're doing.' She was still wearing the green shirt. She can't have thought twice when getting dressed today.

Ruth refilled the water jug. 'I guess they don't want beds clogged up, do they? And there's always the risk of getting an infection.' Her matter-of-fact tone seemed to bring down the temperature. She leaned across the table to place the jug in the centre. Drops of water flecked the wooden surface, little globes of winking light.

Ma looked at my face and folded her arms tight across her chest. 'I'm not so sure I want you going to see Bex today but I suppose I can't stop you. I don't see how it will be good for you, not today.' Ruth put a hand on her arm and Ma's shoulders hunched as if she had swallowed a wasp.

I stood in the garden assessing the wall. It could be finished in a couple of hours if everybody helped. I saw the floor of the ruined house, and the shards of glass in the clitter where rue-leaved saxifrage grew.

As I walked along the track to the road, a wet, black creature leapt between my legs from the grassy verge, mewing faintly. I hardened my heart and walked on. No creature was safe with me. Trying not to picture Marmalade dead in a ditch was so hard that I stooped to pick up a flint from the track and ground it into my palm.

It had turned into a typical Sunday afternoon, with cloud settled on the fells for the rest of the day and every tree and shrub water-sodden. *We could grow gills.* Creatures evolve to fit the habitat. We could all become amphibians together, like two-legged dolphins. My eyes stung from the salt of unwanted tears. I ached to know what had happened so that I could bury him – no, so that I could lay him to rest. Burial meant concealment in the dark earth, a covering over and forgetting. Ma and Pa were used to the reincarnation of Marmalade in the next stray, but this Marmalade had been mine from the moment we moved into the new house, the year we moved from London. Someone had dropped him in the verge, barely able to lap his milk. How do you forget?

Suddenly a car drew up behind me. Noah. 'I'll drive you. Come on.'

'I need to walk.'

Wearily he propped his elbow across the open car window. 'I can take you, easy.'

'I need to think.' His face closed up again and he reversed along the track. I walked on, baffled by the muddled softness in my brother, but soon the only pictures in my mind were of Marmalade. I kept imagining him at full stretch along a windowsill, or bounding across the field towards me, or curled tightly on top of someone's newspaper. To find myself at Bex's gate was shocking. How did I get here? I pinched my arm. There was a cat-shaped space in the crook of my knee for Marmalade by night. You don't choose who or what you love. Maybe in cyborg life you grow out of your emotions or man + machine leaves out everything that hurts. The mist intensified the scent of lavender garden. I struggled to get feelings into place.

Jack opened the door. He looked as bad as Pa, haggard and too small for his rusty-red sweater. He pulled me across the threshold. 'I'm sorry to grab you like this but Caroline's frantic, we're both frantic. She won't talk to us. She asks for Susie and Tess but we don't want them frightened. She's still sedated. They had to give her blood.' Words tumbled out as if all the normal controls had been switched off. 'Susie keeps bursting into tears and Tess hasn't spoken a word since Friday night. Friday night. It's three o'clock, my God, she still won't talk to any of us.'

The kitchen was stark. Nobody seemed to have used the great black range and the table was bare apart from a bread board and hacked pieces of bread. A half-empty bottle of milk stood beside the sink and two or three mugs with protruding spoons sat on the draining board. Someone had dropped an entire packet of butter on the floor.

'Do you want some orange or tea? Water? I'll tell Caroline. Don't go, will you?' His eyes were huge, the pupils dilated, like a man's who has been underground for days.

Left to myself, I shivered, wishing I had brought a fleece. It was warmer outside, walking in cloudland.

Caroline's face was as bleak as Jack's but steadier. She managed a smile. 'Thanks, Joey. Thanks so much. Sit down a minute.'

We perched on the bright chairs, I on one upholstered in yellow and Caroline on indigo. Jack leaned against the range, fretting at his finger-ends.

'I can't ask you to talk to her and then tell us what she says, I realise that. If she tells you what, why –.' Caroline stopped dead, closed her eyes. Her face was white and her black hair looked lank. 'If she talks to you, I'd just be glad if you could ask her permission to tell us if it's something we've done that we didn't realise.' Then she covered her face with her hands. The new wedding ring was a soft, wide silvery band, white gold, they said.

I said that I would try. 'But I don't think it's you.' The doubt in my voice made her look up. She was not crying. 'It might be me.'

Her eyes widened. 'You? Of course not. She thinks everything of you. She thinks –.' She ran her hands over her face, fingers clenched as if to tear off the skin, and covered her eyes.

Jack inched forward to place his hands over hers. It was a curious picture of double blind-folding, colour-coding, his old red sweater curved around the shabby brown fleece she wore for screen-printing. 'She's in her room.' He nodded in the direction of the stairs.

They couldn't imagine that I was the one who had let her down. Ok, I didn't cut the rope, not deliberately, like

310

the climber in the film. But that was only because the invisible cable in me was paid out to Marmalade. It was all wrong, of course. Nobody's supposed to love their cat more than another human being. It wasn't exactly that I loved him more but I knew how to love him. I loved him for his wildness, for winding himself around my legs, for taking over my bed, my face, the hollow in my body. He was fearless. Being friends with Bex was a great deal more complicated. I went online instead.

I hadn't talked to anyone online for days.

Slowly I stepped up the magnificent wooden staircase, stroking the banister, the warm, mellow oak sliding through the palm of my hand like polished rope. I might never come here again. I looked through an open door at the gallery, where clearing up had not been completed. There were still several empty glasses and plates on the floor. At Susie's room I paused, pressed my ear to the closed door, knocked. No answer. The further up the stairs I went, the harder my heart knocked on my ribs. It felt like the end of a very long run.

A small voice fluted ahead. I pushed open the door of Bex's room to find Tess and Susie sitting on the end of the bed. Bex was lying flat on her back in the middle of the floor. She wore only her bra and pants. Her wrists were lightly bandaged and the white scars slicing up the inside of both arms were terribly clear. There were scars at the top of her thighs, too. Some of the scars were red. I knew now that this meant they were recent.

Susie leapt off the bed and ran towards me. I bent to embrace her quivery body, shielding her head in the palm of one hand. The cap of hair was soft and slightly damp. Bex gazed at me with a motionless face. Only her eyes were alive, peering through peep-holes.

'I think Bex wants to talk to me,' I said, freeing myself from the tight hug. 'But maybe she wants you both to stay too. I don't know.'

Susie's voice was higher than ever. 'She's got these marks all over. She cuts herself. She gets a knife.'

Bex sat up, clasping her arms around her knees. 'Would you mind? Could you pass me a shirt?' She was talking to me. She was talking to me. I plucked one of her usual long-sleeved shirts from the bottom of the wardrobe and handed it over. There were goose-pimples on her legs. A short blue skirt, no more than a frill, and a pair of black footless leggings were folded neatly on the chair by the window. I held them out. She took them as if I were serving in the shop. Tess's mouth was firmly shut but her eyes were wide and with a shock I recognised the huge, empty pupils I had seen in Jack's face, Caroline's. Pa's.

Bex sat cross-legged on the floor and gestured that we were to sit too, forming a circle. 'Carpet time,' I said, idiotically. The others slipped into place as if this were regular.

It was unnerving to watch Bex. No muscle of her face moved, except her mouth. 'I'll begin. Yes. The cuts. They are old, you know that.' She pulled up a sleeve, her mouth tightening as the fabric snagged in the bandages. 'Mostly old.' Again she patted at her wrist as if taking a pulse, stroking the scars. 'I started out with compasses from my protractor set. The year you came, Joey. I had wanted to do it before.' I began to shiver again. 'I used to dream about it. I used to dream about getting a knife and slicing into my mouth. I used to dream about getting a knife from our kitchen and slicing across my lips.' She chopped down over her mouth with the side of her hand. Tess's face did not change, but Susie clasped her mouth with both hands.

'Why? Why?' My question burst out. 'It wasn't me was it? Was it my fault?'

'Oh.' Her small, dead white face looked at me as if I were a passer-by. 'It never occurred to me before, but maybe. I didn't have any friends before you moved here. I used to get picked on. Teachers always used to tell me to stand up for myself but I couldn't.' She talked in a flat, soft voice, turning her head like a puppet, a robot, so that Susie, Tess, would come into focus. I felt flat as a picture on a wall. 'Our teacher, that year you came, she told me bullies could smell me being afraid and I needed not to be so they wouldn't smell the fear. But I didn't know how. I was always afraid, even after –.' She fell silent and seemed to be holding her breath. I counted. *Twenty-nine, thirty seconds.* 'Even after Mum ran away with us, I couldn't stop being afraid. She went back once and I remembered. She ran away with me when I was little, I remember that. I remember a little room. She had a friend we stayed with. But he came for her. He's good at that. He made us go back. Everything started again.'

Susie and Tess looked like dolls propped up around a rug for a pretend tea-party. Susie's eyes open and shut mechanically, like a doll's. Her mouth opened and the small voice said, 'Who's *he*? Who ran away?'

Bex's eyes swivelled in her direction. 'Mum ran away with me.'

'But who's *he*?' Despite her toy-like movements, Susie's eyes were determined.

I said, 'Your real dad.'

Tess stuffed both fists into her mouth but Susie's head snapped up. 'He's not our real dad. Jack's our real daddy.' The tears on her cheeks were real and the hands clenched and unclenched around her bent knees, but the voice was that of the teenager-in-waiting.

Bex slowly turned her eyes in my direction. 'Yeah. That

man. Dominic.' She was looking at the ghost again, the shadow in the room.

I needed to help us out, Susie, Tess and me. 'So what started again?'

'He used to slap Mum about. He told her she made him. I heard him. After Susie was born it was worse. I saw it.'

Susie's head reared back. 'Do I remember that, Bex? Do I?' She choked on the question, child again. I wanted to reach across but Bex was talking to the ghost.

'We got away again only this time Mum fixed things better. We moved to our little house here, the one we used to live in. That man went abroad. You came to our school. Tess was born and she never knew him. Never had to know he was our father.'

The little white-washed house. I could picture every room, Bex's tiny room with the sloping window in the roof that you opened with a rope, and the big room downstairs for Susie and Tess with stick-on transfers all around the walls, and Caroline's room next door, her table at the window, the computer alongside, and designs tacked loosely to the walls. Everything was white, to bring in the light, Caroline always said.

I asked the question cautiously. 'You cut yourself because he hit your mum? I can't work out about Susie and Tess.' My mind went whirling round possibilities.

'It was sort of like an offering to the gods,' said Bex unexpectedly. 'You'd come, you were my friend, he'd gone and I wanted to make sure he would never come back.' There was a faint tinge of colour in her face and she looked at me properly again, pleadingly.

'Ok. Ok. But why this? Why now?'

Bex's eyes darkened. The chill in the room was almost solid. 'Maybe you two should go downstairs and see your mum,' I said uncertainly, looking from Susie to Tess. 'We'll be down in a minute. What do you think?'

Susie got to her feet, held out her hand to Tess. 'Come on.' She straightened her shoulders, took charge of Tess's hand and stepped around us towards the door. 'Come down in a minute. I don't like it. Tess and me, we don't like it, do we?' Tess shook her head. The door clicked softly shut. Jack's gentle hinges.

Bex suddenly blurted, 'Check out of the window. See if he's there. You've got to check.'

Mystified, I peered down. 'Where am I looking?' Bex's window looked down upon the garden at the back of the house. 'Who could get into your garden? You don't mean Jack, do you?' The appalling words had slipped out before I could swallow them.

'You'll have to look at the front.' She wasn't listening. The ghost was in the room and the hairs stood up on the back of my neck.

Then she told me.

Zef's Blog

Noah brought me a can of beer. He didn't hang around, just put it on the desk beside the laptop. He didn't try to look at the screen, even.

Work tomorrow seems another world. Someone will have to tell Shirley.

The worst was Jack. He looked wild. I should have come away when Bex was telling them but she wouldn't let me go. She had to practically die before she would tell.

She said, when she was telling Caroline and Jack, that it had been like living in a box.

Caroline sat with her arm round Jack whilst Bex talked and for a while I couldn't work out why, but it was to make him sit still. It's to do with why he left the police. She didn't say anything and he wasn't going to but he was kind of doubled over as if someone had knifed him in the belly. He threw up in their cloakroom. I heard him when I was leaving.

Something's going on with Jack and I'm trying to understand because there's enough going on that I never paid attention to. And he's Bex's dad now. Father.

I found this website, www.ukpolicetalk.org. It's a bit like www.iwannagetoutofhere.co.uk. Policemen go online to try and work out stuff, mostly what to do if something happens that they can't control, or to share experiences. Like what to do if they are off duty and there's a crime happening in front of them and whether anyone will believe them if they do or don't do something. Whatever they do it may be wrong. I get that. I identify with that.

I never thought about a policeman being in agony like Jack. He began a rant about regulations being worse than prison but Caroline stopped him.

I looked up police regulations for custody sergeants and they are impossible.

There's something in this website about stresses on the police, people like custody sergeants. They have to be almost superhuman steady, making decisions.

There's so much to remember, so many variations

> While in police custody, detainees are treated in a way that is dignified and takes account of their human rights and diverse individual needs. Custody staff are respectful in their day-to-day working and are aware of and responsive to any particular risks and vulnerabilities relating to:
>
> - those who have consumed alcohol;
> - those who have consumed or packed drugs;
> - those with mental ill health or learning disabilities/ difficulties;
> - women;
> - black and minority ethnic detainees;
> - children and young people;
> - those with disabilities;
> - foreign nationals;
> - immigration detainees;
> - those with specific religious requirements;
> - older detainees;
> - sexuality;
> - transsexual and transgendered detainees;
> - other factors.

Doesn't this mean treat everyone decently? why are women singled out, not men? what's the difference between a mental ill health disability and 'disabilities'?

On www.ukpolicetalk.org it says if a policeman has a really bad experience he may be off his head with worry and nerves so anything he says shouldn't be relied on. If he's asked to make a statement he won't want to refuse in case they think he's hiding something. But he'll be afraid that anything he says will be used against him, whatever. And all the time he's going mad with worry that he could have made a better judgement. That's what it says on the website.

That's definitely Catch 22. If you make a statement it can be used against you and if you don't make a statement it can be used against you.

Jack said some men can't keep their dicks to themselves. He said some men ought to be castrated at birth. He pushed Caroline away and ran at the wall. He slammed his fist into it so hard that the plaster was dented and she had to shove his hand under cold running water and fetch ice. She wanted him to get checked out at casualty.

Bex talked like a dummy as though everything had happened to somebody else. Caroline did not move until Jack hit the wall. Then she jerked as if he was going to hit her next. Jack didn't raise his voice above a whisper. Caroline said she would take Bex to the police station in the morning. Bex said, 'I'll go when I'm ready' and it sounded like a slap in the face. She can't have meant it to sound like that.

I try not to think about what the father did to Bex. She described it all. I don't want to remember but the pictures won't go away. Like the image Matt created on Bex's phone. I want to look it up but if I do I might get on a porn site by accident.

I don't drink beer but it was a family sort of thing for Noah to bring me some, I guess.

He probably raped Caroline, for Tess to be conceived. The father. I think that's part of what Bex meant to say, because Caroline would never have said yes.

He fucked his daughter, over and over. Total control.

I thought it was Matt's fault, I thought it was me.

20:20 Bex

Log on, chat

2 long for txt

Chat

Bex	Can't say it out loud
Joey	Are you ok?
Bex	He was after Tess, that's why she went for tea.
Bex	He kept saying he wanted to get to know me again.
Bex	He said he was going to get to know Tess better. You don't get away from him.
Bex	Are you still there?
Joey	You thought he'd do the same to her as he did to you.
Bex	He gets into your head.
Joey	You have to tell your mum and Jack.
Bex	Hospital in the morning. Some consultant or other.
Joey	I saw at the wedding, him and Tess, outside, her.
Joey	Do you think Julia knows?
Bex	poor cow, she won't stop him
Joey	you're sorry for her?
Joey	bet she knows
Bex	Like Mum, you mean?

Networking

Narrative: Zenith 22:45

Does anyone know about being no-sex?

Comment: Moderator Sue 23:22

What's worrying you, Zenith?

Narrative: Zenith 23:22

Sex seems to drive people off their heads.

Comment: Cybersnake 23:34

Makes you human, though. Old people give it up don't they?

Comment: Moderator Sue 23:34

Most people would say that sex in a loving relationship brings fantastic happiness. It's no good being driven by sex, though. Sex is part of the engine, not the driver.

Narrative: Zenith 23:35

What about paedophiles?

Comment: Barbarian 23:41

What are you getting into?

Comment: Moderator Sue 23:41

Everything can be twisted. Too much food makes you fat, too much alcohol rots your liver; fighting for justice is a good thing, fighting on its own leads to murder. Like cancer cells – cells in themselves are fine; cancer cells are just the same cells doing the wrong thing

---

Comment: Barbarian 23:42

What?

Narrative: Zenith 23:46

Can you kill the love in the paedophile and not kill the paedophile too?

Comment: Cybersnake 23:48

They make their choices, free will and all that

Narrative: Zenith 23:53

Do you think people are born paedophiles? Or does something horrible happen and they grow up twisted? Do they choose to be paedos or does something else do it to them, make it happen? what about their families? what if they're married, have partners?

Monday August 28

'I didn't expect to see you today.' Shirley's eyes were newly framed by lines of golden glitter along her cheekbones. She looked exotic for a Monday morning on the high street. Ma stood on the pavement with the bulging briefcase at her feet. 'Is this your mother?' Shirley tiptoed down the steps. 'You have a look of your mother, Joey. I heard about her great work in the middle of Friday night. You must be very proud of her, Mrs Wilcox.'

Ma said, 'It was a tough night.'

But Shirley was more interested in her window display. She walked around Ma to stare at it, clicking her tongue. 'That purple ribbon doesn't work.'

I caught Ma's eye and she shook her head. 'I came to talk about Bex. Her mother would have come but everyone's still in a state of shock, as you can imagine.' Shirley shifted, and Ma fixed her with the headmistress look. 'She hopes – we all hope – that Bex will be returning to work soon.' Shirley tried to scoop Ma into the shop but Ma performed a neat sideways step. 'I have to get to school.'

'Yes, but.' Shirley smoothed an invisible hair from the corner of her mouth. 'I don't want to be responsible.' Her voice trailed away. Glancing up, I saw strips of pale blue sky.

'It's all over the town.'

Ma said, 'Rebecca is not ill.'

Shirley could bite. 'She's not been exactly reliable recently.' Then she added, 'I've got my business to look after.' She looked at me, at Ma. 'Well all right then, but I don't want any trouble. Are you coming in, Joey?'

Ma spoke as I was opening my mouth. 'Joey needs a day off. A bit of time to get over the shock herself. Is that acceptable?' and she took me by the elbow, walking me away. Shirley called out that she would expect me tomorrow, and the shop door slammed with an incongruous tinkle.

'Don't be cross,' said Ma quickly, hastening me past the library. 'I know you need the money but really. Anyway, what I said's true. You've got a stretched look.'

Ma had parked defiantly on the double yellow lines by the post office. She felt ready to fight the traffic warden, she said, fumbling in the pocket of the briefcase for the car keys. I watched the familiar scramble for keys with a darkening sense that anything could change. Ma caught my expression. 'It's not so very long since people who attempted suicide were sent to prison,' she said. I gaped. 'It's true.' Ma tugged open the door. 'The legal position was that your body did not belong to you and it was a crime to try to kill it.'

'Whose body is it then?'

'Don't fight me, darling. It wasn't my law.' We got into the car. 'It was a religious thing. Your body belonged to God so suicide was murder.'

'Where are we going?' I could not get rid of the memory of wrapping my body around Bex.

'I thought we might try to link up with Caroline at the hospital. She sounded so tense on the phone this morning.'

'I thought you were going into school.'

'Later. In a bit.'

Ma was concentrating on changing lanes in the one-way system. I watched her hands on the wheel, seeing familiar fingers. Mine were the same. I didn't ask to be born, I didn't choose it. She and Pa had sex, gruesome. They chose. My genes came from her and Pa and their parents. The bubbling, fierce feelings in my head, were they from my genes too?

We were brought to a halt by traffic lights. Alongside, the river roared through the town, brown and teeming and running back on itself in rough, dark eddies. Rain on the fells had filled the becks and gills, swelling now to the unstoppable current that would tear towards the coast. I opened the window, glad of sounds that more than matched the hum of stationery traffic. 'Ma, you know what you said.'

'Which pearl of wisdom had you in mind?'

'About suicides. Who owns your body.'

'What's bothering you?'

We swept over the bridge, glided between the almshouses and the rich green turf of the river bank. I pictured the river's rampage through the flattening countryside until it carved a route across Morecambe Bay to merge with the sea and the wide, enormous sky.

'Who owns you?'

'Me? You? Anyone? What do you mean?' But I had stopped listening. I was a twig on a branch, on a tree, a huge world-tree like in mythology, roots in a system as huge and intertwined as the underground structure of fungi.

And I was me. I was me, I owned me, not like my coat or my shoes, but what nobody else could lay hands on – my spirit, my secret and unsayable awareness. I marked out my own boundaries, I could choose to say or not say. I chose the route that led to the top of the Bradleyfield Allotment. That was me. I went on my own, I went to rescue Bex. Twig, branch, tree, root, seed floating in the wind, all of it me. My heart raced.

'You're talking to yourself, Joey.'

Tess and Susie were dancing up and down under the canopy of the Out-patients department. 'Mummy's gone in with Bex,' said Susie, her face still pale. 'Jack was going to take us out for an ice cream but he's gone over there,' and she turned to point across the slip road towards the hospital car park that we had just left.

'Oh,' said Ma. 'We didn't see him. But I expect he'll be back soon.' She looked at their small faces. 'Shall we go and find seats?'

We walked past the computer terminals inviting you to 'Check Yourself In Online' into the waiting area, where padded chairs, unnaturally high, were set in formation around low tables. A cardboard box, half-trodden down, displayed wooden jigsaws, an abacus, three or four board books and some blunted crayons. They must get all sorts here. Like us. Ma persuaded the girls to sit down and looked about. There was no sign of Caroline or Bex. 'I think I know where they'll be,' she said, looking like Noah. 'I'll nip along and tell them we've got the girls. Must text Ruth too, tell her where we are. I was going to meet her for coffee before going to school. Might be later than I thought. I wonder what's happened to Jack. You stay, won't you?' She headed off along the wide corridor.

I was dragging the cardboard box to their feet, looking for suitable books, when Susie said, 'Look, it's Matt.'

'He can't!' I shot up, overturning the box. Matt stood in the foyer, clutching a large bunch of flowers in one hand and his mother's arm in the other. His mother went to the reception desk, teetering on wedge-heeled sandals. 'What's he doing here? She's not here. How dare he!' I saw the look of confusion on Susie's face and bit the side of my cheek. Something about him looked undressed, newborn. He had shaved his head and the scalp was limestone-white. I felt a pang of pity that I didn't want.

'I don't understand.' Susie stood up, as if ready to run over to Matt.

I grasped the hem of her short skirt. 'They'll tell him she's not here, she's been sent home.'

'Well she is here,' whispered Tess. 'And our other daddy's here too.' My phone skidded under the stiff moulded chair, and I grovelled after it. Her small hand gripped my shoulder. 'I don't want to go with him. I don't want to cut myself. Not like Bex.'

I wriggled free, took one of her hands, Susie's too as I kept my voice low. 'You live with your mummy and with Jack, now. You don't have to go with anyone else ever again.'

'He said I could go if I asked but I don't want to.' Her lip trembled.

'When you said he was here, what do you mean?' I saw with relief that Matt and his mother were turning away, making for the exit.

'He was behind us.' Susie's eyes narrowed as she gave me a sideways, knowing look. 'I saw him. Bex dropped her book and I picked it up and I saw him.' She took a deep breath. 'He was standing on the other side of the road, where the cars are. I didn't tell Mummy.' Her mouth tightened and again she looked older than her nine years. 'I told Jack.'

'What did Jack do?'

'He went across the road,' still giving me the sideways look. I felt clammy as I cast around for inspiration. An elderly woman cautiously hobbled in front of the glassed-in reception desk, where one man sorted slips of paper into piles and another focussed on a computer screen. I joined the small queue, desperate to catch someone's eye. They were busy. The elderly woman patiently folded her gnarled hands over the top of her walking stick.

'Excuse me —,' but he merely lifted a hand to silence me whilst he completed the task. The old woman shuffled and I had to step back, give her the place that was hers. Urgently I rehearsed the lines. *I just have to go outside for a moment. The little girls there – their mother's inside with their sister. My mother's here somewhere too. Could you keep an eye on them?* Too long, they'd never listen.

'You all right love?' The old woman gave me an anxious glance.

'Susie, you're in charge!' She nodded, straightening her shoulders, and I ran.

The forecourt was almost empty. I hurled past a girl reversing carefully into a disabled slot, past two ambulances waiting with open doors and attendants, past a couple of women crossing the slip road from the car park. Matt lurched, open-mouthed, as his mother pulled him out of my way. I leapt across the hospital road, up the grassy bank below the car park and bounded on to the tarmac where I came to a stop, confused by the ordinariness of the scene and the hectic drumming of my heart.

At first there was nothing to see but neat rows of cars and two men at the ticket machine. In the middle was a raised sort of sentry box for an attendant but it was empty. I started to run again, following the arrows on the road as if I were driving. Then I caught sight of Jack, looking this way and that between the parked cars. I desperately did not want him to find Dominic, not after Jack had smashed a hole in the plaster and hurt his fist.

And in any case, I had stuff to say to that man. Maybe he'd caught sight of Jack, was keeping hidden. It was the sort of thing a man like him would do. I ducked behind a car, so Jack wouldn't see me and slid back down the bank, staying low till I reached the road that ran past Outpatients towards the staff car park.

He was there, hands shoved into pockets, shoulders hunched in a heavy black sweater, like a shadow, like a black thief in the night. I don't know why I pictured him as a thief in the night but it told me what I could do. When thieves break and enter you've a right to grab them, call for backup, police.

I meant to approach him directly, but some mad impulse made me creep. I wanted to startle him out of his skin, see him afraid.

'It's only you.' He barely glanced at me. 'I need to talk to my daughter but that ridiculous man came storming out.'

He meant that Jack was ridiculous. I stared at him, at the curl of his lip, the jutting, dark jaw and a sudden urge to smash his face against the hospital wall bubbled up in my gut and I was breathing fast, clenching my fists and he said, 'You a trannie, are you? You don't look right, you don't look like somebody my girl should have anything to do with,' and he pushed me back. I fell into the road just as the bus was pulling away and I thought, he can't do that and I got up and aimed a punch straight for his belly. I thought he'd double over but the big brass buckle of his belt caught me by surprise and the blood on my knuckles, the pain made me cry out but I wasn't going to stop, now I'd started – I was red-hot with rage at all he'd done, at all the men sticking their dicks where they don't belong – and I slammed another punch at him and I connected, I did, I caught his arm and he yelled but then he whacked his fist against my ear and somebody grabbed the waistband of my jeans, hauling me off and the world swung me round and round and Jack was lashing into the man, slamming punches into his gut, his face, his ribs and I would have cheered but for the ringing in my ears but there were men dancing up and down around us, shouting, and a woman screaming, and the thought flashed through me that Jack, Jack might get the blame for starting the fight when it was me all the time and I hurled myself at Jack. 'Jack, don't, stop, Jack don't!' and I hung on to his elbow and for a second the man got free and then, then he pulled a flat shiny something out of his pocket and sliced it at Jack's face and there was blood running down and I grabbed the man's hand and I bit it, I bit into it, I bit its fleshy edge with all my strength and I felt the gristle and tissue of a human hand between my teeth and again I bit, over and over, tasting the metal of blood, was it mine? and I slipped and somebody put the boot in, stamped and kicked with a pointed hard boot, my ribs, my groin and my head cracked against – blackness and roaring and —

— someone was hammering nails into my skull.

Someone had clamped my neck and shoulders to a bed. Someone was trampling up and down my body. Swirling rainbows, murky, swarming spots and —

— after a while I knew that someone was softly stroking my hand. My eyelids had been gummed down but I was determined to prise them apart. Ruth's voice said, 'Hi Joey. You do have a knack of creating plot-lines,' which brought an unexpected grunt of laughter and stab of pain in my side. Ma hiccupped, and my eyelids winched themselves fully open.

They were sitting together on one side of the bed which saved me the agony of turning my head. Ruth's nose was pink.

'Jack?' I still had a voice that worked.

'He's ok.' Ma leaned forward. It was her hand cradling mine. 'They've patched him up but he's being sent on to Lancaster. His eye's a bit of a mess. If you hadn't got involved.' My eyelids fell down again. Her voice continued, 'Shall we get the doctor back? Ruth?'

I heard a rustle, the swish of a curtain. The air moved over my face with a comforting sigh.

Ma said, 'It could have been so very much worse. Dominic Ainsley knocked you out and didn't stop kicking you till Jack grabbed him. That's what the others said. Apparently it took three men to get Jack off him.'

I stared at the theatre of lights behind my eyelids. 'Jack,' I started, cleared my throat, tried again. 'Jack's eye. That man had a metal thing in his hand. He meant to get Jack's eye. Dominic.' I made myself say it. Make him human, not the devil.

'Yes darling. Try not to think about it.'

'Ma,' I said, feeling the weak, salty tears springing out regardless, 'I wanted to kill him.' Tentatively I moved my lower jaw up and down. It felt as if my bite would never be the same again. My free hand moved to the piercing pain in the corner of the jaw.

'Mm,' said Ma. 'I shouldn't worry about it. Let's think about you, let's take care a bit of you, shall we? Leave it alone, love. You probably damaged a tendon or two but it'll be all right. The doctor says we should take you to the dentist. Maybe you'll need one of those bite things to sleep with for a few weeks. Let your jaw relax.'

'Yes, but Jack's eye.' I kept seeing the gouge, the droop of the eyelid, the swollen globule like rotten fruit. I would always want to kill the man. It was a black certainty.

'You shouldn't worry about anybody except you right now,' said Ma, reaching over to lay her cool hand on my forehead. Her breath smelt stale. She had been crying.

I tried in vain to sit up.

'It's a brace on your neck. It won't stay but they're making sure you don't thrash about. Your head struck the tarmac pretty hard. No, leave it alone. Try to be quiet. Here.' A straw was pushed between my lips and automatically I sucked. Cold, clear water rushed into my mouth and down my chin. Ma mopped up with a soft cloth.

The curtains swung back, and the doctor came in. Ruth was behind. Her nose was pink. The doctor was young, a woman with long hair swept into a loose knot on top of her head. She picked up my spare wrist. 'Right. Pulse settled nicely. X-rays next but I think you'll be fine to go home tomorrow.' She looked at Ma. 'We'll just observe her overnight. In case the concussion has consequences. But you seem a very resilient person, Joey. Fit.'

Ruth said in a low voice to Ma, 'There's someone from the police outside. They want a statement, I think.'

The doctor frowned down at me. 'That's up to you right now, Joey. I'd quite like you to have some normal sleep.'

I wanted to sit up but the room twisted and made me feel sick. 'Tess – what happened?'

Ma held tight to my hand. 'She's fine. Everyone is safe. It's a bit of a mess, doctor.'

The doctor sat down carefully on the edge of the bed. 'The local press have been waiting. It sounds like a bit of a drama. You've been in the wars twice now, I gather from the notes. I expect you want to get her home, Mrs Wilcox.' I saw their eyes meet. They nodded at one another.

Ruth said, 'Bex's father has been arrested, Joey, if that's any consolation. I think it's all coming out now.'

'What about Jack?' The air felt chill.

Ma said, 'We'll have to wait. People reckon they saw it all. It was very confusing.'

I muttered, 'I would have killed him.' A small remembered rage ran through my body. 'Evil bastard.'

The doctor slowly stood up, watching me with a strange look on her face. 'He certainly laid into you, young woman. You're going to have some spectacular bruises. I'll leave you to it for a while, Mrs Wilcox. We'll probably discharge her tomorrow and send a note to your GP. I'll come in later, Joey. See about some pain relief.' She nodded. The silence thickened as the curtains closed. I had to let myself go. The stabbing needles in my groin were gradually morphing into an intense and throbbing ache that rose and fell like a great tide, dragging at banks of sand. It was easier to close my eyes, to float up and down.

Ma was whispering, 'She can't be so bad. They'd have taken her to Lancaster or somewhere, like Jack.'

Dimly I heard Ruth's response. 'You heard her say it, she's a fighter. He. Who've you got here, Moll?' and Ma murmured, 'No idea but it scarcely matters, does it? Our kid.'

'They won't charge Joey too, will they?'

'God, I hope not. He's much bigger than Joey. He really hurt her, for God's sake. God, Ruth, what an appalling thought.'

'Somebody said he hit first, isn't that right?' I felt another, cooler hand on my cheek. 'It's a good thing I'm staying around for a while longer.'

Much later, somebody else sat on the edge of the bed. My hand was taken into a firm grip. 'You'll be wanting your Superperson Logo next,' said Bex. Then Noah said something.

Text

17:42 Simon

You were hero, I gather

17:42 Joey

Noah says your mum's sick

17:42 Simon

Relapse. OK now.

17:43 Joey

How's London?

17:4 Simon

OK. Sorry to leave u such short notice

17:45 Joey

Can we chat?

17:42 Simon

Get Noah to bring u to leeds next term.

Noah's v proud of u.

Research Sheets (Private)

The god Jupiter was taking it easy, drinking, cracking jokes with his wife. 'You women have more fun making love than us men.' She said he was talking rubbish so they decided to ask Tiresias what he thought.

Tiresias had made love both as a man and a woman, because of what had happened to him. He had been out walking in the forest when he stumbled on two snakes, mating. He swiped at them with his stick and was miraculously transformed into a woman.

Seven years later, she was out in the same forest and again saw two snakes mating. She was curious and said to the snakes, 'Well, well! Last time I whacked you, you were so mad you changed my sex. I'll give it another go!' So she hit out at them with the same stick (some things don't change). In a flash, Tiresias became a man once more.

When Jupiter demanded that Tiresias should decide between him and Juno Tiresias was very twitchy. He was bound to annoy one of them. But he was stuck with the truth. He had to agree with Jupiter. Juno was so furious that she struck him blind. Jupiter could not change the curse that another god had made, but he could help out. He gave Tiresias the skill to foresee the future.

Maybe Bex thinks I want magic knowledge

Maybe I do

someone online says you can't just put gender off and on every day like a jacket. Why not? does it always have to be what other people think??

Thursday August 31

It's a beautiful afternoon. The little girls are playing by the nearly-built wall, with Noah in charge of some elaborate process involving dragons, a makeshift tent, face-paints and buckets. The tent is an old groundsheet slung from the almost-finished wall and weighted on both wall and ground by old bricks. Caroline and Ruth bend over the garden table looking at catalogues, whilst Bex and I recline like seagoing loungers on the expanding chairs that Ma set up before going to work for the afternoon. We are the invalid corner.

My neck and shoulders are rigid with a dull ache that nothing seems to ease except a hot-water bottle at night and pills. I resent the pill haze. Ma has made the appointment with a doctor for tomorrow. I told her to ask for Dr Hallgrave. She looked but didn't ask.

I dug the grave yesterday morning. The voicemail from the vet said everything. The microchip confirmed it. I wouldn't let anybody else bury him. I cried hot tears into the earth. Ma and Ruth came out afterwards to say the funeral rites and we chose a stone to mark the spot. I'm going to plant meadow flowers on his grave, flowers that grow in the field where he spent so much time. It's funny how peaceful I was at the vet's. When I saw the flattened body I knew it wasn't him anymore. Roadkill. The vet says it usually is. Ruth says he was my familiar. I said I'm a goblin not a witch but she laughed and said he was my familiar anyway.

Last night I put out a plate of sardines for the black stray. He's lying under the rose bay willow herb that Ma lets flourish as a hedge. It's in full bloom, humming with invisible life. The thrushes and finches are squabbling at the feeder and we watch out for thieving seagulls who forget they should be at sea. I'm in no mood to tell anyone where they should be.

Bex sleeps. She's sedated all the time, reads a bit, doesn't say much. Her face is a blank, like she's turned into one of her masks, till she opens her eyes. The first time it made me go cold as stone, the way her eyes peer about, like a cat in a cage.

Sleep seems to help. It's almost like lying in Maude's Meadow, with people doing their stuff, except that now people are watching us. There's something strange going on with Noah. He's here all the time as if there never was Fi. He drifts over to kneel on the grass beside Bex whenever her eyelids flicker, like he's grown antennae and she lets him. He's not touching her, though. He seems to know he mustn't.

I feel stifled by the unspoken anxiety in the air, thick as flying wheat dust. The harvesters have been out all night, and the great golden bales lie up-ended in the fields. I wish Simon were here. Noah would be his bluff and blag self instead of this peculiarly kind person who brings me beer, offers water to Bex. I look up at thin cloud stretched across the sky and wonder if Jack is near a window, and what he can see with his good eye. His wounded eye will probably be ok. He may be prosecuted, maybe not – assault. He might have grounds to get him off but he should have known better, they will say. There might be a way out because of his depression. I can't get used to the idea of Jack and depression. Ma says it's a difficult thing, people don't always look depressed. I am so glad that Dominic Ainsley has two broken ribs. I hoped he would be sitting bolt upright on a bench in a cell finding it hard to breathe but Ma says he's got bail. He has money.

I heard stuff yesterday afternoon in the garden, when they thought I was asleep.

'I can't reach him. He's taking the blame for stuff he shouldn't.'

'It's that lad who died in custody, is it?' Ma's voice, sympathetic, neutral.

'What was that exactly?' I was glad of Ruth's question. Bex had begun to tell me but lost the words.

'When Jack was custody sergeant. There was a joy-rider, the umpteenth time, and the arresting officer wanted him kept in a cell while they sorted out the charge. He'd been cautioned loads. The lad wasn't sick or drunk. He was over eighteen so Jack didn't call anyone. If they're under eighteen you have to give them the option of someone in the cell with them the whole time. And if they're drunk you might take a look every half hour, even. But this lad was in a furious temper about being arrested again, being locked up. Jack didn't think he was the sort to harm himself. But nobody knew he had a bad heart and could just drop dead. When the officer went to check the lad was dead. Jack got the blame.'

'Were you together when this happened, Caroline?'

'I wish I had been.' There was a long silence. I heard the little girls murmuring and hoped they were too deep in their game to overhear. 'If I'd been with him I like to think he wouldn't have got so depressed. He was suspended, and by the time he was cleared and could go back he was blaming himself. He never went back. Three years. And now he thinks he should have noticed what was up with Bex.' Her voice sounded so tight the words hardly got out. 'He hasn't said a word to me about what I didn't notice.'

Nobody said anything about that.

'Is it the same for headmistresses, Moll? Are you responsible for everything even when it isn't your fault?' Ruth tried steering the conversation in another direction.

'You bet.' Ma sounded unexpectedly grim. 'You have to arm yourself. Invisible armour, so you don't frighten the kids, of course.' Then she laughed. 'It goes with the job. It's all right.'

'Yes,' Ruth said. 'I've worked out the armour plating.'

But she wasn't able to distract Caroline for long. 'It was just after he'd been signed off the second time. I thought being with us had made all the difference. I really thought we were happy.' She drew a breath and Ma tried to speak but Caroline's words spilled out with a tight misery that I don't want to remember. 'He says all the time now that he's a bad risk, he doesn't see what's under his nose, he didn't see what was happening with Bex. But it's me, I'm the one, it's my fault.' She struck her breast with both fists until Ma grabbed hold, and Ruth slid out of her chair to sit with the little girls. Truth is, Caroline might have seen it. But he beat her up. That's what Bex says. Bex doesn't blame her mum.

Today, Ruth has been roped into the game again, and Noah is the pirate, apparently. There's something about an evil pirate and a good one, and two princesses. Why are there always princesses? It's a relief to see Tess with dirt streaked down her face. In fact, Ruth is smearing the dirt. I hear her explaining what camouflage means. Noah says the evil pirate has an invisibility cloak but that he, Captain Noah, has the spell for seeing all things as they truly are. Susie asks if it's a spell to drink and Ruth says it's a powder to sprinkle into a drink and she will fetch the drinks.

Caroline follows her into the house, and we are left, Captain Noah and the camouflaged princesses, sleeping Bex and me, waiting for the magic spell. I stretch out along the chair, grasping the metal frame behind my head. I envy their skill at creating an adventure in the corner of our garden. The wall across the slope is part of their island now. Maybe, once we've filled the hollow behind it with topsoil and planted the vegetables or herbs or whatever it is that Pa wants, the wall will be transformed into a castle, a fort, a cliff. At least he's left finishing the wall to me, he's told Harry not to bother. That's something. It's quite a big deal for Pa.

Marmalade would have prowled along the ramparts. A lorry killed him. A lorry driver killed him. The vet said it had to be a lorry because of the size of the tyres that flattened him so completely. I could have made Marmalade stay in all night. Most cats killed on roads die at night, but he would have hated it. He yearned to go outside and I chose his yearning. Like the lad that chose to steal cars. I guess he didn't choose to drop dead with a wonky heart but are we all responsible for how everybody else dies? Choosing is not straightforward and people who go on about the right to choose don't tell you how hard it is because sometimes things choose you. Something is choosing me, something that's shadow and light.

Will I ever forget the sensation of biting down into a living hand? I wish it were a dream but it isn't. My ribs are in agony. The bruises are dark, and there's a sponginess under the skin that bothers me. But I guess it will heal.

Ma said uncontrolled aggression is never to be condoned and I couldn't argue. My head aches. She wasn't telling me off, though. So how do we sort that out?

'You've dropped your notebook.' I shade my eyes, looking up into Ruth's face which is dark against the sky. Slowly she bends, picks up book and pen, glances at the page. 'Remarkable.' Quietly she reads the heading. 'Manifesto for a post-gender world.' I take the book, lay it on my lap. I am going to publish this somewhere, find the right website. 'Fresh lemonade?' she says.

'Ice? Fresh lemons?'

She moves round so that I can see her quiet, pointed face. Who is she, really? What's she doing here?

'Magic powder for the spell coming shortly, I believe.' Two tall glasses froth with chocolate milkshake and Captain Noah appears with a small bottle, tightly corked. He gives a conspiratorial wink and I realise that Bex is awake and smiling up at him. Is she having a thing with Noah? I don't mind. It doesn't seem important.

'Heigh-ho, me hearties!' Noah says, making-believe to scatter the spell over the surface of all seven glasses. 'Seven's a magical, mystical number, my princesses.' Susie runs to swing on his arm, her smeared face full of glee. 'Ma just phoned,' he adds, changing register. 'She'll be back any time.'

Caroline pulls a stool to the garden table and flips the pages of the plant catalogue.

Bex struggles to sit up, glass in hand, smiles again at Noah.

My stomach contracts painfully. Lives fall apart but children play at pirates and gardens get planted. There are more hours to survive before night and sleep.

Bex will have to give evidence in a court against her father. I suppose Julia will be in court too. I wonder if they are together this afternoon in their new house, out on the road to Windermere. They might be sitting in a garden, listening to the traffic on the A591 that leads to Borrowdale and the Bowder Stone and High Spy and Catbells. Poor cow. She guessed at something, I reckon, but poor cow anyway for needing him. She does seem to.

Ruth says she can script-write from here for a few months, apparently – though I am not sure where 'here' is. She might be staying at Caroline and Jack's for a while. So she says. I don't know how to feel about it. Ruth is part of my life, my memory, she's in our family photos. I can't picture her in Bex's new house. Don't want to. I close my eyes.

When I stir it's because of Ma's voice, calling from the kitchen. The others have gone inside, even Bex, and my body is heavy with sleep and painkillers. Words drift like thistle-down, orange frits. I am who I am. The sun has dropped behind the trees and the house martins swoop upon insects, calling with a piercing sweetness. Slowly I get out of the pad-ded lounger and take small steps down the garden to the hedge. A couple of yards away, I halt. Two yellow eyes stare at me through fringes of green.

I say, 'Are you coming out, then?' and I bend down, ignoring the stiffness in my neck. I click at him with my tongue. The ears prick up. Out he comes, slowly, slowly, on his belly, inching forward. I put out my hand. He's very thin and his coat needs serious grooming. We touch, my finger, his nose, which is cold and wet. I wonder whether he's male or female and my heart contracts for my grey tabby in the dark earth, but here's another stray. I sit down unsteadily on the grass, wincing as my bottom touches down. It's a good thing, this time, that I have no balls. No visible balls at any rate. I would have been in far more pain from Dominic Ainsley's elegant boot. The black cat sits up, curls his tail around his body and licks his chest vigorously. He is decid-ing whether or not to choose this as his residence.

A little voice says, 'Will you have the cat, Joey?' Tess leans against my shoulder, her eyes alert.

'If he'll come. He has to choose me.'

'How do you know it's a boy?'

After supper, I sit cautiously on the kitchen sofa with my feet on the sill. I have been chatting to Simon online and now I know that I am a chrysalis. I don't think Pa or Noah will call my new self a butterfly, though. Noah is on the late shift. He sent me a hug ( ). His hug is virtual, texted. It might take half our lives for me to get the real hug but it could happen tomorrow, too. Captain Noah is a new character in my life. In Bex's life as well, it seems. Or maybe he was always Captain Noah and I never noticed.

Ma's head appears above the back of the old brown sofa. 'Are you all right?' I pat the seat beside me. 'Just a tick.' She reappears with two mugs of tea, followed by Ruth.

I ask what has happened to the wine tonight and she gives me a headmistress look to go with the headmistress shirt she hasn't changed out of, green, again, with a small stand-up collar. 'Tell me your thoughts, Joey.' I look beyond at Ruth, who has perched on the arm of the sofa. The sun is shedding colour as it sinks, the high cloud teasing out shades of pink, purple, red, orange, vermilion, more and more refined and impossible to describe. Bex would paint the colours and the words wouldn't matter. The house is quiet. Pa won't be home for another hour, maybe more. He is still uneasy, I know.

My instinctive sense that I was given the wrong gender is as it is. I don't feel that I am male either. Being made to be either/or feels like a trap, a box. I choose the words carefully. 'I want to live as a man. I want to be myself as a man. For a while.'

They speak together.

Ma: 'For a while?'

Ruth: 'Does that mean hormones?'

Ma's face has gone blank like someone pulling the sheet tight on the bed.

'I'm not changing sex.' I try to answer both at once. 'I'm not messing with my brain.' Ma says she might like a whisky after all. Ruth takes her place on the sofa and looks at me intently, tucking her white hair behind her ears. She smooths down the blue shirt, clicking her tongue at dirt-marks, grass stains.

'This gender thing?'

'We don't know what we could be.'

Ma slides behind me so that the three of us are jammed closely together. 'Tell me simply what will happen.'

'If the police arrest you they have to ask what gender you are and you choose. It says whatever you look like, it's your choice. I choose other.'

'Other,' she repeats, still blank. 'What does other look like?'

Ruth says, 'I'm sorry. I'm very sorry. In the UK there isn't 'other' yet. You have to put a gender on your passport, on your driving licence.' She makes speech marks in the air, slopping tea from her mug.

'Ruth, what are you talking about?' Ma's frustrated voice vibrates against my skull. At the moment, she touches me as often as she thinks I can bear.

Ruth dabs at the arm of the sofa with the tail of her shirt. 'I'm not sure but I guess Joey thinks she has characteristics of both sexes and she doesn't want to be tied to one gender or another yet. Is that it?'

I say, 'I'm not a hermaphrodite, I don't have a dick.'

Ma pulls back. 'You looked exactly like a little girl when you were born.'

'But it doesn't feel right.'

Patiently Ruth asks, 'What *does* feel right?' She looks at me over the rim of her mug; the little red mug that we carried up Orrest Head a million years ago when she told me how characters in her scripts all have secret lives. The thought holds me. Whatever I do in public I'll always have a secret life.

'I have to live as a guy for a while. I want other people to see me as a man, treat me as a man. I've tried it out online and that's not enough. It has to be face to face.'

Ma's head snaps away but Ruth fixes me. 'For a while. What exactly does that mean?'

'Like I said before. I want to go back to school next month on the boys' register.'

'Testosterone, surgery, all that?'

'No, no, it doesn't feel as final as that. That would change my brain.'

'You don't mean you'd be a girl again, sometime later?' I begin to visualise all the years ahead as a great forest that I will have to hack through, cutting my way. With a machete? I have never seen a machete for real, let alone handled one. 'If you do,' Ruth persists, looking as if she wished she had not thought of it, 'it's going to be a rare person who wants to have a deep personal relationship with you. Sex. Think about it.'

Ma suddenly puts her hand on my shoulder. 'Sorry, let me get this straight. You want to go into school and tell Peter Jolly that instead of being registered as a girl you want to be boy.'

'No, I want to be other but they don't have a column in the register so I'll have to be boy.' Then I add, as a wild vision of incontinence pads pops up in my brain, 'School loos will be a bit of a problem.' For a second Ma's expression is of absolute consternation. 'I'll show you online,' I say, as my skin prickles with anxiety. 'I'll get my laptop –,' but she holds me down.

'My darling, listen. This is just not possible, it won't be possible. I mean, we'll support you of course.' She catches Ruth's eye and I see her consternation enlarge. 'I mean, I'll come to see Peter Jolly with you. Oh God, worse and worse.' She lifts her hair up tight from her scalp.

I push myself off the sofa and stare up at the garden, the hedge, the dim outline of the fell holding up the sunset.

'There's a whole world of people like me, Ma, even if they're not round here. Websites full of people who become friends online.'

'Is one of your online friends worth a minute of Bex's time? Would you swap her for a laptop and an internet connection?' Ma sounds unexpectedly sharp.

'It's not my problem. It's not going to be my problem. If people only want to be with me if they think I'm *either* male *or* female, I don't want them.' I feel suddenly inspired. 'Did you only love me when you thought you knew I was a girl?' Ma stares up at me, her expression unreadable. 'What difference will it make to you anyway, Ma? It won't change your life, will it?'

Ma's voice says 'Well, it might. School, for instance. My school, not yours.'

'What do you mean?' Ruth's turn to sound sharp.

'Oh, you don't know the independent sector, my friend,' says Ma, slowly getting to her feet and brushing past Ruth towards the kitchen table. 'I'm putting the kettle on again to stop me drinking another whisky.' She halts at the table, even so, pulling the bottle towards her, angling it to see how much remains. 'You can't imagine the social explosion there will be once the school governors get their heads round the fact that one of my children is changing gender or has a gender issue.'

Ruth said, 'Really? You really think that's likely?'

'I've been thinking about it since Joey told us,' says Ma. 'Last year I had a row with the governors about one of our pupils. She's the product of incest, we found out. For God's sake. They were terribly sympathetic but "a child like that in a school like ours" – oh, you can't begin to imagine the things that were said at my last governors' meeting. For God's sake.' She sounds unutterably weary. 'The rest of the country's not like London, Ruth. We love it here but – anyway, some things are commercially sensitive, that's what they will say. They'll say that prospective parents will ask questions about me, what sort of parent I've been.' She fills the kettle and sets it on the hob. Her life at school seems suddenly a dark struggle with forces I do not recognise. 'And God knows what parents will say about us online. About me. Don't look like that, darling, I can cope.' She wanders back to stand beside me at the window, bringing the whisky with her. 'Darling's a great name, isn't it? Gender-free and saying what it means.'

I want to say that she doesn't call Noah darling, but she does say it to Pa quite often, so maybe it's fine. Ruth sits at the table and traces with her little finger the lines of one of Noah's penknife engravings. He was fined a month's pocket money for it. 'I guess almost any school will be just as twitchy,' she says. 'Fantastic plot line, Moll.'

'You don't mean you might lose your job, Ma?'

She snorts, laughs, takes a slug from the bottle. 'Not likely. When we say equal opportunities that's exactly what we mean. I'm not going to be bounced into something just because what's happening is hard to handle. I won't be bullied.'

The back door bangs open. 'I'm always having to switch on the lights,' Pa bursts out breathlessly. 'Joey!' I jump. 'This cat needs feeding, worming, neutering whatever. I haven't investigated its sex yet but let's get on with it.' The new Marmalade is squirming under his arm. I pull his small hot body into my neck, feel his ribs, his palpitating heart, and find the place behind his ears that will make him purr.

Pa stands legs astride, surveying us. He still wears that wary look. 'What's going on in here?' he demands. 'I can almost read the air.' He smells strongly of cattle.

'You're later than I expected,' says Ma, trying to detach him from his old waxed jacket.

'Traffic on the A66, getting back from Ennerdale.' He shakes his arms free of the sleeves. 'You have to come soon. It's beyond what we hoped for. When you think, a few years back we'd have charged in there putting up walls, changing the course of the River Liza, chopping down trees, culling deer. Sorry about the smell,' Ma is wrinkling her nose at his sweater. 'I got a bit close to the Galloways.' The room feels crowded. He might as well have brought the cattle. 'It's a dream – at last it's happening – a bit of cooperation with nature.' He kisses Ma's left ear, turns to me and I see the kiss in his mind. 'Hey, it's too balmy out there to sit in. Come on.'

We follow him into the garden and sniff at the air which freshens as it brushes the fells. The house-martins cling to tiny stone ledges on the side of the house. Swallows take up position on the telephone wires. Neighbours have lit a bonfire and the tempting snap and crackle of burning wood punctuates our silence.

'Our wall's looking good,' says Pa. 'Got a bit of a list, but that's character. As long as it doesn't fall over.'

I say, 'We'll have to build it again if it does, better. We'll know how to do it better.'

Ma says, 'Maybe one of us could go on a course.'

Pa slaps me on the shoulder. 'We don't need a course, not with you around.'

Monday September 4

'He's ready,' says Mrs Patten, walking from behind her reception desk to shake Pa's hand. 'Nice to see you again, Mr Wilcox. Joey did so well, didn't she? Peter's delighted, but I expect you already know that.' Then she looks at me again and shakes her head slightly, frowning, as if she isn't sure what she's seeing. I try not to touch my left ear where a tiny gold stud now sits in the lobe. Noah's idea.

Pa strides through the doorway into Mr Jolly's study and I follow, breathing faster than I'd like. Then Mr Jolly catches sight of me, tries not to stare. 'Good morning, Andrew. We don't see you often enough. Mollie's done well, hasn't she?' They always talk, these headteachers, as if the exam results of their pupils somehow belong personally to them. *Always*. I'm generalising on the basis of two. I have to stop generalising.

Pa says, 'She's pleased with the results, of course. It's good of you to find time this morning. If you're as busy as she is –.' He sweeps his arm around the study as if it were a landscape. I guess it is in its way. I've not often been inside this room but it's a bit like Ma's study. One desk is clear, apart from the laptop, and the other is heaped with papers and leaflets and random books. Ma says there will never be a paperless school.

I become aware of a silence in the room. Mr Jolly has walked to his window and is staring out at the groundsman, who is swooping over the grass on a sit-up-and-beg mower, pursued by excitable birds. I imagine their calls and wish I could be out on the Scar. But this meeting must be endured first. Pa clears his throat. 'Well, it's Joe we're here for today.'

Joe. I dig my fingernails into the fleshy mound at the root of each thumb. Joey's behaviour is probably recorded in the school files that Mr Jolly can summon with a password. What will he make of Joe?

'Joe.' Mr Jolly speaks as if the word comes from some strange foreign language that he hasn't learned how to speak. That's when I know I have to take hold of this meeting before I lose my nerve.

'Mr Jolly, I asked to see you this morning because I –.'

'Sorry, I'm very rude not to offer you both a seat.' Mr Jolly interrupts, and in any case I have already run out of breath. 'Coffee? Water?'

'Not for me, thanks,' says Pa, and I shake my head. Mr Jolly lifts the handset of his phone and starts to ask Mrs Patten for a coffee but thinks better of it. He returns the handset to the cradle, puts both hands on the desk, and looks at me steadily for the first time today. He waits. I notice the tinge of grey in his freshly trimmed hair, the neatly-pressed collar of his polo shirt, a hint of smile. And I realise that he likes me, not just because I'm Ma's child and Noah's younger sibling. We sit down.

'You asked for this meeting because?' The smile is meant to encourage.

'I want to – I need to come back to school on Wednesday on the boys' register.'

He laughs.

Pa starts to rise and my jaw drops.

'Sorry – I'm not laughing at you.'

'Don't you dare laugh —.'

'Please, Andrew – you'll understand —.'

'It's my son you need to convince.'

We are silenced. My son. For one appalling, hot moment I am about to cry. Pa practised 'my son' earlier when he handed me the keys of the Land Rover to drive us both to school. That was another of Noah's ideas. I was sure of it when I saw Noah standing at the front door as we left, Ruth peering over his shoulder. They were going to spend the day at Caroline's, and I thought they'd have more to do than see me off.

It's up to me. I am choosing this. So I say, 'Actually, I want to come back as other but you don't have other on the register, so boy it is. Why did you laugh?'

Mr Jolly rubs his mouth. He's still smiling when he says, 'We had a meeting about it at the end of last week. About what to do if someone came with a request like yours. That's why I laughed. I didn't expect it so soon, that's all.'

'Who were you meeting?' says Pa, leaning forward, chin raised. He is far too ready for some in-depth analysis of mammalian behaviour in organisations.

'Pa, thanks, it's ok.'

'I'll wait outside.' As he stands up I feel hot all over again that he insisted on coming with me. For solidarity, he said.

The door closes with a soft click and it's just me and Mr Jolly.

'I was trying to work out what's different about you,' he says, 'I mean, apart from the –.' He fingers his own ear lobe. 'Do you mind if I ask why?'

'The stud?' He nods. It seems bizarre that this is what we are discussing and not the far more dangerous topic I've brought through the door. 'It was Noah's idea.' Noah said it would confuse everyone even more and he's right. I love it, the whole notion of people looking at me and not knowing which box to stick me in. But I can't tell Mr Jolly I want to confuse him because it wouldn't be true, anyway. He seems ok with it being Noah's joke, so I shut up.

'Well then,' he says, propping his chin on his hand. 'Tell me a bit about how this has arisen – how you've come to this.'

I try to explain that I've felt trapped inside myself for as long as I can remember and now it's time to do something.

'Have you consulted anyone?'

'I went to the doctor.'

'Who said?' He's having to drag it out of me but his face still holds that kindly smile that makes me feel it will be ok, eventually. Of course, all headteachers are great at kidding you they've understood, so they can squeeze out every last drop of what you want to hide. 'What did your doctor say?'

'She said I could have tests, if I want, see if I've got mixed up hormones or a testis inside.' He looks thoughtful. 'I've thought about it and I'm not going to have any tests. I'm not ill, I don't need a cure.' He's as surprised as I am by the vehement way I say this.

'Did she recommend anyone else?

'What, like a counsellor or a psychiatrist?' He nods. 'She said it wasn't really a counselling thing. Anyway, if I wanted to do something really big like have surgery, gender reassignment or hormone therapy, stuff like that, I'd have to live as a man for at least a year before they'd consider it.'

He sits back in his chair. 'You've done your research.' His face straightens. 'But of course you have. I wouldn't expect anything less of you. What about your parents?'

I am so full of emotion that it's a relief to leap out of the chair and run for the door, to get Pa back. Pa stands just inside the door, like a new pupil who's too nervous to walk further into the room. But I know he's trying to establish that it's my interview, not his. He says that he and Ma are fine though Ma's a bit nervous about a couple of her governors. 'She's meeting them now, as a matter of fact.' Pa looks at his watch. Mr Jolly raises his eyebrows and Pa says, 'I'll explain another time.' He backs out of the door. 'I'll leave you with Joe. It's his chat.'

His chat. He can't help hesitating over *his* but my heart lollops in my chest because I do know he loves me. We never say this, the *I love you.* Well, we never used to.

'I'd like to talk to the Head of Sixth,' says Mr Jolly.

My whole body stiffens – he's trying to fob me off – he doesn't want to get committed. 'And your tutor, Joe, if you don't mind. I'm sure you won't. We need to make sure this works smoothly.'

I'm aware that my mouth opens and shuts. I feel completely stupid.

His smile is faintly mischievous. 'I did say we'd been in a meeting last week. We're a team. I can decide something but if they don't approve they'll undermine what I say even if they don't plan to, and I don't want anything bad to happen to you, not after you've made such a huge decision.'

I find myself saying, 'Really, I'm other. I'm not going to change gender. I'm ok the way I am and I'm not girl, I know that.'

Mr Jolly draws a deep breath and leans forward across his desk, arms folded. 'The change in your appearance is really subtle, isn't it? You've got a different hair-cut, and I guess you're wearing boys' jeans. That's a man's shirt. Lots of women cross-dress.'

I am not going to own up to wearing men's boxer shorts, my very own, not Simon's. Ma has insisted on giving me a massive subsidy so I can buy a whole new set of clothes –boys' socks and sandals, trousers for school, shirts and sweaters, everything. Mr Jolly's right. Lots of girls and women wear whatever they want, and they still like their tits sticking out. The tits are the hardest to cope with. And the blood. But if I eat carefully, keep running, I can keep skinny, not bleed much. That's enough for the moment.

Mr Jolly is still thinking aloud. 'We had a talk about the toilets. That's a real issue.'

'I'm not disabled,' I say, stiffening against what I anticipate.

'That's the point exactly. You might have to put up with using the disabled loos in the short run but we are considering a major change. See if it will improve behaviour across the school.' I frown. 'Unisex loos,' he says. 'Properly serviced, with an attendant. We're looking at the budget for the rebuilding programme. In the new block.' I can't help laughing. 'You'll be pleased about that, I imagine.' He's looking pretty pleased with himself.

'That would be great.' I try to picture Matt in a unisex loo queue, and grin wildly.

'I'm sure Rhona will be fine.' Rhona is the head of Sixth. I think of Spikey Todd. He'll be ok if Bex is.

Then I think about what some of my year group will say if I turn up as Joe, with Bex as my best friend. We haven't tackled this yet. I don't want her hurt anymore. Mr Jolly is reading my mind for he says, 'It's your fellow students who may cause more problems. Have you thought about them?'

I say that they've never much liked me so it won't be any different.

He goes quiet for what seems like ages. Then he says, 'It's our job – my job – to make sure you don't get bullied in school. It would help, though, if you had a couple of good friends who'd stick alongside you.'

I've thought of that. I texted Oliver on Saturday and he came round. It was better like that, at home. I told him about being other and he said, it was strange, he'd wondered if there was something. He could understand, just a bit. It made sense, he said. I didn't know what he meant but that didn't matter. He said he would come into school with me on the first day back, he'd sit with me at lunch, he'd sort out Matt.

But I didn't think Matt would be a problem, not anymore.

I tell Mr Jolly I'll be ok. We shake hands and he says he'll ring later, that I'll probably have to come back tomorrow to see my teachers. It's a bit short notice. He'd have liked half a term to prepare the school, not a couple of days, but I'm almost eighteen. I've the right to choose.

When Pa and I walk back to the car, I find myself matching my stride to his, and he laughs, adjusts his own pace slightly to make it easier.

'Are you really fine with this, Pa?'

He sighs. 'I'm doing my best, love.' He is pale again beneath the tan. 'It's like the whole of my history with you, well, Mollie and me. We've been telling the story from the wrong point of view, but it's the same story, isn't it? That's what we keep telling ourselves. Ruth's telling us that. We've got to get used to seeing it from the other perspective.'

I unlock the driver's door, strap myself in. What would I have done if there had been no Ruth to help? Jack's coming home tomorrow.

'Are you going to start the car or am I driving?'

I am still afraid to ask if Jack will be charged, if Dominic Ainsley will talk his way out of going to prison, if Caroline will cope, if Noah and Bex are an item, now, if Bex will ever truly recover. For all those years she was never safe at home. The monster could talk himself back in. Maybe we've all got monsters on the doorstep, just waiting for the chance to come inside. Maybe the monster's already inside. The void isn't empty at all, it's full of nightmares and you have to meet them.

There's a new Marmalade at home who has already decided that my bed is hers.

Pa says, 'What you're going to do, Joe, it's ok. Brave.'

And I say, with a flash of intuition, 'Maybe.'

Research Sheets (Private)

My brain is an exploding star...

Edit? Publish?

Other?

Acknowledgements

I am deeply grateful to Jackie Kay for inspirational guidance; to Linda Anderson for generous encouragement; to Ann Coburn for a rich fund of ideas; to Dominic Quinn, formerly Custody Sergeant in Cumbria Constabulary, who described the stresses of the job; to Matthew Murgatroyd, who shared his passion for climbing; to Jan Wiltshire, who showed me how to get lost on Scout Scar even if you think you know it really well, and where to find the rue-leaved saxifrage; to Tom Witcomb, who persuaded me to write an extra chapter because he wanted to know what happened next; to Steve Wilkinson who let himself be interviewed so that I could write it; to inspiring fellow writers who gave abundant and truthful advice; to Matthew Connolly for his detailed commentary and his faith in the project; to the many young people who were willing to share with me their experiences of life online.

Finally, I have to thank the hundreds of young people – and their parents – whose conflicts of love and hope and aspiration I listened to for many years.